BAD
BLOOD

BOOKS BY ANGELA MARSONS

BAD BLOOD

Angela MARSONS

bookouture

Published by Bookouture in 2023

An imprint of Storyfire Ltd.
Carmelite House
50 Victoria Embankment
London EC4Y 0DZ

www.bookouture.com

ISBN: 978-1-83790-675-8
eBook ISBN: 978-1-83790-674-1

This book is dedicated to my sister, Lyn Allen, also known as the family wrecking ball, who has been a rock and a huge support following the recent loss of our mum.

ONE

By Kim's count, that robin had landed on the windowsill outside eleven times.

For all she knew, it was a different robin every time, but the result was still the same. He landed, bobbed his head, looked inside and then flew away. She didn't blame him. If she could be outside pecking the windowsill for insects right now, she would be.

'Don't you agree, DI Stone?'

The rhetorical question had come from the chief superintendent at the head of the table, and it was a trick. The query had been posed like a schoolteacher challenging a daydreaming pupil.

No, she probably didn't agree, but she did pull her attention back to the proceedings. A meeting that should have been attended by her boss, DCI Woodward, who had been struck by a stomach bug in the early hours of the morning. Pity the same one hadn't rendered her incapable as well. Any speculation about the truthfulness of Woody's illness would remain firmly in her head.

Present were representatives of every department at

Halesowen Station: Lydia Knight from the press comms office, Inspector Plant for the uniforms, Warren Marwood from the control room, Betty from the canteen, Martin Hobbs from community liaison and the chief super who ruled all the land.

From the corner of her eye, she saw the robin land and fly away again.

Yeah, still nothing to see here, buddy, she thought.

'I've taken the liberty of drawing up a shortlist of three potential projects,' Martin said, passing round a piece of paper to each person. Really, they couldn't process three pieces of information?

It had been decided that Halesowen could be doing more to connect with the local community over and above the force-wide initiatives.

The chief super nodded approvingly at the list. A quick glance across the table told her that Inspector Plant was feeling the exact same way she was, and they both had a million other things they should be doing.

'The first contender,' Martin continued, 'and possibly my favourite, is Three Oaks Primary School. A portion of their playground has become overgrown with weeds and brambles. The area needs clearing to make space for a vegetable garden and a mini nature reserve.'

Everyone nodded enthusiastically. Martin talked through the other two options, but the favourite was clear, and neither of the others achieved the same level of eagerness.

Okay, that had been easy enough, Kim thought. A decision had been made and she'd been able to follow Woody's directive of 'don't speak'. That part of his text message had been in capitals. Both he and her working partner, Bryant, would be very proud. She also wanted to win the wager Bryant had offered that she couldn't complete the meeting without offending someone.

She was silently considering how to spend her £5 winnings when the chief super spoke again.

'That's decided then. We'll meet again on Wednesday to discuss the details.'

The eye roll she aimed at Inspector Plant was an involuntary movement. And it wasn't like actual words came out of her mouth so the fiver was still hers.

'What was that, Stone?'

Don't speak.

She shook her head to indicate she hadn't said anything.

'That look you sent across the table. What was it?'

Every pair of eyes was on her, silently thankful that the attention wasn't being aimed at them.

Don't speak, she repeated in her mind. *You are not going to trip me up now. I have a lot riding on my ability to remain silent.*

'Please share your thoughts,' the chief super persisted with a stubborn set to his mouth.

Don't speak. No. No. No. No. No.

'You don't think it's a positive thing to engage with the local community?'

'Of course I do, sir,' she said, unable to hold her tongue and feeling the £5-pound note slip from her hand. 'Give me a date and time and I'll be there with my shears. But that's not how it works. There'll be planning meetings, risk assessments, equipment training and briefings amassing countless work hours that I'm pretty sure Three Oaks School would rather we spent trying to find the little shits that broke in last week and stole their four computers. Sir,' she added as Inspector Plant glanced at his vibrating phone on the table.

Her own silent phone lit up a split second later. She and Inspector Plant shared a look before reaching for their devices.

'Excuse me,' Kim mumbled, grabbing the phone and heading for the door.

On seeing the name of the caller, she became oblivious to

the curious looks from around the table and the thunderous expression on the face of the chief super. Nothing either personal or professional trumped a call from this man.

'What you got, Keats?' she asked, once in the corridor.

'Homer Hill Park. Now.'

The line went dead but she didn't need it repeating.

She also needed no explanation for his summons.

TWO

'This is a first, eh, guv?' Bryant asked, once they were in the car.

She nodded as he headed out onto the road. It wasn't a place they'd been called to before.

The park was in Cradley, Halesowen and was used by families, runners and dog walkers. As far as she knew, it had a toddler play area, a football pitch, a basketball court for the older kids and large areas of flat managed grass for picnicking. Kim couldn't recall a body ever being found there.

'I'm going to take a wild guess and assume that you were unable to keep that mouth of yours shut during the community meeting,' Bryant said smugly.

'How'd you know that?' she asked, wondering who he'd had on the inside and how they'd communicated her slip-up so quickly.

'I'm a detective. I know shit.'

'No, really. How did you find out? Who snitched?'

'No one. If you'd won the bet, that fiver would already be out of my wallet and in your back pocket. I'll take my winnings in lunch, thank you very much.'

She opened her mouth to argue and found that she couldn't.

Bryant shifted in his seat. 'Listen, guv, I don't wanna nag, but...'

'Then don't,' she said simply.

It was a known fact that people who started sentences with such words unfailingly went on to do the exact thing they were saying they didn't want to do. 'I don't want to offend you, but...' 'I don't want to appear unhelpful, but...' The list went on.

'It's just that she's...'

'Bryant, I've asked her twice and she insists she's okay.'

She could hear the accusation in his silence.

'What more would you like me to do, genius? I could always try removing her thumbnail with a pair of pliers to make her talk, but I'm pretty sure the staff handbook doesn't list that as a management tool.'

'You being facetious, guv?'

'Nothing gets past you, does it?' she said before turning to look out of the window as her thoughts went to Stacey. She'd asked the detective constable more than once if everything was okay. It was clear to anyone that knew her that she'd lost around a stone in weight. On a daily basis, Penn frowned at the still half-full Tupperware containers that he was placing into his man bag at the end of each shift.

Something was missing with her. The spark was gone. That natural zest and alertness had been dimmed, though her work wasn't really suffering from whatever ailed her. Stacey operating at eighty per cent was still better than many people at full throttle.

Kim had idly wondered if there were issues between her and Devon, but she suspected not. They were made for each other. But who knew what went on behind closed doors...?

Jeez, she hated it when just one remark from Bryant caused her to re-evaluate her own performance; but she'd asked the girl on two separate occasions if she was okay and, while her work wasn't suffering, she really had no right to try and dig any deeper.

Kim's thoughts were quickly distracted as Bryant pulled into Slade Road and approached the car park.

Her first thought was that everything was as it should be. Almost. There was a cordon in place that was drawing crowds from the surrounding houses. There were squad cars, Keats's pathology van, a forensics vehicle and an ambulance. All perfectly normal for a crime scene.

And yet something was off, Kim thought as Bryant brought the car through the cordon and pulled to the left, away from the other vehicles.

Energy, she realised.

Normally when she arrived at a crime scene, everyone present had downcast expressions, quiet respectful demeanours as though scared of waking the dead. People were standing in small groups discussing and pointing, thinking and assessing, logging.

But here everyone was alert, expectant, engaged. There was a buzz in the air that she'd never witnessed before at a crime scene.

The puzzlement on the face of her colleague told her he was thinking the same thing.

They got out of the car as a booming voice called for everyone to move out of the way.

They headed towards the voice, which came from a police constable sprinting up the path to the car park.

Behind him, two paramedics were manoeuvring a wheeled gurney along the gravelled path.

Keats followed closely behind, his face ashen.

She watched as the paramedics opened the ambulance door and expertly transferred the gurney into the back.

'Keats, what the hell is going on?' Kim cried.

'He's not dead,' Keats said breathlessly as the engine of the ambulance started up and the siren kicked in.

She turned to face the pathologist. 'Jesus, Keats, how the hell did you fuck that one up?'

THREE

'I mean, I suppose it's easy enough to miss,' Kim continued as she followed the pathologist to either the scene of the crime or the spot where the guy had taken a nap. Right now, she wasn't sure which one it was. 'Just minor details like a heartbeat, pulse, breathing. Totally understandable.'

Keats turned so that she almost walked into him. 'How long am I going to have to endure this?'

'Until retirement,' Bryant offered.

'Ha, why would I stop there?' Kim asked, walking past Keats and taking the lead. 'I'll be happy to ring you every day after you retire to remind you of this little beauty.'

'Stone, I'm warning—'

'I mean, you're a pathologist. You had one job,' she said as she approached the head forensic techie.

'Hey, Mitch, did you hear the one about the pathologist who—?'

'Inspector, I swear...'

'Oh, come on, Keats, if the situation was reversed, you'd be dining out on this for months.'

Despite his thunderous expression, Keats knew she spoke

the truth. He also knew that if anyone outside of their tight professional circle dared to criticise him, she'd roast them alive.

'So, what exactly are we talking about?' she asked, taking a look around. The uniforms had done a good job of clearing the area, and only a woman with a young boy remained just outside the fenced-in recreation park. A police officer was at the child's level, showing him something on his radio.

Keats followed her gaze. 'Little boy found him when his football went into the trees. Ran and told his mum, who had a look and called it in as a dead body.'

'But it wasn't, was it, Keats?' she asked with a sideways grin. Oh, she really shouldn't be having this much fun at his expense.

Bryant headed straight over to the witnesses.

Keats ignored the jab and continued: 'We arrived. No life signs detected. I called you. Checked life signs again. Detected the faintest pulse and instructed the paramedics to get to work.'

She looked down at where the dead body should have been, but instead all she saw was a deep, scored line in the dirt that she guessed had come from the paramedics' gurney.

'A passed-out drunk?' she asked, trying to get Bryant's attention so she could signal him to return. This wasn't a job for them and was worth only a few more minutes of her time to roast Keats.

The pathologist shook his head. 'No amount of alcohol will mask life signs.'

'What will?' Kim asked, wondering briefly if Keats was going to try and find an excuse to cover his tracks.

'There *are* drugs that can mimic death.'

'Yeah, in the movies,' Kim argued, wondering why she was still here, staring at an empty space that had once held a not-dead body.

'We'd started taking photos and everything,' Keats said, rubbing his bald head as though still trying to understand what had happened.

'To be fair, he did look proper dead,' Mitch said, supporting his colleague.

'Overdose?' Bryant asked, returning to her side and matching her thoughts, even though there was no evidence of any drug-taking paraphernalia.

Drugs could have been ingested elsewhere and he'd staggered here to die, she supposed.

Keats shook his head. 'You'll soon realise that's unlikely.'

'Well, did he say anything at all?' she asked, looking back along the path. Right now, she was looking at someone who had either taken a few too many drugs or was possibly suffering the effects of a sex game gone wrong.

'Inspector, I don't think you're getting it,' Keats said. 'The man did not move one muscle. He didn't budge an inch. There was no flicker, no twitch, no blink, and when the paramedics moved him, they were lifting a dead weight.'

'Not seeing a crime here yet, Keats,' she said, taking a step away. It didn't currently look like a case for CID.

'Show her,' Keats said, nodding at Mitch.

Mitch approached her with his digital camera. An image lit up the screen.

'What the...?' Her words trailed away as she took the camera from his hands.

Initially, her gaze went to the man's face. She zoomed in and there was no question that he looked dead. She almost couldn't compute that this man had been alive in this photo. There was a slackness to his flesh that only came when every single muscle had been relieved of its duty. The gaze was unseeing and vacant, glazed and lifeless.

'Okay, Keats, I can forgive the visual error,' she said as Bryant took a look over her shoulder.

She zoomed back out and guessed she was looking at a male in his late twenties with dark hair and a bit of stubble.

She zoomed out further to take a better look at the photo.

The man was wearing tracksuit bottoms and a beer-logo tee shirt. His arms had been stretched up either side of his head so that they were flat against his ears. His fingers rose to a point as though about to perform a pirouette. From the waist down, his legs were spread apart with a good three-foot gap between his feet.

'Not your normal overdose position,' Mitch noted as she handed the camera back.

'Not at all,' she said, fighting the curiosity that was growing inside her. She'd attended many overdose scenes and the one thing they all had in common was the distinct lack of position-ing: their bodies had fallen haphazardly into disuse as the muscles relaxed. This man had not got into this state on his own.

'Can you get anything forensically?' she asked Mitch.

'Nothing that's gonna stand up against a decent defence lawyer,' Mitch said as Keats's phone began to ring.

Kim understood the problem. The scene had been trampled by paramedics who had only one priority – to save lives. Foren-sics and evidence were not their concern.

Okay, maybe she'd take a trip to the hospital to question this guy when he came out of his stupor. Just to satisfy her own curiosity.

'Thanks for letting me know,' Keats said, ending the call.

She waited.

'He didn't make it. Declared dead on arrival at the hospital.'

'They're sure?' she asked, even though she'd never had cause to question a DOA assessment before.

'Oh yeah, they're sure he's gone.'

Kim looked to Bryant, who shrugged in response. He was as bewildered by the whole thing as she was.

They had a dead body with no obvious signs of violence. They had a location that might or might not be a crime scene.

No witnesses, no obvious cause of death and no real proof that any crime had been committed.

'What now, Inspector?' Keats asked.

'Probably about time we all got to work and solved this thing.'

FOUR

It was almost lunchtime when Kim finally rested her backside on the edge of the spare desk.

Since returning to the office, she'd spoken to the hospital, confirmed the man's death, gained his identity and details, and despatched Inspector Plant to inform the family.

She'd also replied to Woody's shouty text message about her sudden disappearance from the earlier meeting. He was somewhat mollified when she explained there had been a body, not a body, and then a body again, and had demanded a full explanation by email. As the hours of the day wore on, she had become more convinced that her boss really was unwell and hadn't just been trying to avoid the meeting.

'Okay, folks, our man is thirty-year-old Eric Gould from Colley Gate. Inspector Plant is with the family now, and his personal belongings have been collected from the hospital by Mitch for forensic examination.' She took a sip of coffee. 'And before you ask, yes, Keats pronounced him dead a little prematurely, and if that fact leaves this room, someone will be looking for another job.'

Nobody spoke.

'I'm sure you're all wondering how that could have happened, and I'm sure Keats is too. Hopefully, the post-mortem will tell us more. Until we're told any different, Eric is our victim and we want to know exactly what happened to him. It's clear that he was incapacitated in some way.' She paused. 'My biggest question right now is why. It's safe to assume Eric didn't put himself into that state or that position. So what's it all about?' Kim asked, trying to imagine what it must have felt like for the young man if he'd been conscious.

Had he heard the police officers approaching? Had he thought he was going to be saved? Had he felt hope? Had his mind been unimpaired even while his body was useless to him? She shuddered at the thought. It was like being buried alive – the frustration, the futility. The feeling of trying to make yourself known, of trying to communicate while being talked about as though you were already dead.

'Stace, get on to his socials. I want to know what kind of man he was.'

'Will do,' Stacey said, sliding her notepad over her mobile phone. Despite it being on silent, Kim could see the screen was alight.

'Do you need to get that?' she asked, more so that the constable didn't think these things were going unnoticed.

Stacey shook her head. 'Getting a lot of nuisance calls, life insurance and stuff. My number is obviously on someone's database.'

A simple 'no' would have done fine. Bryant's words rang in her ear again, but she had to trust that if Stacey needed anything from her, she'd ask.

'Penn, head over to Keats,' she said. 'He's going to want to interrogate this one pretty quickly.'

'On it,' Penn replied, opening his drawer for a tie.

'Oh, and don't even—'

'Not a chance, boss,' he answered, assuring her he'd make no mention of the pathologist's mistake.

Only she was allowed to enjoy that pleasure.

FIVE

Stacey let out the breath she'd been holding, and as she did, some of the tension flowed out of her shoulders.

She allowed her head to fall into her hands and rubbed at her face vigorously, fighting away the fatigue that was like a constant shadow looming behind her.

It was hard to remember a time when her stomach hadn't been full of anxiety, sometimes so overwhelming that she struggled to force breath into her lungs. Often the fear of not being able to breathe brought forth a panic that made her heart race and her vision blur. She'd taken to reciting the phonetic alphabet over and over in her mind until her breathing regulated. Once that had stabilised, the fatigue would sneak up on her, taking back the energy expended from the fight-or-flight state her body was being propelled into countless times every day.

Tears threatened to spill out, but she gulped them back. She'd been forced to lie again when her phone had lit up. It was an unknown number, which only meant Birch had bought yet another phone after she'd blocked every number he'd used. Lies on top of lies, every single day, which made her feel even shittier. Why hadn't she spoken to the boss when it all started a couple of months ago, when she'd realised her confrontation with Terence Birch hadn't done her any good? She thought she'd made it abundantly clear that she had no interest in him and that he should leave her alone. But it only seemed to have made him worse.

She wondered how many times his previous victim, Charlotte Danks, had felt the exact same way she did now. How often, during her ten-year ordeal, had she hoped and prayed he'd just leave her alone? His relentless pursuit of the woman through letters, messages, phone calls and following her everywhere she went had driven her to move halfway around the world. Even prison hadn't dampened his passion, and within a day of being released, he'd been back to his old tricks.

Stacey's own experience in the last two months had given her a full understanding of Charlotte's actions, as her torment seemed to escalate with every passing week. Deliveries of flowers at work had increased. The first few times they'd arrived she'd been alone and no questions had been asked, but she'd since been forced to leave an instruction at the front desk that any further deliveries were to be binned immediately or sent back to the florist. In response to Jack's questioning gaze, she'd told him that she was being pranked.

Terence must have been watching the florist return the blooms to the van because the deliveries had pretty much stopped. But the constant messaging to her phone and social-media accounts hadn't. The minute she blocked him, he just found another way to contact her. His most recent attempts were via the post, knowing she couldn't block that.

His letters were long and wordy. He poured out his heart and spoke of their connection. So far, she'd been lucky enough to get the mail before Devon, just one more pressure on top of all the things running around her mind. A mental checklist of everything she had to do to keep it all secret.

She'd never before kept anything from Devon. Their entire relationship had been founded on honesty, but the whole thing had snowballed. In thinking she could handle it herself, she'd foregone Devon's input at the beginning. When it had become clear that Terence had seen their confrontation as encouragement, she'd been ashamed to realise she'd made the situation worse. She couldn't bear the thought of the hurt and reproach she'd see in her wife's eyes at her secrecy, and with each day that passed, that fear grew worse.

The whole thing had affected her entire life. She wasn't sleeping, she could barely eat, and she hadn't gone to bed at the same time as Devon for weeks, choosing instead to sit in the dark silence worrying about what was coming next.

They hadn't been out in ages. She always made some excuse to stay in, preferring the safety of her own home and avoiding the double fear of leaving the house. The first fear was being followed and the second that Devon would find out what was going on.

Recently, Devon had urged her to accept Alison's invitation to try rock climbing for a few days in Shropshire. Stacey had flatly refused, knowing she would feel almost as guilty about not sharing her predicament with her best friend as she did with Devon.

And she couldn't even imagine telling the boss. Her legs trembled at the very thought of it.

There was no question the boss already knew there was something wrong. They all did despite her efforts to hide it. Just the simple task of eating her lunch or Jasper's delicious offerings had become a lesson in deceit.

She would wait until the office was empty before dumping her lunch in the bin, always making sure that the empty container or wrapper was left on her desk long enough for one or two of them to see it and assume she'd eaten.

The truth was that food held no pleasure for her. The

second she put anything in her mouth, the saliva was stolen by anxiety, making every mouthful an effort to chew and swallow. Everything had the taste and texture of cardboard and just wouldn't travel down her throat.

Workwise she knew she was just about managing to keep her head above water, in itself a miracle seeing as it took every ounce of willpower she had to force herself into the shower in the morning.

Existing was the word that often passed through her mind. She had forgotten what normality was. It was hard to remember a time when the foremost thing on her mind wasn't Terence Birch and what he had planned for her next.

She functioned; she ate enough to fuel her body for part of the day before she was running on fumes. She knew her clothes felt looser every day, but she took no pleasure from the weight loss. It wasn't worth it by any means. She'd explained it away to Devon by saying she was trying to drop a little weight, but her partner hadn't been convinced.

She got herself to work every day, but by mid-afternoon, she could barely keep her eyes open. She was managing to keep her workload under control, but if she hadn't been able to do that, she was sure the brief welfare chats with the boss would have had a different tone entirely.

With that in mind, she pushed back her chair, grabbed the photo of the victim from the printer and stuck it to the board.

She took a good look and had to agree that Eric Gould had most definitely looked dead.

Next, she went to work on his socials. Profiles on every platform filled her screen.

She viewed his TikTok first and found seven videos, all of him flexing at the gym. He appeared to be in reasonably good shape. He wasn't body-builder standard, but he had good muscle definition. For some reason, he liked to make short videos of his activity: bench presses, weights, push-ups, nothing out of the ordinary but all set to the 'Eye of the Tiger' song. His videos attracted a couple of hundred views and a few comments here and there, some positive, some negative. The good ones came mainly from girls and the negative from guys. She read every comment on every video to check for repeats but saw few people commenting more than once, and while the comments were a bit insulting, there was nothing threatening or suspicious. Eric interacted with none of them. His account had only been live for a couple of months, and it was like he was just trying to work out what to do with it.

She switched to his Twitter account. He followed fewer than five hundred people and only about half of those followed him back.

'Ooh,' she said, realising he might have lost a fair few followers after his last tweet hailing Andrew Tate as his hero. Championing raging misogynists didn't do a lot for your general popularity. Most of the responses were negative, and he'd been called a few foul names. Again, he'd not responded to any of the comments, and that had been his last tweet two weeks earlier.

His Facebook was pretty stagnant with only family and friends, but his Instagram was completely different.

That account was full of photos, personal information, chauvinistic jokes, pictures of food, gym photos and videos. There were a few posts about jobs he'd attended, especially to the homes of lone females, with innuendos about not only the boilers needing servicing.

Amongst the many photos and videos of himself, she found a tag from the account of a woman named Teresa Fox, who was proudly showing off her engagement ring. It took Stacey a minute to realise she'd tagged him because that's who she'd become engaged to. He'd liked the post but made no comment. Not the overly sentimental type, she thought.

The man had obviously found the forum that suited him.

From his posts, she could determine that he was a bit immature, a show-off with a healthy dose of confidence.

Yeah, he might be a bit annoying, but she couldn't see any reason for someone to want him dead.

She'd report back to the boss that he was just your average typical bloke.

SIX

'Nothing to see here,' Kim said, reading the text message from Stacey as Bryant negotiated the many traffic stops through Colley Gate. 'Eric Gould appears to be clean. A little immature with a hint of misogyny thrown in, but nothing to warrant his death,' she went on as Bryant finally found the street they wanted.

The home of Eric Gould was situated in a short row of six houses behind the West Midlands private hospital.

Kim was surprised to see a squad car still there. Inspector Plant met her at the door.

'She's in a bad way,' he offered quietly. 'Didn't want to leave her. Parents should be here any minute now.'

'Okay, we've got it,' Kim said, indicating it was fine for him to go. It was a small house and too many strangers in it was just going to overwhelm her more.

Kim stepped through the front door straight into the living room. A woman she assumed to be Teresa Fox was sobbing on an armchair in the corner.

Her reddened eyes looked hopeful.

'We're sorry for your loss,' Kim said, taking a seat on the sofa.

Bryant also took a seat while introducing them.

The small room was functional and centred on a television that was too big for the space. It was as though the room had been forced to sacrifice additional furniture for the sake of the TV. A coffee mug on the floor to the right of Teresa's chair demonstrated that fact. Kim took a few seconds to note that the only pictures on the wall were of the dead man.

She guessed the woman to be in her mid-twenties with long brown hair that tumbled over her shoulders. Despite the reddened eyes and blotchy skin, she was attractive, with an innocent, elfin quality.

'We're sorry for the intrusion, but may we ask you a couple of questions?'

'O-okay,' she answered, choking back a sob. 'But can you tell me how he died first? When? Was it an accident? Was it a car? I don't know anything.'

Due to the confusion at the crime scene, Kim could understand why Inspector Plant had shared little detail, because he hadn't known any. They didn't know much more themselves at this point, Kim thought, but she said nothing to that effect.

'We're currently trying to get all of those answers, Ms Fox, but we need to know a bit more about Eric. We understand he was your fiancé,' Kim said, glancing at the ring.

Teresa's right hand moved away from the watch strap she was touching to twiddle the engagement ring around her finger.

'Just last month,' she answered tremulously, like the time frame mattered, as though she hadn't been engaged long enough for this to happen.

'We don't have all the answers, but we do believe that someone else was involved. Is there anyone that Eric had issues with?'

She shook her head vehemently. 'No, everyone loved Eric. He was outgoing and friendly, always up for a laugh. I mean, some people were jealous of his body, but he just ignored the haters.'

'Eric had lots of friends?' Bryant asked.

She thought for a second. 'Not loads. I think even friends used to be a bit intimidated by his fitness. He'd sometimes mention names of people at the gym, but I never met any of them.'

'How about old friends?' Kim asked.

Teresa dabbed at her eyes before her hand returned to fussing with her watch strap. 'No. He didn't have any old schoolfriends or anything. He never talked about his past. I don't even know where he went to school.'

'Family?' Kim asked.

Teresa shook her head.

'He doesn't have family or he wasn't in touch with family?' Kim tried to clarify.

'Doesn't have any.'

'Mates at the pub?'

'Not really. He hardly drinks. He takes very good care of his body,' she said, twirling the watch strap faster.

Kim couldn't help but wonder who the 'everyone' who 'loved Eric' actually were.

'Was he close to his colleagues?' Bryant asked, clearly trying to find the same group of admirers.

'I don't think so. Plumbing is a bit solitary, isn't it?'

There were many solitary professions, but people still had colleagues who became friends.

Right now, there was no one else to talk to about Eric other than the girl sitting in front of her. She needed some sort of clue to understand why he'd been found in that state earlier that morning.

'What else can you tell me about him?'

'He was just a really nice guy. He was generous and warm. He took his fitness seriously, loved to watch sport.'

As she talked, the watch was being twirled like a hula hoop.

'What a lovely watch. Reminds me of one my mum had. May I?' Kim asked, holding out her hand.

Kim took the watch and turned it around, while in her peripheral view, she could see Teresa still fussing at the exposed skin, which was reddened and raised.

'Yes, it's very much like my mum's. It's lovely,' Kim said, handing it back. She stared pointedly at the wrist as Teresa fiddled to put it back on.

The woman caught her gaze just as Kim had intended.

'Laser surgery,' she explained. 'Recent. Old boyfriend's name. Eric doesn't—' She stopped speaking as the front door opened and a huge hulk of a man entered the room.

'Daddy,' Teresa cried, launching herself into his arms.

'It's okay, pumpkin, it's okay,' he soothed her, holding her tightly.

A blonde woman followed the man in and closed the door behind her. She reached around and patted the girl reassuringly on the back but couldn't get any closer.

The two extra people in the room had made it unbearably cramped.

Kim stood, realising that both father and daughter were now oblivious to her presence. She produced her ID and introduced herself and Bryant to the woman who was negotiating the tight space to greet them.

'Jackie and Rufus,' she said, pointing to herself and her husband. 'Mum and Dad.'

She took off her jacket. 'I'll make tea,' she said, leaving the room.

Kim stepped around the sobbing girl and her dad and followed Jackie to the kitchen. Bryant, she suspected, was trapped for the time being.

'Thank you for coming so quickly. She needs you,' Kim said.

'She needs one of us, Officer,' the woman said, filling the kettle. She turned but her expression gave no indication to her feelings. 'I have lots of questions, but I'm sure you'll only share what you're able to. Teresa was incoherent when she called her dad at the surgery.'

Kim had detected a smell of disinfectant and dogs when she'd passed the bear of a man in the living room. 'I'm very limited with what I can tell you,' she said honestly. Not least because right now she had no idea herself. 'But we're sorry for your loss.'

'He was no loss to me,' Jackie said honestly.

'Oh,' Kim said.

'Or I could lie because he's dead, if you prefer.'

'No, please don't,' Kim said, still waiting to meet anyone from the Eric Gould fan club Teresa had told them about. 'Your daughter seemed to love him very much.'

'Of course she did. She's barely into her twenties. He's older, reasonably attractive, full of muscles and he paid attention to her. She was besotted.'

'But you didn't like him?' Kim asked as Jackie took down three mugs from the top shelf. She paused before reaching for more.

'We're fine, thanks.'

'Don't get me wrong. He was pleasant enough to us. It was just the odd thing here or there. They came for Sunday lunch. I was taking out the plates. I saw him pointing to his watch in the reflection of my glass cabinet. Ten minutes later they were gone. She'd only been in her own flat for six months before he persuaded her to move in with him. Sometimes he'd answer on her behalf. That kind of thing. Probably just being overprotective, but she's our only one.'

'You're saying he might have been a bit controlling?'

'From what I saw.'

'And your husband's thoughts?'

'He agreed completely, although he did admit to being a little biased. He was very close to Teresa's ex-boyfriend, Curtis. No one will measure up to that boy.'

'I noticed the scarring on her wrist.'

Jackie's face tightened as she used the teaspoon to squeeze colour from the teabags. 'A tattoo. Curtis's name. I'm pretty sure that was the proviso to the engagement.'

Kim remembered Eric's name had been on Teresa's lips in connection to the tattoo when her parents had walked in the door. 'Do you think his controlling behaviour went beyond that?' Kim asked.

'You're asking if he was ever violent?'

Kim nodded.

'I won't say it hasn't crossed my mind.'

'Did you ask her?'

Jackie shook her head then nodded back towards the living room. 'If there'd been anything like that going on, it wouldn't have been me that she'd have told.'

SEVEN

Penn was met at the doors to the morgue by something he'd never seen before: warning signs printed and taped to the wall – AUTHORISED ENTRY ONLY.

Keats's second assistant, Andy, a man rarely seen, was standing in front of the double doors that led into the anteroom. From what Penn knew of him, he was a dour, humourless man who perhaps spent too much time around dead bodies.

'Doctor Keats instructed me to advise you this one is full protection.'

'Okay,' Penn said, following him through the doors. He normally wore the disposable white suit and goggles so what more protection did he need? And what exactly was he being protected from?

Two piles of PPE were laid on the countertop to the right of the sink.

'Follow my lead,' Andy said, reaching for the white suit.

'You're going in as well?' Penn asked. He could already see Keats and Jimmy in the room.

'For this one, yes,' he said, stepping into his white suit.

Penn did the same. Next, he put on the protective shoes and then a second pair.

'Double shoes and double gloves,' Andy instructed.

'Is this really...?'

Andy's look was delivered straight from Keats. It left him in no doubt that if he didn't comply, he'd be made to leave.

Andy reached for a roll of tape and dropped to his knees. He wound the tape around the point where the boiler suit met Penn's protective shoes.

'Arms?'

Penn slid on the gloves then held out his arms, and Andy repeated the process around his wrists before passing the roll of tape to him.

Penn returned the favour, now wondering if he was being pranked.

He laughed as Andy reached into one of the units and produced two respirators.

Andy pushed one towards him while putting the other on himself. He indicated for Penn to pull up the hood of his protective suit. A quick glance into the room showed Keats and Jimmy donning their respirators.

If he was honest, he could feel his bum cheeks starting to clench a little bit. He'd never before attended a post-mortem fearful for his own safety.

Andy pushed the door open for him to enter, came in behind him and stood in front of the doors. No one else was getting in.

'No closer than five metres,' Keats called over.

'Overkill maybe?' Penn asked bravely. It was like a scene from the film *Contagion*.

Keats fixed him with a hard stare that was obvious despite the respirator. 'My apologies, Doctor Penn. Clearly, you've identified the toxins in the man's body and have determined that it's nothing that will vaporise and poison us once we make incisions into the flesh. Please explain why you haven't shared this knowledge and saved us all this bother.'

Two words. He'd only uttered two words and now he felt like a primary school kid who'd misspelled a word he should have known.

'Sorry, Keats, never done this before,' he muttered, trying to get himself out of the naughty corner.

'Then it's a good job I have,' Keats said, turning back to the body.

Penn hadn't considered that whatever had killed Eric Gould might be waiting to wreak further havoc, and he was kind of relieved that Keats had forced him to take the necessary precautions. He couldn't afford to be so blasé about his own well-being. He had Jasper to think of. He also now had Lynne in his life, and his current concerns in that department were another story completely.

'As you can see, Penn, we're going to be doing this one a little differently. Only the four of us will be allowed in the room. If anything needs to leave, it will be transported by Andy, who will remain clean of any potential splashes or spillages. All equipment will remain on the tray or in my hand. Jimmy will hand me anything I need or move anything that's in my way. You will not step forward, and if I tell you to leave, you'll do so immediately. Understood?'

'Absolutely. Am I allowed to ask questions?'

'Of course.'

'Do you have any idea what you're looking for?'

'Not at all. It may be nothing, but since Litvinenko was poisoned by the Russians in 2006 with a radioactive compound, we have to be as careful as we can be.'

'Was he injected?' Penn asked. He knew the name but he couldn't remember the exact circumstances.

Keats shook his head as he removed the sheet covering Eric's body. 'It was administered in a cup of tea. Equally as creative was the attempted murder of the Skripals in 2018 with the nerve agent Novichok.'

'Perfume bottle?' Penn said. He'd watched documentaries.

Keats nodded.

'You think the Russians killed Eric?' Penn asked with a smile.

'I'm ruling nothing out at this point.'

'Why the elaborate methods though? The tea, the perfume bottle. Why not a simple injection?'

'The people sent to murder the victims I've mentioned had no connection to them. They were hired killers, paid to do a job. There was self-preservation in not getting too close or being recognised by witnesses. Injecting someone is both risky and personal. It's like stabbing. It requires an intimacy, a desire for physical contact, maybe even a need for recognition, like wanting the person to know it was you. I'm no psychologist, but in this case, it feels like our killer wanted Eric to see him.'

Penn pondered that thought while Keats began his external examination of the body. Eric wasn't a small guy. He would have taken some overpowering to be made to do something he didn't want to do. Unless he knew the person who'd caused his death.

He continued to watch as Keats meticulously searched the body literally one inch at a time. He motioned for Jimmy to assist him with turning Eric very slightly onto his side. He bent in closer with the magnifying glass focussed on the left hip.

'Got it,' Keats said, turning his way. 'Puncture wound in the left thigh. So now we know how it got there, we need to find out exactly what "it" is.'

'May I?' Penn asked, motioning towards the door.

Keats nodded. 'Andy will assist.'

Most times Penn stayed for the whole event, but he needed

to contact the boss and he couldn't do that while he was tied up like an Egyptian mummy.

She would want to know that Eric's death had been confirmed as murder and possibly by someone he most likely knew.

EIGHT

'So, what's up?' Bryant asked, driving into the car park.

They'd only travelled a mile from Teresa Fox's home when Kim had asked him to pull into the McDonald's.

'Dunno,' she said, opening the coffee they'd just collected from the drive-thru.

She placed the open cup on the dashboard just because she enjoyed the mild panic that crossed her colleague's features. His furtive glance gave her a stab of satisfaction.

'I'm uneasy,' she said.

'Yeah, me too,' he replied, stealing another glance at the cup.

She completely understood Rufus Fox asking them, very politely, to come back later because his daughter was distraught. But there were questions that she would have liked to slide into the conversation.

There was no single thing that was bugging her. The news from Penn about the puncture mark found on Eric's body, with the indication that this was a deeply personal attack, had just added to the list. Okay, so the parents hadn't been overly keen on the fiancé, but that wasn't unusual, especially for an only child with overprotective parents, particularly her dad. But it wasn't like Eric had been lazy. He'd had a good job; he'd had a trade. He wasn't a heavy drinker, no drugs, and he took care of himself. Many parents would have been delighted. But not Mr and Mrs Fox. So what was it about him they didn't like?

'You reckon they thought he was a bit controlling and she wouldn't listen?' she asked after taking a sip of her drink.

'Not sure any guy would have been good enough for her dad. Although if I was dating his daughter, I wouldn't have put a foot wrong.'

Yeah, Kim got that. Rufus Fox appeared to be a big character in every sense of the word.

'What's your view on the tattoo?' she asked.

'Damn, I knew that question was coming. I'd like to say that it wouldn't have bothered me, but I'm not sure,' he said, shaking his head. 'Your girlfriend having the name of another man on her body...?' His words trailed away as though he knew the answer but didn't want to say the words.

'But would you have issued an ultimatum?' Kim pushed. 'No engagement until it was removed?'

'No, I don't think I would have done that,' he replied, answering that question much quicker.

'Okay, daddy question now. What if you found out Josh had put his hands on Laura?' she asked, referring to his daughter and her boyfriend.

The rage that filled his face was instant. 'I'd grab the little bastard by the—'

'But you're a police officer,' she reminded him.

'I'm a dad first, and don't even say stuff like that. They're coming for dinner tonight and I don't want that picture in my head.'

'You like him,' she pointed out. She suspected he liked Josh as much as he was going to like anyone who was dating his daughter.

He shrugged. 'He's okay. Anyway, we may be jumping to conclusions about Eric cos Stacey had a good look and said there were no red flags.'

'Hmm...' Kim said, taking out her phone. She logged into the desolate wasteland that was her Facebook account. She had profiles on all the platforms even though she never posted or even accessed them unless she was looking for someone. The fascination of social media was lost on her. It demanded work, interaction, maintenance. She wasn't the slightest bit interested in what anyone else was doing, and she had no wish to share her own activities.

'You phubbing me again?' Bryant asked, sipping his coffee.

'Am I whatting you?'

'Phubbing. It's when you ignore a friend or significant other in favour of your phone. It's a combination of snubbing and—'

'Bryant, I swear you gotta stop trying to get down with the kids. How long you been waiting to use that one?'

'Heard it on the radio this morning.'

She shook her head in despair as she typed Teresa's name into the search field. The woman she was seeking was in the top five results.

She clicked on the profile, and the first picture she saw was Teresa smiling broadly, holding out her left hand.

Kim scrolled through the comments, which were all congratulatory except for a couple of jokey ones about the size of the stone. Jokey or not, she couldn't disagree. It wasn't an extravagant purchase, but Teresa's smile was no less gleeful because of it.

She continued scrolling through the feed until she came across a statement piece. She loved it when people screen-grabbed quotes from the net and just posted them on their page. They were rarely random and more often aimed at someone in particular.

The quote was about everyone being entitled to a second chance.

Hmm... who deserved a second chance and for what? she wondered.

Two posts down was a photo of Teresa with a bruise on her cheek and an overly detailed explanation about the cupboard door in the kitchen. Was this a genuine injury or had she been assaulted? Had she posted on social media as a cry for help, or a veiled warning to Eric that it couldn't happen again?

The unease in her stomach tightened as she passed the phone to Bryant. 'Oh yeah, no red flags at all.'

Puzzlement settled on his features as he scrolled. 'That's weird. How'd Stacey miss...?'

His words trailed away as her phone rang in his hand. On seeing the caller ID, he all but threw the phone back at her like it had suddenly burst into flames.

She groaned as the name Frost screamed out at her.

'What?' she answered.

'Stone, where the fuck are you?' Frost bellowed into her ear.

'At work. Unlike some folks, I have a proper job. Sorry, did I miss our anniversary dinner or—'

'Quit the comedy act. You might want to get your ass back to the crime scene instead.'

'For what reason?' she asked, sitting forward.

'Cos it's absolute bloody mayhem down here.'

Kim reached for her drink as Bryant started the car.

NINE

Luckily for Stacey, the gym frequented by Eric Gould was part of a national chain with over two hundred branches.

Once she spoke to the right person and proved her identity, she was granted a login and password for their CCTV system that would expire in one hour. After agreeing to their user protocols, she was able to access all seventeen cameras on the property.

Stacey wasn't old enough to remember the old VHS recording systems, but she had been sent many times as a constable to locations to burn CCTV footage to a CD. It was much quicker and far more efficient to email videos, and being granted access to a company intranet was the five-star service. Their co-operation had saved her hours of work.

A quick flick through the system confirmed that there were very few black spots and that the quality of the footage was exceptional. So far they were scoring pretty high on the wish list for searching CCTV.

Although Eric's Instagram hadn't included a picture of him at the gym that morning, the usual time stamp of his flexing muscle posts was between 7 a.m. and 8.30 a.m., so she needed to rule his gym visit in or out to confirm his movements.

She easily located him entering the gym at 7.01 a.m., dressed in black Adidas joggers and a plain black tee shirt with short sleeves that looked stretched to their limit around his biceps.

She was able to track him into the changing room, where he emerged three minutes later in shorts and a vest top that showed off all his muscles.

First, he headed for the treadmills beside a row of bikes. Only one bike was occupied and no greeting took place between the two men. Eric donned earbuds before starting his run. Fifteen minutes later, he stepped off the treadmill and headed for the weight room. As he entered, two men glanced at each other and left shortly afterwards.

Stacey went backwards and surveyed the scene again. They didn't appear to have had any intention of leaving until Eric had come in.

She switched to the previous camera and wasn't surprised to see that both men were in the next room, one heading to the treadmill row and the other to the bikes, as though they hadn't wanted to enter while Eric was in there.

She went back to her target, now aware that he wasn't particularly popular. He had the room to himself.

She took a moment to evaluate his lack of interaction with other people. She'd already noted that he possessed what she called the 'cock' walk. Shoulders pulled back, torso and genitals thrust forward in a slow swagger, as though announcing the arrival of his privates before the rest of him caught up. She had no idea if it was his normal walk or if he saved it for the gym. It emanated an arrogance, a superiority that was probably off-putting to people who didn't know him. And to people who did know him, perhaps it was just another distasteful element once added to his boastful, sexist and misogynistic traits. Stacey was pretty sure she wouldn't have wanted to get to know him any better. It remained to be seen if, either singularly or collectively, those traits had been responsible for his murder.

After the findings of the post-mortem, she was looking for anyone that came close to him, but she wasn't having to work very hard.

By 7.50 a.m., Eric had worked his way around most of the equipment and was heading back to the changing room. He hadn't spoken to a soul, and no one had engaged him in contact.

At 8.05 a.m., he left the locker room and headed for the exit.

Stacey accessed the footage of the locker-room door. No one had entered in the fifteen minutes prior to Eric going in, so it was safe to say he'd been in there alone.

To make absolutely sure that Eric hadn't been approached at the gym, she followed his route back to the front door.

He swiped his membership card and left.

She was about to press the exit button when something caught her eye.

Just outside the automatic doors, as he strode out onto the pavement, a passer-by collided with him.

She could see nothing above the waist of either of them, but she already knew what Eric was wearing.

She played it back slowly and zoomed in.

After watching it again, there was no doubt in her mind that the hand of the passer-by had made contact with Eric Gould's thigh.

TEN

'What the bloody hell...?' Kim said as they approached the road to the crime scene.

Traffic was at a standstill and cars were parked bumper to bumper. Crowds of people were heading towards the cordoned-off area as though arriving for a concert. Residents were on their doorsteps watching the commotion.

Bryant slid into a spot on double-yellow lines.

'Frost wasn't kidding, was she?' he asked as they got out of the car.

'More accurate than most of her news stories,' Kim observed.

As they neared the entrance to the park, the chaos worsened, and they had to fight their way to the front of the crowd, where she found the reporter.

'They're doing their best to contain it, but a few have broken through,' Frost told them.

'To the crime scene?' Kim asked.

'Well, two officers weren't gonna stop the hordes.' She held up her phone. 'Luckily, I have plenty of footage of the chaos to add colour to my online story tonight.'

'Yeah, that'll help the situation,' Kim snapped.

'Not my monkey, not my circus. You should have had more people here to fight this off.'

'Fight off what?' Kim asked, hearing sirens in the distance. Support, she assumed, but it was going to take some manpower to disperse this lot.

'The call to action.'

Kim said nothing.

Frost's face scrunched up in disbelief. 'You're telling me you don't know about the Twitter account?'

Kim fought down the rage that was building inside her.

'Have you had your head up your ass for the last few hours or were you just taking a nap?'

'Enlighten me without enjoying yourself too much.'

Frost unlocked her phone as the sirens grew louder. 'The account name is "Sentinel" and... oh my goodness.'

'What?' Kim asked as Frost turned the screen towards her.

'Well, when I called you twenty minutes ago, he had around one thousand followers and now it's up to five thousand. He's going viral.'

'With what?' Kim took the phone from Frost's hand.

'Telling people to come here, to cause a nuisance, to get in the way. I've followed his links and he's a member of lots of neighbourhood groups. He's built a bit of a following by commenting on local crime and slamming the police, but he's gone up a few gears in the last couple of hours.'

Kim scrolled through the Twitter feed as officers worked through the crowd, advising people to go home.

But why? Kim wondered. Why was this person encouraging mayhem, and why was he getting so much attention?

She finally found the first tweet of the day, posted around the time she'd arrived at the crime scene.

Homer Hill Park. Dead man found. Bad man. Waste of life.
Coward. Violent. Deserved to be punished. Deserved slow
death 1/6.

Following the tweet were tags to the Twitter accounts of
local groups and communities. Every tweet after that was
written in the same jarring manner, inciting chaos and disruption. More than two hundred people had replied, and the tweet
had been shared by double that.

She scrolled down. 'Where are the rest?'

'The rest of what?' Frost asked.

'Tweets. He's indicated there are more tweets to come.
Look, it says one of six.'

'Maybe later, like a running commentary,' Bryant offered.

'Jesus, Stone, you really dropped the ball on this one,' the
reporter said.

Unable to argue with the facts, Kim thrust the phone back
into Frost's hand and headed back towards the car with two
questions in her mind:

What was this idiot's game; and why the hell did she have
to find out about it from Frost?

She had her phone in her hand before she was in the car but
waited until Bryant slid in beside her to make the call.

Stacey answered on the second ring. 'Hey, boss.'

'The Sentinel, Stace?' she barked.

'The wh-what?'

'Twitter account inciting chaos at the crime scene,' she said,
trying to keep the rage out of her voice and failing miserably,
judging by her partner's face palm.

Kim could hear the constable tapping furiously in the
background.

'Oh Jesus, oh my God. Is this our guy?'

'Same question I was just asked by Frost, the reporter, who

enjoyed every minute of being the one to inform me what was going on.'

'Boss, I'm sorry. I was—'

'Finding out how Teresa Fox got that whopping bruise on her face? I'm guessing you missed that too,' Kim said. She realised how snarky she sounded, but they were only hours into a major investigation, and her colleague had already dropped the ball twice.

'What bruise?'

'The one that wasn't hard to find on her Facebook page. Does Eric have form for this behaviour? Is he known to us? All relevant questions, don't you think?'

'Boss, I was busy checking—'

'Stace, there is nothing you can tell me that's going to excuse this lapse. Whatever it is that's distracting you from your work, I suggest you get it sorted before you and I have a very different kind of conversation.'

She ended the call abruptly and hoped she'd made her point.

This had gone on for long enough.

ELEVEN

'You okay, Stace?' Penn asked as he took his seat and removed his tie.

She was placing her phone into her satchel and hadn't yet met his gaze. 'Can you let the boss know I've gone home? I don't feel very well.'

'Of course. Is there any—?'

'Thanks, Penn,' she said, hurrying past him.

If he didn't know better, he'd swear she'd been crying.

He pushed his chair back and approached her desk. To the right was her wastepaper bin. He lifted up the top piece of paper and there it was. Today's lunch looked like some kind of pasta salad, thrown in unopened.

She wasn't as clever as she thought she was. He'd first become suspicious when he'd noticed her leaving empty packets and containers on her desk. Something her fastidiously tidy habits had never allowed her to do before. The very obviousness of the act had prompted him to go looking and this was what he found most days.

It definitely explained the weight loss. He'd asked her many times if she was okay, and every time she'd assured him she was fine. He knew she was lying, but what more could he do? He'd considered messaging Devon, but if she was part of the problem, then he could end up making it worse. And even if she wasn't, it was a colleague/friend boundary he wasn't comfortable about crossing.

He wasn't sure what had prompted her sudden exit from the office, but he suspected it had nothing to do with feeling unwell.

He sighed, knowing that whatever it was would have to wait until she was ready to share. For personal reasons, he wished she hadn't left so abruptly. He'd have liked to ask her advice on a tricky situation he had with Lynne at the moment, but it would have to wait.

He fired up his emails and was surprised to see the top one was from Stacey. There were no words, no explanation, just a link to a Twitter account.

He clicked it and began to read the tweets of someone with an account called 'Sentinel'.

'Oh shit,' he said, realising the impact of something like this on the investigation. Having spent the last few hours in the morgue, he'd had no clue of what was happening in the outside world. He was guessing it might be time for a catch-up with the boss, but there was something he wanted to look at first.

Seeing the man laid out in the morgue in the usual position had reminded him of the strange pose of the body at the scene.

It had to mean something.

He took down the photo and studied it. The boss had said something about a line in the dirt at his feet. Medical personnel tended to drop their kit where they were working, but he couldn't imagine they were contemplating CPR on his knees.

He turned the photo the other way. What if the line had been nothing to do with the medical equipment? Had the killer left it as a line telling them which way the body should be viewed? What was the killer trying to say? Was his message connected to dance? The pose only looked like a pirouette from the top half. And how was that linked to the haphazard placement of the tee shirt, positioned so that a single line of flesh was visible around his midriff?

What's your message? Penn wondered, and then considered the Twitter account. *And why are you so eager to talk?*

He pulled his thoughts away from the puzzle when he remembered what Stacey had asked him to do.

He picked up the phone to call the boss.

TWELVE

Kim ended the call from Penn as Bryant parked once more outside Teresa Fox's house in Colley Gate.

A part of her hadn't wanted to leave the crime scene at Homer Hill Park. She'd wanted to wade in with the uniforms and get the place cleared, but Inspector Plant had assured her that his team had it under control, and after scrolling through Teresa Fox's social media, she knew exactly where she needed to be.

Less clear in her mind was Stacey's reason for ducking off home early.

It wasn't like the girl hadn't had bollockings before, and normally she just sucked it up and came back stronger. Kim knew the time was coming for a different kind of chat with the constable.

'Do you think I was too hard on her?' she asked Bryant as he switched off the car engine.

'Ooh, tough question.'

'Really?'

'No, you weren't too hard on her, for you. I mean, you being you, it could have been a whole lot worse, and she has dropped the ball today.'

'Okay, I'm happy with—'

'But,' he continued, 'you might be the straw that broke the camel's back. We know something isn't right at the minute, so your disapproval might have just tipped her over the edge.'

'Jeez, thanks for your support, buddy,' she said, getting out of the car.

He hadn't quite given her the answer she'd been after, so she was more than likely going to disregard it.

She wasn't surprised when Rufus answered the door. She suspected that nobody was getting near his daughter without his permission.

'Back so soon?' he asked, stepping aside for them to enter.

Teresa was sitting at the far end of the sofa. She offered them a wan smile. Jackie appeared in the doorway from the kitchen, and Rufus sat next to his daughter.

'May we speak to Teresa alone?' Kim asked as Rufus took his daughter's hand.

'She has no secrets from me, Inspector. It's fine.'

Kim said nothing and waited.

Teresa got the message. 'It's okay, Dad. I'll be fine.'

He hesitated but tapped her hand and headed for the kitchen. Jackie closed the door behind them.

'Teresa, I'm sorry to have to ask this, but did Eric ever get physical with you?'

Her face reddened as she quickly started shaking her head. 'Of course not.'

Instant and passionate denial.

Kim left a silence she hoped the girl would fill.

'Eric would never hurt me. He was loving and kind. I mean we had some good old arguments, lots of shouting on both sides, but what couple doesn't?'

Kim nodded but still didn't speak.

'We both have quick tempers, so we'd clash about small stuff sometimes. I never was one to back down. We both got angry with each other, but for you to accuse him of being violent—'

'I didn't say that,' Kim corrected. 'I asked if he ever got physical with you.'

'The answer is no,' Teresa said testily. 'Eric would never have punched me.'

And there it was. Given enough time, the truth would reveal itself.

'You do know that domestic abuse isn't just about punching and kicking?'

'Yes, but—'

'Firstly, it rarely starts out that way, and secondly, abuse can take many forms. Can you be honest with us? We have to consider if it could be related to Eric's murder.'

Teresa's mouth fell open in surprise. 'Eric can't be dead because he pushed me a couple of times.'

'How many times?' Kim asked.

'Three, maybe four. I wouldn't back down. He did it just to get me away from him, but he would never have hit me.'

Kim wondered if Teresa actually believed that, or if she just wanted Kim to believe it.

'And were those pushes the only time Eric was physical?'

'Well, no, but the other time it was an accident.'

'Go on,' Kim urged, sensing she was about to hear the kind of story that had become very familiar to her during her years as a police officer.

'It was accidental. He was trying to swat me away. It was just a slap.'

It was an escalation as far as Kim was concerned.

'He was mortified. He bought me flowers and everything. He couldn't say sorry enough. He was so loving. It was no big deal.'

Until the next time, Kim thought.

Teresa's acceptance of the abuse saddened her, but that

wasn't her concern right now. Her abuser was dead and was never going to hurt her again.

'Did you tell anyone about the violence?' Kim asked.

Teresa recoiled, but Kim refused to change the wording.

'Well, it wasn't really violence. I mean it was just—'

'But did you tell anyone?' Kim pushed.

'I m-might have mentioned it to my dad.'

'Anyone else?'

Teresa shook her head miserably, as though this was something she really hadn't wanted to share.

Kim rose and stepped into the kitchen for the second time that day, closing the door behind her and leaving Bryant with Teresa.

Rufus got up and moved towards the lounge door, eager to return to his daughter.

'One second, Mr Fox. May I just confirm whether or not you knew that Eric was abusing Teresa?'

'Excuse me?'

'You heard me, Mr Fox,' Kim said, ignoring his play for time. 'Did you know?'

Jackie was staring at the back of her husband's head as though she too was waiting for an answer.

He sat back down. 'Yes, she told me recently.'

'Rufus, what the hell?' Jackie cried.

'She didn't want you to know,' he said, facing his wife. 'I urged her to leave him, to come back home. I threw every statistic on domestic violence I could find at her. She swore he'd change. I told her he'd only get worse, but she wouldn't hear it.' His face was flushed. 'I'm not even sorry he's dead. He had no right putting his hands on her.'

Kim didn't disagree, and she couldn't even imagine the parental protection gene that would have kicked in on learning the news. She could only liken it to someone hurting Barney, and that alone incited a white-hot rage within her.

'Did you speak to him about it?' Kim asked. She had trouble visualising this man being able to keep quiet.

He shook his head. 'She swore she'd have nothing to do with us if I breathed a word to him. And she'd have done it too. She gets her stubbornness from her mother.'

Jackie nodded her agreement, although she still looked shaken at learning the true nature of her daughter's relationship.

'You must have been pretty angry when she confided in you,' Kim said.

'That may be the biggest understatement of your career, Inspector. I wanted to tear him apart limb by limb with my bare hands.'

And that probably would be possible with those hands, Kim thought.

'But not at the risk of losing my daughter,' he continued. 'I had to just bite my tongue and hope it was a one-time thing.'

Kim opened her mouth to say that it didn't appear to have been just one single incident and then bit back her words. It wasn't her story to tell.

'Did you share the information with anyone else?' she asked.

He looked up and to the left before shaking his head, and immediately Kim knew he was lying.

'Are you sure about that, Mr Fox? It's important that we know.'

'Why?' he asked, frowning.

Jackie turned her way and waited too.

'I can't say right now. So, could you have mentioned it to anyone?'

'Well, maybe Curtis, in passing, perhaps.'

'Curtis as in Teresa's ex-boyfriend?'

'Yes. We're still friends. I see him a few times a month.'

Maybe a little strange but not unheard of.

'He's a nice lad,' Rufus offered. 'Both Jackie and I took the breakup quite badly. He's a good boy. He didn't have it easy growing up, but he's made something of himself. He became the son we never had.'

Jesus, even without the violence, Eric hadn't stood a chance.

'And where might we find Curtis?' she asked.

Rufus checked his watch. 'He'll still be at the hospital. He's on lates this week and doesn't finish until nine.'

'Hospital?'

'The one around the corner. He's a nurse,' Rufus said proudly.

Kim thanked him for his time and collected Bryant on the way out.

Somehow, she couldn't picture Rufus on the other end of the Sentinel social-media account unless that was some kind of ruse.

More troubling to her was that both of the men who appeared to love Teresa very much had access to a wide variety of drugs.

THIRTEEN

It was after seven when Bryant pulled into the hospital car park, and it was almost empty.

She'd updated her colleague on Rufus's admissions during the short car journey.

Bryant had admitted that he'd been giving serious thought to the situation and that he'd come to the realisation that if it were Laura and Josh, there was no way he'd have been able to leave it alone, even at the risk of losing contact with his daughter.

His words and the passion behind them had caused Kim to wonder if she was writing off Rufus's involvement too soon. She'd already stood Penn down for the night, but she'd have him delve deeper into the man's background tomorrow.

'So, according to Rufus Fox, our boy Curtis is the prodigal son who can do no wrong, eh?' Bryant asked as they approached the hospital entrance.

'Oh yeah, definitely the preferred son-in-law.'

The woman behind the desk offered them a welcoming smile that had obviously been aged by a long day.

'Are you visiting?' she asked, ready to give them instructions on where to find the overnight patients.

They both held up their IDs.

'May we speak to Curtis Jones?'

'Umm, he'll be on the ward right now. Can I give him a message to—?'

'We need to speak to him,' Kim insisted.

'Okay, please take a seat,' she said, nodding towards a sofa as she reached for the phone.

Kim stepped away to offer privacy but didn't sit down.

'They'll send him down,' she said, replacing the receiver.

Kim moved back towards the desk. 'Has he worked here long?' she asked casually.

'Around three years. He's wonderful. The patients love him.'

'And the staff?' Bryant asked.

'Oh yes,' she said with a smile that seemed to have discovered some of its vitality. 'Every ward sister requests him for post-op care. Nothing is too much trouble. He takes such good—'

She stopped speaking as the ting of a lift arriving sounded along the corridor.

The unmistakeable sound of Crocs on floor tiles headed towards them.

Kim guessed Curtis to be around five feet ten with sandy blonde hair that was cut in a short but fashionable style. He was dressed in matching navy tunic and trousers. Two pens peeped out from his chest pocket. His arm was outstretched, and Bryant shook his hand.

His smile was warm if a little puzzled.

Kim stepped away from the desk, and he followed.

'We're here to talk to you about Eric Gould.'

It took a second for the name to mean anything to him. 'Isn't that Teresa's boyfriend?'

Boyfriend not fiancé, she noted.

'He was, but he died earlier today.'

'Wh-what?'

'Did you know the man, Mr Jones?'

'Curtis, please,' he said. 'No. The first time I heard his name was when Rufus told me the real reason Teresa broke up with me.'

'Go on.'

'I'm not sure how this helps, but after three years together, she said she wanted some space. I got it, even though I had no wish to end it. I thought we were happy.'

He raised his shoulders in a shrug, and Kim caught the sight of some ink beneath his watch. She guessed they'd had matching tattoos. She had to wonder if he knew that Teresa no longer had his name on her wrist.

'I was on the cusp of asking her to marry me; I was so sure.'

And another man had managed to put that ring on her finger.

'It must have hurt that you had such different views of the relationship.'

'Of course. Little did I know she'd already met Action Man and she was introducing him to her parents two weeks after the breakup.'

Ouch, Kim thought.

'But you kept in touch with her parents?' she asked, trying not to find that a bit weird.

'Of course. I'd been part of their family for years. Teresa broke up with me, but they didn't.'

Tricky around Christmas though, she thought, wondering why he hadn't backed off.

'My dad died when I was fifteen. Rufus is a big character.'

'Father figure?' Kim queried.

'I suppose so. We get along well. We have things in common.'

'Because he's a vet?' Bryant asked.

'Not only that. We like the same sports; we're both committed Albion supporters. A pint and a game of pool.'

Kim was beginning to wonder who he'd been having a relationship with.

'I didn't want to lose that even though Teresa and I were on a break.'

'Is that how you felt? That the two of you would get back together?'

He hesitated and then nodded. 'And Rufus agreed that she'd come to her senses eventually.'

Sounded to Kim as though Daddy was keeping his preferred boyfriend on ice while waiting for Teresa to change her mind.

'And Rufus told you about the abuse?'

The man's jaw tightened. 'He did.'

'And how did that sit with you?' she asked.

'How do you think?' he shot back as the calm control slipped for just a second. She was willing to bet that the ward sisters didn't see this side of him very often. 'I wanted to jump him in a dark alleyway and get him to pick on someone his own size.'

'But you did nothing?'

Such strong emotions normally demanded an outlet.

'I tried to speak to her, advise her that this wasn't right. She told me to mind my own business. There was nothing more I could do.'

'You're sure you didn't take matters into your own hands?' she asked.

'Absolutely not, Inspector. I'm not stupid, however much I wanted to hurt him.'

'Okay, Mr Jones, thank you for your time,' she said, heading towards the doors.

Right now, she was finding it difficult to believe that the two men who had loved Teresa the most had stood idly by knowing that another man was putting his hands on her.

And the relationship between the two men was very unsettling indeed.

FOURTEEN

Stacey felt her heart lurch at the sound of the front door opening. She pulled herself tighter into the corner of the sofa, aware she had just a couple of minutes until Devon came into the lounge.

She knew the jig was up. She'd barely been able to stop the tears that had forced themselves from her eyes in the back of the taxi.

The harsh words from the boss about the social-media account and her other failings had rocked her to the core for two reasons: the boss had never had cause to come down on her so hard and so she wasn't used to being on the receiving end of her sharp tongue; but secondly, and worst of all, she knew the boss was right. She wasn't performing to her ability, and that was true of everything in her life. Only this time it had affected her work. She should have been the one to discover Teresa's bruise and the Sentinel's Twitter account, and normally she would have been the first to spot it. Instead, the boss had heard about it from Frost of all people. The harsh words were justified, and she sensed she'd be called in to a formal meeting tomorrow.

The fight-or-flight response in her body had opted for flight, and she'd barely been able to pay the taxi driver before getting inside and having a full-blown panic attack.

For just a few minutes, she'd thought the pounding in her chest was going to kill her. While she'd been terrified at the idea, a part of her had been relieved, even hopeful, and those thoughts had terrified her more than the panic attack.

She knew she didn't want to die. She wanted peace, a rest from her own head. She wanted to return to a time when her fear of Terence Birch wasn't the most dominant thing in her life. A time when she'd known there was no one watching her from across the road as Birch was sure to be doing right now.

As the panic attack had subsided, leaving her body weak and shaken, she'd given in to the tears that were never far from the back of her throat. She'd allowed the sobbing to wrack her defeated body while wondering how her once enviable life had been reduced to this.

And as the sobbing had begun to subside, she'd known that she no longer had the strength to fight this on her own.

'Hey, babe,' Devon said, switching on the centre light. 'What the hell?'

Devon immediately rushed to sit beside her and clutched her hand. 'What's happened? What's wrong?'

Stacey took some steadying breaths. She had no idea how this was going to go.

'Is everything okay? Is your mum...?'

'She's fine. Everyone is fine,' she said, squeezing her wife's hand. The concern on Devon's face was doing nothing to ease the ball of anxiety in her stomach.

'I need to talk to you, Dee. You're not gonna like it.'

'Hey, come on. I've told you before that nothing can break us.'

Stacey hesitated, not quite knowing where to start.

'Come on, babe, you're really scaring me now. Have you met someone else?'

'God no,' Stacey said, squeezing her hand. 'Nothing like that.'

Devon's face instantly expressed relief before resetting right back to concern.

She had to find a way to get it out. She couldn't cope on her own for one more minute.

'Do you remember our last big case, the psychics?'

Devon nodded.

'I had to interview the man who found the first body in the graveyard, Terence Birch. It didn't go well,' Stacey said, wishing she could go back to that day and ask Penn to question him.

'He had form, for stalking. Do you remember when we got home after that driving lesson and someone jumped out from behind the bushes?'

It took Devon some time to recall, but she eventually nodded.

'That was Birch.'

Stacey could see that a hundred questions were forming on Devon's lips, but she held them back.

'During that week, he turned his attention on me. I started seeing him everywhere. At first I thought I was imagining it, and then I thought it was some weird coincidence, but then he started sending me messages, flowers, more messages.'

Stacey gulped as the emotion caught in her throat.

Devon looked horrified. 'You didn't tell me, babe?'

The tears gathered again at the hurt in Devon's voice.

'I couldn't. I felt guilty, like I'd done something to invite it. At first, I wasn't sure, and by the time I confronted him—'

'Jesus Christ,' Devon exploded, releasing her hand and launching herself up from the sofa. 'You confronted him and you didn't even tell me?'

Stacey nodded, feeling the sickness grow inside her.

'I thought if I was just direct with him and told him to leave me alone, he'd get the message.'

Stacey was tempted to explain what Charlotte had been through but knew that wouldn't help her.

'You spoke to him on your own?'

Stacey nodded.

'Jesus Christ,' she said again. 'You confronted an unhinged man alone and never thought to mention it. Bloody hell, Stace, anything could have happened and I wouldn't have had a clue. What if he'd attacked you or... oh my God,' Devon said, pacing around the room as though it might all make sense in a different spot.

'I know and I'm sorry. I've made a lot of mistakes, but I just didn't know what to do.'

'How is it still going on? What did Kim say?'

Stacey choked back a sob.

'You have got to be joking me? You didn't tell her either?'

Stacey shook her head.

'Babe, what were you thinking?' Devon asked, opening her hands in exasperation.

'I thought it would just stop. After confronting him, I thought just ignoring him would work, that he'd get bored. Nothing worked. He won't leave me alone. He's getting worse. I can't eat, I can't sleep, I'm constantly tired and anxious, and I'm not even doing my job, but he just won't stop.'

'Don't you see that you gave him everything he wanted? You gave him intimacy.'

'I never did—'

'Not that kind of intimacy. Because you haven't told anyone, it's been just you and him locked in this twisted relationship. The sick bastard has had you all to himself. Clearly, he's been the biggest thing in your head for weeks.'

Stacey couldn't argue.

'This is the reason for everything, isn't it? Why you stopped the driving lessons, why you never want to go out, why you refused to go away with your best friend for a couple of days. You've stopped everything because of him?'

'I know... I know... I don't know what to do.'

Stacey could see that Devon was torn between comforting her and continuing to process what she'd heard.

Suddenly, Devon's head whipped round. 'Hang on, you said you confronted him. Where?'

'Over the road.'

'He was watching the fucking house?'

'He's always watching the house.'

'He's here now?'

Stacey nodded.

'But I've just come in,' Devon said, heading towards the window.

'He hides behind the tall conifer.'

'This is sick, Stace,' Devon said, drawing back the curtain. 'He's fucking standing right there,' she exclaimed in horror.

Of course he was. He was rarely anywhere else.

Devon pushed open the window. 'Oi, fuck off, police are coming,' she shouted before pulling it shut again.

She turned back towards Stacey. 'How long has this been going on?'

'Two months,' Stacey admitted, moving towards her.

'I just don't know how you could have kept something so terrifying and creepy to yourself. This is beyond disturbing.'

Stacey took a step closer. 'Dee, I'm sorry I lied.'

'Too soon, babe,' Devon said, stepping out of her way. 'I need some space. Too many emotions, and I don't wanna say the wrong thing.'

Devon headed for the hallway and grabbed her jacket.

'Dee, please, let me explain,' Stacey begged, following behind.

'Babe, I know you need my support and understanding, and you'll get it, but first I've got to get some space to blow out the lies and deceit. Something in you couldn't trust me enough to share this, and I gotta see how that lands.'

Stacey heard the catch in her wife's voice and understood the level of hurt she'd caused.

She knew there was no point in trying to prevent her leaving, but as Devon reached the front door, Stacey couldn't hold back.

'You told me nothing could break us. You said we could put anything back together.'

Devon hesitated in the doorway.

'Every type of glue needs time to dry,' she said before closing the door behind her.

FIFTEEN

The conversation with Curtis was still on Kim's mind when she poured her second coffee from the machine as the clock hit 10 p.m. All the way home, she'd been trying to recall any situation where a father and his daughter's ex-boyfriend had remained so close after the breakup. She couldn't help wondering if Eric had known all about that weird dynamic. It might have been one of the reasons he hadn't relished spending time with Teresa's family, or maybe he really was just a violent bully who liked to smack women around.

'Okay, boy,' she said, patting the sofa. 'Come and tell me all about your day.'

Barney looked at her, looked at the sofa and was about to jump when his ears perked up and he headed for the door.

'Buddy, you're losing it. Ain't nobody visiting at this time of—'

Her words were interrupted by the barking which immediately preceded a knock at the door.

'Who the hell is that?' she asked no one as she got up.

She didn't need to look through the peephole. The figure was recognisable even through the distorted glass panels.

What on earth was he doing here at this time? she wondered, opening the door.

'Bloody hell, Bryant, shouldn't you be tucked up in bed with your Horlicks by now?'

'Hate the stuff,' he said, stepping past her and offering Barney an apple.

The dog took it to his chewing rug, happy for their visitor to stab her and take all their possessions as long as he'd brought the favoured fruit.

She did a quick assessment in her head as she walked towards the kitchen. Normally, visits to her home, where she was Kim and not guv, were preceded either by them having had words or from her having done or not done something he didn't agree with but was professional enough not to raise in front of the team.

Ah, there it was. She knew why he'd come.

'Bryant, I'm not talking to Stacey again,' she said, taking his mug from the cupboard. 'I know you're concerned for her, but after today's fiasco, it wouldn't be a welfare chat so...'

'I'm not here about Stacey. I know you've done your best there. We'll know when we know.'

'Oh, okay,' she said, running the rest of the day through her head. Who else had she pissed off?

'It's not you, for a change,' he said, taking a seat on one of her breakfast stools.

'Cool,' she said, sliding his coffee towards him. On closer inspection, the man looked utterly miserable.

'Jeez, Bryant, who died?'

'No one, thank God. And... and... anything I say is going to sound anti-climactic now, isn't it?' he puffed.

There was something about his demeanour that was making her want to laugh. She knew there was nothing wrong with Laura or Jenny because he wouldn't be sitting here if that was the case.

His hunched deportment and scowl was amusing her.

'Bryant, are you sulking?'

'Bloody hell, Kim, give me a break. Of course I'm not sulking.'

'So what's wrong?'

He took a sip of coffee and then sighed heavily. 'I told you Laura and Josh were coming for dinner.'

'You did.'

'Well, the minute they came in, I knew something was different. They were all smoochy and googly-eyed with—'

'Googly-eyed?' she asked, raising an eyebrow.

'You know what I mean. And then right before dessert, they dropped the bombshell.'

'She's pregnant?' Kim asked.

'God no. I wouldn't be here right now. I'd still be chasing him with a sharp knife to cut off his—'

'She's twenty-five years of age. Gotta break it to you, buddy. She's had sex.'

'Ugh, shut up. They're... they're engaged.'

'To each other?' she asked, trying to detect the cause of his misery.

'Of course each other. Who else?'

'Still looking for the root of your distress,' she said honestly.

'It's too soon.'

'They've been together for almost three years and you like the guy.'

'It's too... it's too permanent.'

'Oh, I see. So, actually, you are sulking?'

'I'm not sulking. It's just so sudden. I wasn't expecting it. I wasn't ready for it.'

'So what did you do, just leave in the middle of dinner?' she asked. This wasn't a problem they couldn't solve.

'No, I shook his hand and all that and wished them both

well, but I didn't mean a bloody word of it. The minute they'd gone, I told the missus I was going to grab a late pint.'

'What did she say?'

'Tell Kim I said hi.'

Kim chuckled. She loved that Jenny wasn't for one second threatened by their friendship. She also knew that Jenny would expect her to talk some sense into him.

'Okay, let's break it down. Is he a drug addict?'

'No.'

'Is he homeless?'

'No.'

'Decent job?'

Bryant pulled a face.

'He's a solicitor. Grow up. Ever see anything to cause you concern?'

He shook his head.

'Laura still keen to advance in her career? She still got a good circle of friends she sees regularly?'

'Yes, of course. She's not stupid. She won't allow anyone to tell her what to do.'

'Of course she won't. She's had a good example. Jenny's done a great job.'

'Funny.'

'But she does know what she's doing. You've given her all the tools. She met a guy, she fell in love, she hasn't rushed anything and now she's ready to share her life with someone. But of course you know all that.'

He nodded. Took another sip of his drink.

'She was never coming back, Bryant. She hasn't been your little girl for a very long time. You've been dead proud of everything she's done and the way she's done it. Why change that now?'

'It'll just be different. I won't be that man any more.'

Kim completely understood. He'd always been the constant

male figure. The one Laura could turn to. The one who would never let her down. It wasn't that he resented Josh for being the man who would now take that place in her life. He resented that anyone would take that place.

'Thing is, you'll always be that man. You'll never judge her, you'll never undermine her and you'll provide a safe space for her for the rest of your life.'

'Shit, Kim, I'm welling up here.'

'Yeah, not bad, eh?' she said, taking back his coffee. 'Now piss off and go tell Laura and Josh how happy you are for them. And mean it this time.'

'Okay. Thanks for the chat,' he said, grabbing his keys and heading for the door.

He took a quick detour to rub Barney's head before making his way out.

Kim poured herself a fresh cuppa.

Oh well, at least she'd been able to help one member of her team. She just hoped that whatever was bothering another would be sorted out before more mistakes were made.

SIXTEEN

'No way,' Kim said to no one as the alarm sounded on her phone. Every sense was telling her it wasn't yet time to get up.

It was only once she sat up that she realised two things: it was still dark outside, and that wasn't her alarm, it was her ringtone.

'What the hell?' she said as she saw the name of the caller, right below the clock that told her it was 4.37 a.m.

'Bloody hell, Keats, sorry I took the piss, okay?'

She waited for him to apologise for hitting the wrong button and revenge would have been served.

'You might want to get on your way towards Gornal.'

She was upright and alert. This wasn't a retaliatory prank.

'You got something for me.'

'I have, Inspector.'

She threw the quilt to the other side of the bed.

'Just one question. Is this one dead?'

'Oh yes. This one is definitely dead.'

SEVENTEEN

It was almost 5.15 a.m. when Kim pulled up at the cordon in Upper Gornal. Situated south of Sedgley, the area had been the target of three bombs by the German Luftwaffe during World War II, but no buildings had been damaged, and there were no civilian casualties. There had been many jokes about people from Upper Gornal having the luck of the devil.

She felt not so lucky being summoned at the crack of dawn. After letting Barney outside, she'd made an instant cup of black coffee that she'd sipped while texting Charlie.

Leaving the house so early before their normal routine had taken place meant Barney would be wondering what was going on. Charlie would feed him, walk him and take him home for company.

Still, she didn't like hurrying off and leaving him. She'd text Charlie again later and make sure her boy was okay.

She showed her identification and ducked under the tape.

Immediately, she got the sensation that she was late to the party.

There was always an initial sense when arriving at a crime scene as to where they were in the process.

Often, there was a respectful buzz as information was being shared for the first time: the circumstances, the timing, the witness details. Everyone was busily conveying information to the next person along the chain.

As she made her way to the scene, there was less chatter, as though everything had already been done.

She found Keats in conversation with an inspector from the traffic division.

He excused himself as he saw her approach.

'Keats, what the...?'

'You'll see,' he said, walking straight ahead.

This crime scene bore no resemblance to the one she'd visited the previous day. That one had been organised, planned, calm. This looked like some kind of traffic incident.

Her suspicions were confirmed when she saw a crumpled figure in the middle of the road.

As she drew closer, she saw that it was a male wearing jeans and black trainers. His upper half was covered by a navy fleece. His body was formed of impossible angles that in life would have given the best contortionist a challenge.

Pools of blood had dried around him, confirming her suspicion that this scene was already a few hours old.

'Keats, this is nothing like my case.'

As tragic and horrific as this was, it was clearly a traffic accident and had nothing to do with her. There was no doubt that to sustain those injuries, he'd been hit by something big or something fast or both.

'Why am I here?' she asked, wondering if the prank was still being played.

'Definitely nothing linked to yesterday,' he said, nodding to his team that the body could be moved. 'But I still thought you'd want to know.'

The team gently turned the man onto his back and as the

gasp left her mouth, she understood why Keats had made the call.

They had both met this particular man before.

EIGHTEEN

Stacey wished she could stop the trembling in her legs.

Having made the decision to come clean to the boss, she now wanted to get it over and done with as quickly as possible.

She'd crept past Devon sleeping on the sofa on her way out, taking care not to wake her. Stacey had no idea what time Devon had finally come home, and she hadn't ventured out of the bedroom to take a look.

She completely understood Devon's anger towards her. Had the situation been reversed, she would also have been deeply hurt. But now the cat was out of the bag with Devon, she had to find the courage to face everyone else. She wondered if she could have handled the situation any worse if she'd tried.

Of all the things Devon had said, the hardest to hear was that she had allowed Terence Birch to create this intimacy, this shared situation that excluded everyone else. Her embarrassment, shame and weakness had given him exactly what he'd wanted.

Telling Devon was unlikely to change his behaviour, but it did mean that she was no longer alone. However angry Devon was, Stacey knew that would give way to support and love.

That point had been proven ten minutes ago when her phone had tinged a text message while she'd been sitting in silence waiting for the boss to arrive.

The message had said:

I love you more than life. We'll talk tonight.

The words had been followed by a dozen heart emojis, and the message had strengthened her resolve to come clean with everyone, but her nerves were weakening now.

She'd hoped to catch the boss before the rest of the team arrived, but that plan was out the window, she realised as she heard Bryant's and Penn's voices outside the door.

'Hey, Stace,' they both said.

'You didn't bring the boss?' she asked.

'Nope. Text message to say she'll be—'

'You talking behind my back again, Bryant?' the boss asked, entering the room.

'Only good stuff, guv,' Bryant said, glancing over at the coffee machine.

Stacey was well ahead on that one. It was the first thing she'd done. The boss was going to need it.

Stacey stood and reached for the boss's favourite mug.

'Good call, Stace, and before we begin the business of the day, some news. Unconnected to our case, but Terence Birch was killed in a hit-and-run incident last night.'

Stacey felt the world come to a stop around her as the coffee pot fell from her hand.

NINETEEN

'What the hell was that all about?' Bryant muttered to Penn as they threw paper towels over the spilled liquid.

Stacey had been stricken with horror at the guv's announcement and then made a hoarse, mumbled request for a private word.

They all knew that Stacey had been acting strange for a while, but why would the death of a witness from a previous case have had such a profound effect on her?

As Penn stood to grab more kitchen towels, he stole a look into the Bowl.

Stacey was sitting down, and the tears were rolling over her cheeks.

The guv stood with her arms crossed, wearing an expression he hadn't seen in a while but knew very well.

Right on cue, her voice boomed out of the Bowl. 'Stacey, are you fucking kidding me?'

Bryant stood. 'Hey, Penn, wanna go get some breakfast?'

'Oh, hell yeah,' he said, grabbing the carrier bag full of coffee-soaked paper.

Bryant closed the squad-room door behind them.

Whatever was going on between the two of them did not need to be heard by him and Penn or the rest of the station.

TWENTY

Kim saw the tactful exit of her two sergeants, but it didn't defuse her temper enough not to repeat the question.

'No, really, Stace, are you kidding me?'

Her rage wasn't being eroded by the tears falling from the constable's eyes either.

'I couldn't tell you. I thought I could handle it. I thought he'd get bored. I thought I'd invited it.'

'That's an awful lot of thinking for someone who seems to have taken a stupid pill. What the hell were you really thinking? How could you not tell me? How could you not report it?'

'I don't know. I don't know,' Stacey said, burying her head in her hands.

'How long?' Kim asked.

'About two months.'

'So right after the investigation tied up?'

Stacey nodded. 'During it.'

'And you knew exactly what he'd done to other women and still took no action?'

Stacey sniffed and shook her head.

Kim couldn't allow the girl's misery to soften her anger. Her actions were unforgiveable. She was a police officer. She knew better.

'Did Devon know?'

'Not until recently.'

Kim guessed the immigration officer was currently feeling even more pissed off than she was.

'Jesus, Stace, anything could have happened, and we wouldn't have had a clue.'

'What can I do to make this right?'

'You can start by sending me everything you've uncovered about Birch.'

'Okay.'

'And then sort out the archiving. Go,' Kim said, needing Stacey not to be anywhere near her.

Archiving was done in a basement room when they had nothing else to do.

Kim let out a long sigh once the constable had left the room. Her anger hadn't diminished one bit, but her control of it had returned. Right now, she couldn't look at the girl without wanting to tear her head off, so it was best that she stayed out of sight.

'Damn it,' she roared, banging her first on the table. She wasn't going to allow herself to think about what Stacey had been through in the last couple of months. Her performance and weight loss were good indicators, but she wasn't there yet. She was still focussed on the deceit, the lack of trust and the poor judgement.

And now the man was dead.

An hour ago, this case had had nothing to do with her. Terence Birch had been no more than a witness. But now he was a dead man with a connection to one of her team.

If Stacey's name came up anywhere near this investigation, she'd be instantly suspended, possibly worse. If she even so much as got questioned in relation to the man's death, the details would be attached to every job or promotion she applied for.

Whatever her current feelings towards Stacey, she knew one thing for certain: she had to discover any links to her colleague before anyone else did.

TWENTY-ONE

'No way,' Bryant said once Kim had recounted Stacey's admission. 'I mean, it explains a lot, but bloody hell.'

'Is she okay?' Penn asked.

'Feel free to ask her once I'm out of the building, but right now my mind is on other things. And this stays with us, got it?'

They both nodded, and she hoped they asked her no more about it.

'Okay, back to Eric Gould. Penn, I'm not convinced that either Teresa's father or ex-boyfriend are in the clear. If we're right about when contact was made outside the gym, there's no way we can identify either of them from that footage, so for now focus on what dad and ex-boyfriend were doing yesterday morning.'

'On it, boss.'

'Also, see what they're like on social media. Could either of them be this Sentinel?'

'Okay.'

'And try and get details for the account. The Sentinel has to be registered somewhere. Chase Keats for toxicology results.

We need to know what Gould was injected with and how easy it is to get.'

'Yep.'

'And look at transportation. Our guy didn't teleport Eric Gould from the gym to the park. Check CCTV in the area.'

Penn did raise a questioning eyebrow at that request. Unless there was footage of their killer physically bundling Eric into a vehicle, they could be looking for anything bigger than a motorcycle.

'I know, but something might jump out. Finally, what's Eric's background? Find out if he's known to us. I know it's a lot of work, and how you choose to delegate these jobs is completely up to you.'

She was aware that many of the tasks she'd given out should have been completed yesterday, and that Penn was now bearing the brunt of Stacey's distraction.

'Got it, boss.'

'Just one sec, guv,' Bryant said. 'Are we not going to take a minute to talk about what Stacey's been going through?'

'You two can sit here and chat about it as much as you like. I've got a murderer to catch,' she said, reaching for her coat.

TWENTY-TWO

'You wanna come back up now?' Penn asked when Stacey answered the archive-room phone.

'Has she gone?'

'Yep.'

'On my way,' she said.

He got why the boss was angry. Keeping something as huge as this to yourself was a hell of a blunder. She would have taken the news badly both professionally and personally.

Professionally because no matter how much of a victim Stacey was in this situation, she hadn't reported it. She hadn't logged it with her boss or any of her colleagues. The timeline of her telling Devon was a question he had no business asking. The boss knew that if Stacey's name came anywhere near this, it would thrust her into the spotlight, and God forbid the press ever got hold of it.

On a personal level, the boss was protective of them all, but especially Stacey.

He'd seen the bond between them the moment he'd joined the team, and it had only grown and strengthened in the years since. He knew that the boss would feel betrayed by Stacey's actions.

None of those things were of interest to him when Stacey walked through the door.

'Hey, buddy, are you okay?'

'Don't be nice to me. I don't think I can take it right now,' she said, sliding into her seat.

'Can't even imagine what you've been going through.'

She held up her hand and shook her head. 'Penn, I just can't.'

'Got it, but I'm here if you need me.'

'I know,' she whispered, blinking back tears.

'Right, let's crack on and tackle our tasks, eh?' Penn said, prepared to give her every bit of space she needed.

TWENTY-THREE

'What part of I don't want to discuss it do you not understand?' Kim asked as Bryant headed towards the address she'd given him. He hadn't stuck around to chat with Penn, just followed her straight out the door to the car.

'The part where you don't want to discuss it,' Bryant answered. 'I mean, everything else aside, can you even imagine what she's been going through?'

And that was why she wasn't open to talking about it. Bryant would guide her towards empathy, and she wasn't there yet.

'Did you call Laura yet?' she asked.

'Wow, nice attempt at diversion and the answer is no. I haven't had the time.'

'The longer you leave it, the worse it's going to be. If you're as close as you think you are, she's going to know there was something off about your reaction last night despite the handshakes, hugs and congratulatory toast. Don't let that be the thing she remembers about this special time in her life.'

'Cheers, guv. I'll think about it. At the same time, I'll consider whether I should ask you a question when I already know the answer is no, because your mood would be way worse than it is.'

'Wow, way too early. What are you talking about?'

'Yeah, I thought not,' he said. 'Frost has published an article online. You're not going to like it, and why I'm telling you this while we're in the confined space of my car I have no idea.'

She groaned as she took out her phone. It took her less than three seconds to find it. She read it and then read it again.

She switched from the internet back to her contacts and scrolled to the appropriate number.

'What the fuck, Frost?' she bellowed when the reporter answered.

'Morning, Inspector. You're late. I expected your call five past the second the article went live.'

'I've got two issues here. First is that you're making the Sentinel sound like a bloody hero.'

'That's not true. I've condemned his actions.'

'While asking if he had a reason to take Eric Gould's life. You use words like "bold" and "confident", making the readers think he's out there doing good things. It's about the tone, Frost, and you bloody well know it.'

'Luckily my editor's opinion overrules yours, and he was happy with the tone. What's your other problem? I'm just dying to know.'

'Don't be coy. It doesn't suit you. You know that when you use words like "lacklustre" and "distracted" in relation to the police investigation, you're not only going to hit a nerve but also diminish the public's confidence in us.'

'It's my objective observation. You should be thanking me that I didn't detail just how you found out about the disruption at the crime scene. When were you going to turn up if I hadn't called you?'

'Frost, you—'

'No, Stone, you should have been all over that. You had the

victim's name, and you didn't immediately check to see if anyone was talking about him. I was reading the post two minutes after the Sentinel had written it, and you should have been too. I'm interested to know why you weren't. Someone in your team is—'

'Shut it. I want you to take down the article and—'

'Not a chance. There's nothing in that article that isn't the truth, and what's more you know I'm right.'

'That damn woman,' Kim cried as the line went dead.

'That's a fiver I'm getting from Penn. We spotted the article in the canteen while you and Stacey were having your one to one.'

'You were betting on my reaction?'

'Ha, not your reaction. We both know you well enough for that. We bet on how long it would take you to call her and chew her ass. I won.'

In spite of herself, she chuckled. She had no idea if he was telling the truth, but it had eased some of the tension from her body.

'We're never going to control her, guv. Her own agenda comes before anything else. Best spend our time on something we can affect.'

He had a point. She unlocked her phone and scrolled to the name 'Vikram Shah'.

'Hey, Vik,' she said when he answered. The two of them had partnered up in their uniform days before she'd applied to CID and he'd moved to Traffic.

'Yo, stranger.'

'Just calling about that hit and run in Gornal last night. Who's heading it?'

'That would be me. What's your interest?' he asked, avoiding any small talk. It was one of the reasons they'd got on. Neither of them had felt compelled to fill the silences that inevitably occurred during a twelve-hour night shift.

'He was a witness on a recent case,' she said, not yet lying. 'We got our guy but just making sure there are no loose ends.'

'Got you. You absolutely sure you got the right guy?'

Her stomach turned. 'Yeah, full confession, but you know how I feel about coincidence. This guy's accident coming just after...'

'Yeah, a bit premature there, Inspector. We're definitely not ready to rule it an accident yet. We've got conflicting witness reports.'

She said nothing, hoping for more.

Nothing more came, but he'd said enough to tell her this wouldn't be going away as quickly as she'd hoped.

'Okay, thanks for that, Vik. Any chance of an update?'

Hesitation. 'Not sure how tight you want to sew up this previous case but sure, why not.'

She thanked him and ended the call right as Bryant pulled up at the address.

'Err... where are we?' he asked, turning off the engine.

'At the home of Terence Birch. Wanna take a look around?'

'I go where you go,' he said as they both got out of the car.

The street in Coombs Wood was quiet, and she was pretty sure no one saw her as she nudged her foot against the front door. It didn't budge.

Bryant said nothing as she headed to the back of the house.

A quick appraisal told her two things: there were no open windows, and the back door lock wouldn't be too hard to jimmy open if she wanted to.

She thought for a moment before turning to her colleague. 'Bryant, I feel that I may be about to make some bad decisions. You might want to go wait for me in the car.'

He snorted. 'And where's the fun in that?'

She took her credit card from her phone case. If luck was on her side, the latch would be facing her way.

She slid the edge of the card between the door and the

strike plate. Once the corner was in there, she straightened the card so that it was perpendicular to the door and the entire edge of the card was between the door and the strike plate. She bent the card towards the doorknob and wiggled it back and forth until she heard the tell-tale click.

The door sprang open, and straight away Kim detected a stale, musty odour.

It was nothing as insidious as a dead body, but it was unpleasant just the same. She guessed if you lived in it, you didn't notice it so much.

She stepped inside the kitchen, which on the face of it wasn't a shit tip.

Bryant followed her in and said nothing as he closed the door behind him.

She moved through the house. It wasn't a huge space. The stale smell followed her.

She poked her head into each room as she passed, not quite sure what she was looking for but feeling sure she'd know if she found it.

She reached the foot of the stairs by the front door. There were bits of food and fluff gathered in every corner throughout. As she looked closer, she saw everything was coated in a millimetre of dust. That was most likely the cause of the smell. Although the house was being kept tidy, it wasn't actually being cleaned. She recalled Stacey saying something about the loss of his mother when she'd interviewed him and wondered if that was the reason why. It was hard to devote time to keeping a place show-home ready when you were on your own.

The first upstairs door she opened was the bathroom. Nothing offensive jumped out at her. It was dated but reasonably clean.

Next was the box room, which was filled with piles of women's clothes, which she guessed had belonged to his late mother.

The next room was the biggest room and looked out onto the road. It was furnished with a king-size bed, one bedside cabinet and a built-in double wardrobe.

The smell of neglect continued to follow her, even as she opened the wardrobe doors and confirmed that this was where Terence Birch had slept. He'd paid no more attention to this space than anywhere else.

Just one more room to check before taking a closer look in one or two drawers.

She pushed open the door of the final bedroom and stopped dead.

Bryant looked into the room over the top of her head. 'Jeeesus,' he said, before letting out a low whistle.

The sickness in her stomach was immediate and almost overwhelming.

She swallowed it down as she approached the largest wall in the room.

Stacey's image met her from a hundred spots. Photos of her entering her flat, coming out, getting off the bus, sitting in a café doing something on her phone, walking round a supermarket. The photos varied in size and shape. The thinner ones were likely where he'd had to cut Devon out of the picture. Some were small and some had been blown up to A4 size.

Pinned within and around were receipts, phone bills, leaflets, wrappers; some that had been scrunched and then flattened out.

The nausea wasn't helped by the realisation that he'd been going through Stacey's rubbish.

'He's been this fucking close to her,' Kim snarled, approaching the wall.

Before she could stop herself, she started tearing at the photos, pulling them off the wall, ripping Stacey's face from what had been his viewing gallery.

'Hey, hey, hey,' Bryant said, grabbing her arm. 'That's more than looking, guv, that's tampering, which is a whole worse pile of shit to land yourself in.'

'Aaargh,' she growled, stepping back. 'Fuck's sake.'

If Birch had been in front of her, she'd be digging her fingernails into his face. How dare he do this to one of her team!

Seeing this wall of obsession, she was glad he was dead, and she made no apology for that thought.

She stared at the ripped photographs on the floor. More than anything she wanted to gather every piece of paper that linked this man to Stacey so that her name came nowhere near the investigation into his death. She wanted to erase the girl's name from the psycho's life to protect her. But that meant doing something she'd never done before.

'Bryant...'

'You can't, guv. You know that.'

Her conscience had spoken. But still...

'Guv, go to the car,' he said, throwing her the keys. 'I'll put these back up.'

She hesitated but knew she had no choice.

She headed down the stairs without needing to check anywhere else. Her worst fears had been realised, and Stacey was front and centre.

She got into the car and sighed, wondering how well she'd be able to protect Stacey once her name was plastered all over the press in connection with a dead man.

The ringing of her phone startled her from her thoughts. She experienced that immediate stab of relief when the caller was anyone other than Keats.

'Go ahead, Penn.'

'Got him, boss.'

'Who?' she asked, giving her brain time to catch up.

'The Sentinel. Got his address. Managed to get a direct chat with a Twitter—'

'Where are we going?' she interrupted, not needing the details.

'It's thirty-two Sandy Lane, Wollescote.'

'Got it,' she said, ending the call as Bryant got in the car.

'Sandy Lane, Wollescote,' she repeated to her colleague. 'We have the address for the Sentinel.'

'That was quick,' he said as he put the details into the satnav to find the quickest route.

She took one look back at the house.

'They're coming, aren't they?' she asked, knowing the traffic investigation team would have to search Birch's house for clues.

'Oh yeah.'

'What the hell are we going to do?' she asked, more of herself than him.

'We'll cross that bridge when we come to it,' he said, pulling the car away from the kerb.

TWENTY-FOUR

The bad feeling already forming in Kim's stomach worsened as Bryant pulled up outside a row of bungalows at the end of a road in Wollescote.

The one they wanted was last but one. A walking frame that doubled as a seat was beside the front door with a carrier bag attached.

As they got out of the car, a man in his seventies appeared and locked the door behind him.

It was clear that this man was not the Sentinel.

'Excuse me, may we have a word?' Kim asked, intercepting him at the end of the path.

'Of course, young lady, but I ain't buying anything.'

'We're not selling. Can you tell us your name?'

'Hey, hang on a minute. You came to me. What's this about? I've been told by the folks at Age Concern not to give out any personal information. Just one snippet and the crooks can do all sorts.'

They both held up their IDs. 'It's okay, we're the police.'

'Not sure that makes you any better to be honest. You ain't all clean.'

Kim was saddened by his view but couldn't argue against it. Every cart had bad apples, and the police force was no exception.

'Sir, we think—'

'Donald,' he said, opening up his frame and taking a seat. 'Don to such a pretty lady as yourself, and the last name is Beattie, but you ain't getting my bank details. I only give them out to the Nigerian princes that email me about my inheritance.'

'Don, you don't really—'

'Oh, that one always gets folks going,' he said with a sparkle in his eye. 'Age Concern keep us updated on the latest scams, which is a shame cos I wouldn't mind the eighty million pounds the one guy was promising me.'

Kim was beginning to learn that Don was quite the handful, but he'd already answered what would have been her next question.

'So you do have internet access?'

'Yeah, my daughter insisted on getting the interweb fitted. Came cheap with some telly channels or something. To be honest, I reckon she only wanted it in there to check I wasn't inviting ladies round after her mum died. Said something about having different programmes to watch, but I think it's a ruse for her to spy on me.' He lowered his voice. 'And I think I've got her sussed. Sometimes the green light on the machine flashes and that's when she's watching me from up in York. But she ain't gonna catch me doing anything with ladies in my house.' He paused. 'I always go to theirs.'

He roared with laughter, and Kim couldn't help but laugh with him. It was the first genuine smile she'd had all day.

'Talking about your interweb, has anyone asked you for any numbers?'

'What kind of numbers and where are they?' he asked.

That was a solid no then.

'And you've had no overnight guests or visitors?'

He eyed her suspiciously. 'You sure my daughter didn't send you?'

She smiled. 'Don't know your daughter, Don. Just need to make sure your interweb hasn't been tampered with.'

He shook his head. 'Ain't nobody touched it. My daughter would have my guts for garters if I did anything to it. I was hoping the fecker the other week had taken it, but—'

'What's that now, Don?' Kim asked.

'I was broken into last month. Weirdest thing. Burglar didn't take a thing. I was at the old folk's tea dance. I only really knew cos my lock was a bit messed up. Must have realised I didn't have much to take.'

Or he got exactly what he came for, Kim thought.

'What did the police say?' Bryant asked.

'Well, they said that due to the severity of the incident, they were putting all their best people on it. Not sure what they were going to charge him with, but perhaps they were gonna make him apologise.'

'You don't seem very bothered by it,' Kim observed.

'I wasn't hurt, I wasn't even home, and nothing was taken. My daughter got a bit worked up about it, but I've been dining out on the story for weeks, especially with the ladies.'

The devilish wink he gave her made her think he must be the life and soul of the club he frequented.

Kim had the brief thought that if she'd ever had a granddad, she would have liked him to be like Don.

'And has there been anything else to cause you—'

She stopped speaking as her phone rang.

Her heart skipped a beat when she saw the name.

She gave Bryant the nod and moved away while her colleague thanked the man for his time.

She gathered all her hope to pray that Keats was calling her with the toxicology reports.

'Stone,' she answered.

'Belle Vale.'

'Another one?'

'This one's worse.'

'He's dead?' she asked.

'Not yet – paramedics are working on him now.'

'Worse how?'

'You'll see for yourself when you get here,' he said before ending the call.

TWENTY-FIVE

'What the hell is fentanyl?' Stacey asked as Penn typed it into Google.

The toxicology reports had literally just landed in his inbox. Moira at the lab had rushed it through cos she had a thing for curly hair, she'd said.

The email had distracted him from being able to prove for certain where both Rufus Fox and Curtis Jones had been at 8 a.m. yesterday morning.

Rufus claimed to have arrived at the veterinary practice early to prepare for a major surgery on a Doberman. Unfortunately, none of the nurses could verify the alibi, as they hadn't arrived until just before 9 a.m.

Curtis claimed to have been out jogging until 7.45 a.m. when he'd returned home to shower and prepare for work, even though his shift hadn't started until midday. Unfortunately, Curtis didn't use anything like a Fitbit that would have enabled them to track his route. Unable to prove them right or wrong, he was happy to pass that information back to the boss later and move on to trying to discover the origin of the drug used to kill the man.

He knew he'd heard the name fentanyl but normally in connection with American politics.

He read aloud from the screen so that Stacey was learning at the same time he was.

"'Fentanyl's growth from its original design as an effective surgical pain-management tool to a leading cause of overdose death has happened quickly. It's a synthetic opioid created in laboratories in the 1960s as a potent pain reliever for very specific circumstances. It's fifty times more potent than heroin"... Jesus,' he said and whistled. 'The last bit was from me.'

'Keep reading to yourself, then give me the edited version,' Stacey instructed.

He did as she asked and learned it was good for surgery – injectable for use in operating theatres.

He skimmed the information about it being easy to synthesise from a couple of precursor molecules available from Pakistan, India or China. But his attention was fully restored on learning it was simple to order over the dark web and easy to ship due to its potency. Very small amounts could go a long way. Just two milligrams could be fatal depending on a person's body size, tolerance and usage. The onset of action could be as little as sixty seconds, and it had a duration of thirty to sixty minutes.

The most common drugs substituted with fentanyl were oxycodone or Xanax tablets, and a small side article informed Penn that San Francisco appeared to be drowning in the stuff.

'Not a highly volatile compound so doesn't turn to vapour,' he read, meaning that although Keats had taken every precaution at the post-mortem of Eric Gould, they had all been safe.

Reading on, he could easily understand how Keats had made the mistake of presuming the man dead. The main signs of a fentanyl overdose included severe respiratory depression, extreme decrease in the level of consciousness, floppy arms and legs, inability to speak, unresponsiveness. There had been more than one reported case where the victims had been pronounced dead due to their limp bodies and almost undetectable pulse.

His thoughts turned back to Rufus Fox and Curtis Jones. A quick internet search told him that most hospitals stocked fentanyl. A further search confirmed that it was also used by most vets.

As hard as he'd tried, he was still unable to rule out Teresa's father or her ex-boyfriend.

TWENTY-SIX

Belle Vale was the name of a road and area in Cradley, Halesowen and had once been called Cradley's beautiful valley. Evidence of that plaudit had long since been destroyed by the foundries and forges that had replaced the many watermills along the stream that led into the River Stour.

Bryant headed past Clancey Way, a development of more than eighty homes built on the site of G. Clancey's foundry over ten years earlier, and joined the other vehicles parked in the Corngreaves Nature Reserve car park.

Kim sprinted down the path towards the River Stour and the men in high-vis jackets, but Keats emerged from the pack shaking his head.

'He's gone. Lost him a few minutes ago.'

'Damn it,' Kim said, stepping around one of the paramedics collecting together his equipment.

The crime scene was an absolute mess with equipment bags, wrappers, footprints, knee marks in the ground. Again, Mitch was going to get nothing from this chaos.

'Couldn't save him even though we knew what he'd been

injected with?' she asked, assuming he'd received the same email from the toxicology lab she'd seen.

'Fentanyl is an opioid. It binds to and activates opioid receptors on cells located in the brain, spinal cord and other organs in the body. There are opioid antagonists like naloxone which, if used quickly, can reverse an opioid overdose. It's unlikely that even a couple of doses would have saved our victim even if the paramedics had had it on board. This isn't an accidental overdose. This dosage is being administered to kill. The quantity detected in Eric Gould's system would likely have killed an army.'

She raised an eyebrow.

'Okay, not quite, but definitely between five and ten men.'

She turned away and took a good look at the victim while Keats completed the handover with the paramedics.

She guessed the man to be early thirties and around two stone overweight. He wore navy jogging bottoms that had a small hole at the knee. His trainers were a decent name but well worn. The paramedics had pulled his plain red tee shirt back down once they were done, and she could see his stomach straining against the fabric.

Her gaze travelled up to the rugged skin on his cheeks that looked like old acne scarring. His lips were slightly parted to reveal a couple of missing lower teeth. His brown hair was untidy and long.

This man bore no resemblance to the honed perfection of their first victim.

Bryant had taken a quick look before heading over to two runners in the company of a constable. He'd guessed they were the ones who'd found the victim.

Keats approached once more as the paramedics headed back up to the car park.

She gave him no chance to speak. 'Please tell me you have—'

'Jimmy,' he called, beckoning over his assistant.

'Boss?'

'Show the inspector the photos.'

Jimmy took out his phone and scrolled to the first one. She moved from frame to frame. There were seven photos, all from different angles, trying to get a decent picture around the paramedics.

She forced down her frustration at not seeing the scene before it got tampered with. Of course the paramedics had no choice but to try and save the man's life.

She flicked back to the first photo. 'Had they moved him at all in this one?'

Jimmy shook his head. 'The paramedics actually took that picture before they started work on him.'

She disregarded the other photos and focussed on this one. It was the only one that mattered.

'Did they touch him?' she asked, nodding towards the runners.

'No,' Keats answered.

So this photo was the closest to how the killer had left his victim.

The image showed the man lying on his left side. His head was pushed down into the ground. The left arm had been raised in an arc that brushed the side of his head, and the right arm had been stretched out to meet it, forming a perfect circle. His left leg was straight, but his right was positioned as though he was about to kick something.

She turned the phone a few times to try and get a clearer picture.

'You told me this one was worse,' Kim said.

'It is. You see that perfect circle formed by the arms?'

'Yeah.'

'Try and replicate it. It's not possible.'

She tried to do it as Bryant headed back towards her with a questioning expression on his face.

She thought she had it pretty close.

'Not really,' Keats said, pointing at the photo.

The circle made by the arms on the photo was much smoother and appeared much larger.

'No,' she said, hoping her suspicions were wrong.

'Oh yes. Two dislocated shoulders and a hammer to the elbows.'

'While he was still alive?'

'Yes.'

'Bloody hell,' she said, trying to imagine suffering that level of pain while being unable to defend yourself or even cry out.

Kim instructed Jimmy to send the photos to her and the team, then took a final look at the battered body on the ground and wondered what the hell they were dealing with.

TWENTY-SEVEN

Stacey couldn't remember any time in her life when she hadn't known what to feel.

Her emotions felt as though they'd gone a full ten rounds with Tyson. Her brain and heart weren't working together, and although the boss had told her that Terence Birch was dead, her system hadn't yet computed that her ordeal was over.

It was hard to recall a time when the fear hadn't lived somewhere within her, when she hadn't feared looking out the window or getting on the bus. When she hadn't been terrified to scroll through Facebook or answer her phone. They all seemed like inconsequential actions that shouldn't have provoked deep anxiety. It was hard to believe that she was free of the terror that had been attached to her for months.

And what would happen when her brain and heart did start working together to process the information he was dead? Would it be a slow, long exhalation, like letting down a bouncy castle? Would her emotional state decompress gradually, or would it be like using a pin to pop a balloon and suddenly she'd jump up and dance with joy? Would she really be able to take so much pleasure from a man's death?

She'd texted the news to Devon. She'd offered no explanation or details, and Devon hadn't asked for any. She'd simply replied with:

Thank God

Followed by a couple of praying-hands emojis.

A second text had followed with some kisses. Like an afterthought.

Another anxiety was growing within her. Just how much damage had she done to her relationships? In addition to Devon's anger, the boss hadn't yet communicated with her once. Penn's phone was the hotline, the last call informing him that they had a second victim. Normally those calls would have come to her, but apparently the boss couldn't even stand to hear her voice.

'Well, that's that then,' Penn said, ending the call from Lloyd House. She knew he'd been speaking with tech support. Somewhere within West Mids Police HQ were people dedicated to the relationship between the police and social-media platforms. They knew the best way to get an answer that didn't include the *contact us* options where you might get a standard answer within forty-eight hours.

'No go?' Stacey asked.

'Not a chance. That Twitter account is registered to Don Beattie at that IP address, and seeing as Don Beattie does indeed have that IP address, they're happy that no rules have been broken and have no plans to shut down the Sentinel's account.'

'But the boss said there's no way that the man who lives there is our guy.'

'Tell that to Elon and his mates. Account stays active.'

Penn drummed his fingers on the desk. 'Stace, how hard is it to try and track down where he's diverting out of that IP address?'

'Depends on the proxy server and the VPN and how he's obscuring it.'

'Hmm... that's what I thought you were gonna say but in a language I can't understand.'

'Yeah, it's— Ooh, hang on,' she said as something flashed on her toolbar.

She maximised the tab which she'd kept open on the Sentinel's Twitter account. She wasn't going to miss it again.

She'd already been dismayed to see that his followers had almost doubled overnight.

She read the tweets aloud as they appeared.

'"Hello, fellow watchers. You'll be pleased to know that once again, justice has been done. The bad man met his end in Belle Vale and will do no further harm. His name was Paul Brooks and he doesn't deserve an ounce..."'

'Oh shit, he's named him,' Stacey said while waiting for the next tweet.

'The boss won't even have spoken to the family,' Penn said, reaching for the phone.

Stacey returned her attention to the screen.

'"... of your sympathy. My sources tell me that forensics will be a bust so the police are going to be looking for witnesses and passers-by. Feel free to offer duff info just to make the game interesting 2/6."'

'Oh shit,' Stacey said again, realising what he was trying to do. Not content with causing havoc at the crime scene itself, he was now encouraging people to offer information they didn't have. He knew they'd never be able to tell the difference between bogus or genuine tips until they'd checked them out, using up valuable resources and wasting massive amounts of time.

'Penn, I think you'd best pass this to the boss as well.'

TWENTY-EIGHT

'Bastard,' Kim said after ending the call from Penn.

'Narrow it down,' Bryant said, heading towards Hollytree and Paul Brooks's address.

'The Sentinel. He's shared the name of the victim before we've had a chance to inform a single family member, and he's encouraging false leads.'

Kim rubbed at her temple. This was turning into a very long day. Any tips called into the station now would likely be useless.

They pulled up beside a squad car. Two constables were looking through the window of the flat.

'See anything you like, guys?' she asked as Bryant went to talk to the woman watching proceedings from over the road with a cigarette in her hand.

'No answer, marm. Lives alone and no spare key, according to the neighbour. Permission to use the big key?'

'Yep, get her open.'

Kim realised that giving authorisation was pretty rich coming from her after her own performance earlier at Terence Birch's.

Two minutes later, she was stepping over the threshold of Paul Brooks's home. She found herself pleasantly surprised by the sweet floral aroma that greeted her.

She stood in the hallway for just a second, waiting to see if any household pets came forward.

There was nothing so she moved further into the property.

Being a ground-floor maisonette, the front of the building was made darker by the covered walkway that fronted the row of six properties, rendering the kitchen gloomy even on a bright day.

It was barely three o clock, and the light would need to be on to cook a meal.

Despite the gloom, the space was reasonably well taken care of.

She moved through to the lounge, which was a similar picture. While dated, the furnishings were clean and tidy. The television was small but up to date.

His appearance at the crime scene had given her the impression of a slovenly man, but that didn't seem to be the case.

She headed upstairs and entered the first bedroom on the left. It was the smaller room and held only a couple of wardrobes.

She approached and opened the first.

'Hmm...' she said to herself, surprised to see his clothing washed, ironed, sorted and hung. There were no expensive designer labels, but all the items appeared to be in better condition than the ones he'd been wearing. A curious observation that probably meant nothing.

'No family that the neighbour knows about,' Bryant said, startling her.

She waited for more.

'He lived here when she moved in five years ago. Not really

seen any visitors. Says he's been on benefits for years. Not a lot else, but she didn't talk to him if she could avoid it.'

'Why's that?' Kim asked, moving to the master bedroom.

'He gave her the creeps.'

'Is that it?'

Bryant nodded.

At the minute, Paul Brooks appeared to have been one of life's invisibles. He made no impact at work as he had no job, and had no great effect on his neighbours either. He collected his money, kept his home clean and was just treading water through life. Or he had been until someone else had had other ideas.

Like the other room, his bedroom was tidy with an old-fashioned eiderdown on top of the double bed.

A television occupied the opposite wall with more wardrobes either side of it and three drawers beneath.

The man sure liked his clothes, Kim thought as she pulled open the wardrobe door.

'Oh,' she said as she found herself looking at shelves that weren't filled with clothes.

'Same this side,' Bryant said, opening the other door.

Both wardrobes were filled top to bottom with videos and DVDs.

Kim's gaze fell on some of the titles as Bryant opened the drawers beneath the TV. It had to be one of the biggest collections of pornographic material she'd ever seen.

'Oh well, each to their—' She stopped speaking as her gaze continued across the titles. Phrases like 'She had it coming' and 'Let her have it' were some of the tamer ones, but others were full-on revolting.

'Kick her in the tits,' Bryant said disgustedly.

'Looks like this guy liked his porn with a good measure of violence thrown in,' Kim observed.

'Against women,' Bryant added as her phone began to ring.

It was the station main number.

'Stone,' she answered.

'I've got a couple of guys here,' Jack, the duty sergeant, said.

'Get a couple more and you got yourself a boy band.'

'They both want to talk to you, and it's getting a bit busy in here.'

'Sudden crime wave, Jack?'

'Nah, sexual assault just come in. So if you could see your way to emptying my reception area, I'd appreciate it.'

'You sure they both want me?' she asked.

'Oh yeah, the one guy is saying he murdered someone, and the other guy says he knows both of the men who died. Definitely sounds like they want you.'

'On my way,' she said, heading for the door.

TWENTY-NINE

Kim took the time to check the news headlines on the way back to the station, in lieu of checking the PNC once she was back in her office, to see if there had been any updates about Terence Birch.

The nagging voice in her head urged her to contact Vik, but she wasn't sure how to do it without raising suspicion.

Ah, sod it, she thought as she took out her phone. Her need to know by far trumped her fears of how it might look to her old colleague.

He answered on the second ring.

'You again,' he said. She couldn't tell if his voice had a touch of humour or an edge of irritation. 'You always were like a dog with a bone.'

'Yeah, just at a loose end and wondered if you'd found anything at his home I should know about?'

'Like what?'

Jeez, he wasn't making this easy for her.

'I dunno. Just anything out of the—'

'I'm just messing with you. I get it. Sometimes we get

attached to witnesses during big cases. I get your concern, and you know we're going to do everything we can to find whoever did this. We're actually on our way over to his place right now,' he said, and Kim's heart skipped a beat. 'I'll give you a call if there's anything to report.'

'Cheers, Vik,' she said, knowing their next conversation was going to be very different.

'Shit is about to get real,' Kim said as Bryant pulled into the station car park.

'As we knew,' Bryant said quietly.

They got out of the car, and although Kim had said little to Bryant about the two men awaiting them, she was already pretty sure these were the first of many false leads that would be coming their way thanks to the Sentinel. She'd deal with them swiftly and get back to the investigation.

'Go check in with the others while I get rid of these time-wasters,' she instructed as they entered the building.

'Got it, guv,' he said, key coding himself through the door.

She approached Jack's glass partition. 'Okay, which one killed someone?' she asked, taking a look at the two men who sat with two spare seats between them.

The man on the left was in his early twenties, wearing jeans and a blue tee shirt. A sports jacket lay on the seat beside him. His curly black hair brushed the top of his collar. He was leaning forward with his arms resting on his knees.

The man on the right wore black trousers and a white shirt and hadn't looked up from the book he was reading.

'Guy on the left,' Jack said, pointing with his pen. 'Name's Philip Drury.'

'Thanks,' she said, heading over and standing between the two of them.

'Mr Drury?'

Both men looked up, and the man on the left nodded. She turned to the other one. 'I'll just be a minute.'

'Take your time. I've just got to the good bit.'

He held up a book entitled *The Adventure of English: The Biography of a Language*.

Kim wondered what the good bit was actually going to be.

She said nothing and motioned for Drury to follow her through the locked doors.

She passed interview room one which was engaged – with the sexual assault, Kim guessed. She guided Drury into interview room two, and indicated for him to take a seat as she did the same.

She wondered how much patience she was going to be able to muster for these two timewasters. After her early morning call, it was already feeling like a very long day.

'So, Mr Drury, there's something you'd like to share with us?'

'A-am I going to lose my job?'

Fair play to him. He was really taking on the part. Beads of sweat were forming on his brow, and he was wringing his own hands like a dish cloth.

'My colleague out there tells me you killed a man,' she said, trying to keep the boredom out of her voice.

'I d-didn't mean to. It happened so quickly.'

Speed wasn't a factor she'd considered. Had he been running, tripped over and accidentally injected someone with a lethal dose of fentanyl on two separate occasions?

Suddenly the man burst into tears and buried his face in his hands. 'I'm going to lose everything; my girlfriend, my job.' He raised his head, his face contorted with fear. 'Will I go to prison?'

He was either an Oscar winner or genuine, Kim thought, sitting forward in her chair.

'That depends, Mr Drury. What exactly did you do?'

'I hit him with my van. The man on Gornal Road. It was me that killed him.'

Kim couldn't help the quick surge of elation that surged through her as she headed for the door.

THIRTY

'Forget something, Bryant?' Penn asked as he entered the squad room. Alone.

'Damn, I knew I'd left something at the crime scene,' he said, removing his jacket. 'Talking of which, did you get the photos the guv sent?'

'Just printing them now.'

'Got some updates on Eric and Paul for the boss,' Stacey said as Penn retrieved his sheets from the printer.

'Got a bit of a traffic jam downstairs,' Bryant said, noting the tension in Stacey's face. 'She'll be up once she's sent a couple of timewasters on their way.'

She visibly deflated with relief, giving him a clear answer on how she was dealing with the tension between the two of them.

He wasn't sure that he and Penn were dealing with it any better. The normal axis on which their team dynamic relied was off kilter. The rift between his boss and Stacey affected him more than if it was with himself. He'd watched the bond grow between them, and it had been based on trust and respect. One of those had been totally obliterated.

He was in agreement with the guv that Stacey had dropped

the ball a few times, but if you weighed her contribution to the team over the years, she had credit in abundance. There had been cases that would never have been solved had it not been for the constable's tenacity and skill in data mining. Her gut instinct was pretty reliable too.

He knew that Stacey put in so much effort not only because of her faultless work ethic but to maintain the boss's approval. She enjoyed being MVP, and she deserved the accolade because she often *was* the most valuable player on the pitch. The guv's faith in her only gave her more confidence and enthusiasm to do her job even better.

Being sent to Siberia would be a heavy cross for her to bear, and knowing the guv as he did, he couldn't see her warming up any time soon.

He couldn't solve it, so damage limitation was the best he could bring to this particular party.

He wheeled his chair across the office and leaned on the desk right next to her. 'You okay?'

She turned and nodded.

'Anything I can do to help?'

She shook her head.

He touched her arm lightly. 'We care about you. All of us. If there's anything—'

'Bryant, come and take a look at this,' Penn said, looking up. 'Oh, sorry.'

As ever when concentrating, Penn had no clue as to what was going on around him.

Bryant rolled his eyes, wheeled back his chair and went to stand behind the sergeant. His colleague was unique, and they were never going to change him.

'These photos. I was thinking dance for Eric and football for Paul, but I think we're looking at something else.'

'Go on,' Bryant said, looking from one photo to the other.

'I think they're letters.'

'Letters?' Bryant and Stacey asked together.

'I'm probably completely wrong but I think Eric was posed as an A and Paul was posed as an R.'

Bryant frowned. 'I can kinda see what you mean, but I don't think—'

'Not so fast,' Stacey interrupted. 'With what I've just discovered on the PNC, that would make perfect sense.'

THIRTY-ONE

'That's him,' Kim said, bumping into Bryant as she stepped out into the corridor.

Her colleague was holding a steaming cup, which she took gratefully, feeling as though she'd been playing a game of caffeine catch-up all day.

'Who?' Bryant asked.

'The man who killed Terence Birch.'

She took a sip of the coffee and handed it back to him to take out her phone.

'Hey, Vik,' she said, when the man answered.

'Bloody hell, Stone. Any more calls and I'm going to have to explain you to my wife.'

'I've got your man, Vik. Here at the station. Walked straight in and admitted everything.'

'You're joking?'

'Nope. I'll even put a bow on him if you like.'

Kim knew she shouldn't be so flippant, but the relief was flooding through her. She just hoped she'd got to him in time.

'Okay, keep him warm. We're on our way. Nothing to see here anyway.'

'Where?' she asked as her blood ran cold. She'd been hoping to catch him before they searched.

'Birch's address. All clear.'

'Oh, o-okay, good to know. See you shortly,' she said before ending the call.

She fixed her gaze on her colleague. 'They searched his house and found nothing at all.'

He shrugged. 'Weird. Must not have been looking hard enough.'

'Bryant...' she said as he handed her coffee back to her.

'Look lively, guv, you've got another timewaster to interview and we're making good progress upstairs.'

He turned and walked away, ending the conversation.

THIRTY-TWO

'Okay, sorry about the wait,' Kim said as the second man took a seat across the table in the meeting room. Interview room one was still busy with the sexual assault victim, and Philip Drury was waiting nervously for Vik in interview room two.

'No probs. I'm sure you're pretty busy. Let me introduce myself: Ryan West, English teacher.'

'My colleague at the front desk said you know both of our victims?'

Damn the Sentinel for revealing their second victim's name so soon.

He nodded, and she took a good look at him. He was around five feet eleven with muscles that didn't strain at his shirt but hinted at their presence. His dark brown hair was cut shorter on the sides but with more volume on the top. He sported a full beard, and a couple of faint lines visible at the corners of his eyes when he smiled put him in his mid-thirties. He was good-looking and well presented and wasn't showing any signs of being a typical crackpot. For now she'd give him the benefit of the doubt, while watching closely to see if he was here to take the piss and try to send her on a wild goose chase.

'Ah, well, know is a bit of a stretch and use of the present tense is not totally accurate either.'

'Okay,' she said, feeling the benefit of her doubt starting to slip away.

'Sorry. I'll try and explain. I know what they have in common.'

'Go on,' Kim said, feeling the doubt grow stronger. She couldn't imagine any situation where these two men had anything in common. Eric was employed, fit, engaged, health conscious and organised. Paul was none of those things.

'I thought I recognised the name of the first victim, but I couldn't place it initially. Seeing the second name on social media today blew away the cobwebs and I came straight here.'

Kim waited.

'I knew them both at Welton. They were part of a bigger group.'

'Ahh,' Kim said, needing no further explanation.

To use its full name, Welton Hall was a young offenders institution situated on the outskirts of Wednesbury.

It had once been a borstal, if she remembered correctly, and had been a threat levelled at her many times during her years in care. 'Do that again and you'll be sent to Welton' were words heard by every kid that had spent time at Fairview Children's Home. The words alone had incited a fear so strong that many of the kids wet the bed for days afterwards.

It was only much later that Kim had understood the emptiness of the threat. Welton had been for kids aged fifteen upwards who'd committed crimes. Teens who weren't old enough for prison but too old for secure training centres.

'And you were there as...?'

'A teacher. First job out of university. Idealistic, wanting to break the cycle, at the very least help these kids to understand that the terms would of, could of, should of don't actually exist.'

Kim couldn't help the smile that formed. Oh yes, he was an English teacher all right.

'So you planned to save them with superior sentence structure?'

'Very clever, Inspector. I saw what you did there. Nice bit of alliteration, and yes, kind of. I suppose it's all about the basics, isn't it? There are few jobs that don't need people to read and write at a basic level. Did you know fifty per cent of fifteen- to seventeen-year-olds have numeracy and literacy levels of seven- to eleven-year-olds? I wanted to change those numbers.'

'Very altruistic of you, but I'm seeing regret in your face, so I'm guessing your sensibilities were tested.'

'If you're asking how long until I lost my nerve, I can admit that it wasn't very long at all.'

'Wanna give me a rough number?'

'Seven months, two weeks and three days.'

'You know I'm going to ask why now.'

'Happy to share. There's a lot of lip service paid to the regime in a place like that. They stress the priority of time spent on education or in programmes to help offenders get a job or return to further education. The words look great on the literature or the website but are less impressive in practice. I know where the problem lies. The staff aren't really interested and neither are the offenders. To make a change, at least one of them has to give a shit. I couldn't handle the despondency. I went there full of energy and enthusiasm, but as the days and weeks passed, I could feel it ebbing away. I was twenty-two years old and didn't want to face my twenty-third birthday devoid of hope.'

'And was that the problem with all the kids? Were they all disengaged?' she asked, uncomfortable with the generalisation. She'd fought the stigma of being a 'care kid' all her life, and as was the case with any set of people, there were good and bad.

'Not all of them. There was the odd one who wanted to take advantage of every educational opportunity.'

'What about Eric and Paul? Did they want to do better?'

'Hell no. Those two were a pair of little shits.'

'You say they were part of a larger group?' Kim asked as a rock started to form in her stomach.

He scratched his head. 'Yeah, there was Eric, Paul, Leyton, Nathan, Dean and an older lad named Ian. I don't remember their last names, but that was the group I think.'

Kim had counted the names on her fingers. 'You're sure that's all of them?'

He studied her for a second then nodded.

Kim thought about the numbering on the tweets. It had nothing to do with the number or order of the messages. One of six. Two of six.

Their killer was giving them a progress report.

THIRTY-THREE

It was almost six when Kim escorted Ryan West to the front of the building.

He'd left her with his address and phone number and an offer to help further. She'd thanked him for his time, knowing that it was a link they would have found eventually, but now it was a line of enquiry they could pursue straight away.

Right now, she could think of nothing better than getting home, taking a red-hot shower and spending the night with her boy. Regular texts to and from Charlie throughout the day had reassured her that Barney hadn't suffered one bit in her absence. Just a quick briefing with her team and she'd call it a night.

She headed for the stairs, feeling lighter than when she'd come down them. Her ankles had been pulling the weight of getting Stacey's name away from Terence Birch. And somehow that had happened. She wasn't going to think about the shrine wall in his house too much. Ultimately, Vik and his team had entered the property of their victim and found nothing. She didn't know for sure how that had happened and she didn't want to. She suspected the photos had been creatively hidden, but the question would never leave her mouth. But now they had their man and Stacey was in the clear. The day was turning out better than she'd imagined.

'Hey, Vik,' she said, seeing the traffic officer at the bottom of the stairs. 'Hope you liked your present.' She was trying not to let her relief shine through. Her colleague was out of the crosshairs.

'Absolutely,' he said, smiling. 'And if you want to carry on and solve the whole thing for us, I'll book me and the missus a nice long weekend away.'

'What's left to do?' she asked, feeling the weights creep back towards her ankles.

'I told you there were conflicting witness reports, but there was one thing they all agreed on. That a car was speeding towards Terence Birch on the other side of the road, causing him to run forward into the path of Mr Drury's van.'

'Okay, and what was the conflict in the reports?'

'Whether the speeding car was light blue or silver, but Mr Drury has settled that for us.'

'And?'

'It was something small like a Clio or Focus, and it was definitely light blue.'

'Okay, Vik, thanks,' Kim said, holding on to the banister as she climbed the stairs.

She knew someone who drove a light-blue Ford Focus.

Stacey was right back at the centre of the crosshairs.

THIRTY-FOUR

'Okay, neither visitor was a timewaster and I stand corrected,' Kim said, entering the squad room. 'And before anyone consults the history books to see the last time I was wrong, it was some-time back in the nineties.'

She took the cup that Bryant had brought her and refilled it. 'For anyone who's interested, the first person I spoke to admitted that he was the man who killed Terence Birch. He has no known link to Birch, and it doesn't appear to have been intentional. Vik has spoken to him, but it appears another car was involved and may have been responsible for forcing Birch into the path of the oncoming van. More on that as it comes.'

From the corner of her eye, Kim saw Stacey's relieved expression turn pensive, and even though Kim still couldn't look at Stacey directly without the temperature of her blood rising, she wasn't prepared to offer the details of the car. Not until she'd done some digging herself.

'Second guy gave us a link between the two victims. Both spent time at Welton Hall.'

Kim readied herself for the surprised expressions and

excitement they got from making such a discovery. Neither came.

'We already got that, boss,' Penn offered, nodding towards Stacey, who took over the narrative.

'According to the PNC, our first guy, Eric Gould, was convicted of actual bodily harm when he was fifteen. Made quite a mess of his victim. Broken nose, split lip, two front teeth knocked out and bruising all over the body.'

'Who was his victim?' Kim asked.

'Cheryl Gordon, his girlfriend, except she didn't want to be that any more, which is why he smacked her around,' Stacey said before tacking a Post-it note on the edge of the desk. Cheryl Gordon's address.

Kim held her feelings in check. She hoped Cheryl Gordon had seen the news and recognised the name.

'And Paul?'

'Paul sexually assaulted a girl after a school disco. She'd danced with him once and didn't want to dance again. He followed her home and assaulted her about twenty metres from her house.'

Kim's gaze went to the single photo of Paul Brooks that had been added to the board. She tipped her head.

'They're letters,' she realised.

'Yep, we got that too, boss. Our guy formed Eric into an A for abuser and Paul into an R for rapist.'

'Bloody hell, what a pair. Either of them re-offend?'

Stacey shook her head. 'Not that we know of.'

'Address of Paul's victim?'

Stacey tacked another Post-it note on the edge of the desk. 'Her name is Daisy Hobbs.'

'So if neither of them have re-offended, this has to be some kind of punishment for the crimes they committed back then. But obviously it's not the same historic victim, so do we have more than one killer?' Bryant asked.

'We have exactly the same MO, which would be difficult for two different people to replicate,' Stacey said as the puzzlement grew.

'Hmm... okay, finally, did anyone work out the numbering system on the Sentinel's tweets?' Kim asked.

The blank expressions told her they'd forgotten all about that.

'It's his progress. One of six, two of six. He's talking victims.'

'We have another four to come?' Bryant asked.

'Not if we can help it. Their old teacher, Ryan West, gave me another four names who made up a particularly nasty group of six at Welton.'

Stacey took out her notepad, but Kim waved it away. It was getting late and they all needed some rest. 'Not tonight. Get gone, all of you. See you back here at the normal time.'

They all gathered their things and offered the usual 'good-nights' as they walked out the door.

Unfortunately it was unlikely to be a very good night for her.

THIRTY-FIVE

For the first time ever, Stacey didn't know how to act or feel walking into her own home. It felt alien, tainted and not like the safe haven she'd known. It was almost like Terence Birch was present in every room, even though he'd never set foot in the place.

The habit of him hadn't yet left her. She'd spent the journey home searching every face, every half-turned figure to see if it was him. Her heart had beat a little harder at every bus stop in case he'd boarded the vehicle.

It felt as though the fear had become a part of her being, that her muscle memory now included searching pavements and shops. It was as though she couldn't allow herself to believe he was gone. That he'd tricked her somehow and that the minute she let down her guard, he would reappear outside her bedroom window. Even now, after walking into her home, her stomach was telling her to go to the window: to be certain.

Surely her ordeal couldn't end just like that.

She knew that part of her discomfort came from feeling unsure around Devon. They'd had many fights over the years, but they'd always resolved never to go to sleep on an argument.

Their like for like stubbornness had sometimes dictated that they were still sitting in silence, neither prepared to relent, when the sun came up.

It had been easy enough to communicate by text message and emoji throughout the day, but where did they go from here?

'Hey, babe,' Devon said, appearing in the doorway.

Stacey hesitated.

Devon opened her arms, and Stacey fell into them.

They both started apologising at the same time.

'Oh no,' Devon said, taking her by the hand. 'You have nothing to apologise for.'

Stacey allowed herself to be led to the sofa.

'Listen, I reacted badly. I should never have got angry with you. I should have listened and let you explain. I should have been there for you instead of blowing up. You're the victim in this, not me, and it breaks my heart that you've been suffering alone.

'It's all I've been able to think about. That bastard put you through hell, and I'm not even sorry he's dead.'

Stacey leaned into her, feeling the safety and security of the Devon she knew.

'It doesn't seem real, Dee. I can't seem to accept it's over.' She tapped the side of her head. 'It's like he's still in here.'

'Of course he is, babe, cos he found a place in there to live. The threat of the man was always more powerful than the man himself. It's like an echo. The voice is gone, but the memory of it remains.'

Stacey moved in closer, already finding comfort in Devon's reassurance.

'And like any echo, it'll fade. The space he's been occupying will gradually be filled with something else.'

'Do you think so?' Stacey asked, wondering if she'd ever feel like her normal self again.

'Of course, but it's going to take time. You've settled into a way of life. A horrible, stressful, anxious existence. Your body has adapted itself to be ready for fight or flight at a second's notice. It's an elastic band that's got to find its shape again.'

'Not sure my boss sees it that way. They've got the guy that ran Birch over, but she still can't look me in the eye.'

She felt Devon stiffen slightly at the mention of Birch's name.

'They got him already?' she asked.

'Yeah, he came in and confessed. Case closed. But I'm not sure things with the boss will ever get back to normal. She calls Penn instead of me,' Stacey said, knowing that Devon would understand just how cutting that was. 'I don't think she trusts me to do my job.'

'She will, babe,' Devon reassured her. 'She's not like normal people when it comes to feelings. Let Penn take the strain a bit. Gives you more time to get your head back in the game.'

'I love you,' Stacey said suddenly, feeling the relief wash over her. The tears fell from her eyes, and she didn't try to stop them. It felt good to let them out.

'And I love you, babe,' Devon said, pulling her close. 'Which is the first thing I should have told you last night. I'm so sorry for the way I acted, but it's important for you to know that I always, always have your back.'

THIRTY-SIX

Kim had just answered the last email and closed down the computer ready to leave for the night.

'Ah, Stone, just the person,' Woody said, filling the doorway to the squad room.

As most of their meetings took place in his office with him sitting behind the desk, she often forgot her boss's sheer size and stature.

He entered the space with a nonchalance she didn't buy. His hands were in his pockets, and his tie had been removed. He looked every inch the boss just taking a stroll to see who was still around. Except for the fact he never did that.

As was her habit, her mind automatically began searching for reasons for this unexpected visit. Surely if the chief super was pissed off about her attitude at the Monday meeting, she'd have known about it before now. And that would have been a summons to Woody's office on the third floor not him having a casual meander down to the squad room.

She'd been keeping him up to date on the case by email, text and phone calls so it couldn't be that.

'Just ran into Vik in the corridor. Good officer,' he said, resting his behind on the edge of Penn's desk.

'Yeah, pity he went to the dark side.'

'Hmm... nasty business with Terence Birch. A former witness of ours,' he said.

'Absolutely. Tragic.'

Woody crossed his arms. 'He tells me you have a keen interest in the details of the incident.'

Kim found herself wondering what actual words Vik had used. She knew Vik well and anything would have been said in jest, but it had still highlighted her interest to Woody.

'Just curious,' she said, shrugging. 'We have had previous dealings with the man.'

Not a lie.

This wasn't sitting comfortably with her, but she knew that if she told Woody the whole truth, he would be forced to take formal action that would most likely include a full interview with Stacey and an official report. That report would be like a tattoo on her permanent record.

'No other reason,' he pushed.

'No, sir, just professional curiosity.'

Okay, that was a lie.

'I've also heard rumblings there was a shouting match in here earlier today.'

She forced a frown onto her face. 'Heated debate maybe. Always the same when we start a new case.'

And that was another lie.

'Anything going on here I should know about, Stone?' he asked, fixing her with his stare.

'Absolutely not,' she said, meeting his gaze and holding it despite the fact she was now in uncharted territory. Direct questions from her boss were normally met with truthful answers.

'I think you'd agree that I've shown on more than one occasion that I can be trusted to offer you total support.'

'Yes, sir.'

'And I'd hate to think you were lying to me.'

'Of course not, sir.'

He didn't need to know about the wall of fame at Birch's house.

'Because if you broke that trust, I'm not sure how the future would look.'

'Absolutely, sir,' Kim said.

He didn't need to know about the small blue car.

'Okay, Stone, I won't keep you any longer. Time you got off home.'

She had a couple of things to do on her way home, but he didn't need to know about those either.

Kim tried to ignore the sinking feeling that was growing in her stomach as her boss left the room.

Great, she'd now lied to one of the only people that had ever truly had her back.

THIRTY-SEVEN

'Ella...?' Kim asked as a woman with short brown hair answered the door. Stacey's notes had mentioned Charlotte's sister, who visited her mum every day.

She nodded, and Kim produced her identification. 'Have you got a minute?'

'For what?'

Stacey's notes had been spot on in relation to the woman's hostility towards the police. Her view that the police had done little to help her sister, Charlotte, wasn't too far from the truth.

She'd spent the last hour reading every detail about Stacey's interactions with Terence Birch and anyone involved with him.

Charlotte Danks had been pursued relentlessly by the man, forcing her to move home, change jobs and then move again after her mum had been tricked into revealing her new address. This family had suffered terribly, and they deserved to hear the news in person.

'It's about Terence Birch.'

'Jesus Christ, if I'm not sick of that bloody name. Come in,' she said grudgingly.

'Is that our Charlotte?' Kim heard called from the lounge.

''Fraid not, Mum, not today.'

'Ella, they're doing it again. Make them stop.'

'It's okay, Mum, I'll sort them out.'

Kim watched as Ella entered the lounge and stood with her hands on her hips in front of the sofa.

'I've already told you two to pack it in. Mum doesn't like it, and if you don't knock it off, you're gonna have to go.'

A woman who appeared to be in her late fifties watched Ella shouting at the sofa. The empty sofa.

'They're going to stop whispering now, Mum. I'll just finish the cuppa, but call me if they start again.'

'Thanks, love. Is Charlotte coming for tea?'

'Not today, Mum,' Ella said with a catch in her voice.

Kim was beginning to understand the effect Terence Birch had had on this family.

Ella indicated for Kim to come through to the kitchen. She pushed the dividing door but didn't close it fully.

'Your Mum's unwell?'

'She has dementia. Her particular type is called Lewy body. It's where Lewy bodies, abnormal protein deposits, affect chemicals in the brain. Symptoms started a couple of months ago – REM sleep disorder, restlessness, delusions, hallucinations. She sees things that aren't there. At first, I tried to explain to her that the figures weren't real but that scared her even more. She couldn't understand why she could see them and I couldn't. Now I tell 'em off and she's happy. She phones me at home, and I have to tell her to put me on loudspeaker so I can shout at them for her. She doesn't need full-time care yet, but eventually I'll have some difficult decisions to make.'

'Sounds like a lot.'

'Not really. Not yet. She has good days. The worst thing is she knows exactly what's happening when she's lucid. She nursed her own father through it.'

'You deal with this alone?'

'Don't have much choice, do I?'

'You do now,' Kim said.

Ella turned from the teapot she'd been stirring, and Kim couldn't prolong her misery for another second.

'Terence Birch is dead; Charlotte can come home.'

'Wh-what?' Ella asked, gripping the worktop for support.

'He's dead. Killed by a hit-and-run driver.'

Ella took a seat. 'You're sure?'

'Saw his body with my own eyes.'

'Oh my God,' she said, covering her mouth. 'I've prayed for this for so long. I know how that sounds, but I can't lie. That man destroyed my sister. He destroyed our family. Our own mother doesn't even know where Charlotte is. Birch tricked her one time, and she's blamed herself ever since.'

Ella stared at the table and started shaking her head. 'I can't quite believe it.'

Kim was reminded of the scene from the film *Scrooged* where the lives of many were improved due to the death of one man.

'Seriously, you have no idea what that man did to my sister. As if that wasn't bad enough, he robbed both me and Mum of time with her. He is the—'

'Was,' Kim corrected, reaching across and touching her arm. 'Past tense. It's over. Charlotte can come home.'

Tears started to fall even as a smile played around Ella's mouth. 'I'm sorry, I just don't know how to act. Oh my God, I can't wait to tell Charlotte. She'll get a train and be back with us tomorrow. Mum will be—'

'Tomorrow? I thought she lived in Australia or...'

'No. My lie was deliberate. I've had years to practise it.

'After the time Mum got tricked, I swore that no one would get any idea of her whereabouts. Since then, Charlotte won't even drive a car because she'd have to be registered on the DVLA site, and she didn't trust that Birch wouldn't find her through that somehow. I've said the same thing to anyone that's asked about her. She would never have moved so far away from Mum. She's in Newcastle, and we speak briefly every two months. Come with me to tell Mum.'

Kim followed an excitable Ella through to the lounge. Kim wasn't sure of the woman's age but she seemed to have dropped ten years at the news.

'Mum, guess what?' Ella asked, sitting beside her mother and taking her hand.

'What, love?' the woman asked, opening her eyes wide.

'We can all be together again. Terence Birch is dead. Charlotte can come home.'

Mrs Danks patted her daughter's hand. 'Oh, that's nice, love. Now who on earth is Charlotte?'

THIRTY-EIGHT

Kim swallowed down the sickness in her throat as she walked past the building where Stacey and Devon lived. The curtains were drawn so she was in no danger of being seen.

As she'd suspected, the light-blue Ford Focus was parked at the end of the road.

She didn't expect it to bear any damage. It wasn't the vehicle that had struck Terence Birch, but it was possible that it was the car that had caused the accident in the first place.

Kim wasn't proud of her actions, skulking around in her colleague's neighbourhood. But there was an itch in her mind that had to be scratched.

She walked slowly along the pavement, looking carefully on both sides.

On the third house away from Stacey's, she saw what she was after.

The Ring doorbell was sited just inside an open porch, and she was guessing it had a good view of the road.

She knocked on the door and got her identification ready. She pushed away the feeling of doing something wrong. She was a police officer wanting to view some CCTV.

A woman in her mid-fifties answered the door with glasses pushed up onto the top of her head.

'Sorry to bother you,' Kim said, showing her ID. 'But I see you have a camera here.'

The woman looked at the device as though confirming that yes, it was there.

'I'm investigating a robbery from last night that happened a couple of streets back. Maybe between the hours of 8 p.m. and 1 a.m. I'm trying to see if our suspect passed by this way.'

'Come, come,' the woman said, beckoning her in. 'Do you want my phone?'

'If you don't mind.'

The woman took her phone from her handbag and opened the app.

'I didn't have any callers during that time, but it does catch the pavement and part of the road.'

That was what Kim had been hoping for.

'Here you go,' she said, passing her the phone. 'Do you need anything else?'

'No, that's fine, thank you,' Kim answered, pressing play on the footage.

The camera was motion activated so it bounced from motion to motion.

Her mind viewed and discarded the cat that walked across the wall and the dog that paused to pee up the woman's plants. She prayed that was going to be the worst thing she'd see.

9.21 – Car passing – not Devon

9.37 – Car passing – not Devon

9.49 – Car passing – not Devon

10.01 – Person appears in shot

Her heart jumped as she realised the person she was watching was Terence Birch.

He stopped and turned.

Kim's mouth went dry.

Devon came into shot. She got in his face, pointing and gesticulating.

Terence Birch appeared to be saying nothing. He wasn't responding to her rage; instead appeared to be amused by it.

Kim watched as Devon raised her hand and punched him in the face before turning and walking away.

It wasn't what she'd expected to see, but the punch hadn't killed him, however damning it was.

Birch rubbed at his chin and then walked out of shot. Kim continued watching. Let that be an end to it, she prayed.

10.17 – Car passing – not Devon

10.21 – Car passing – not Devon

10.23 – Car passing – Devon

Shit, that's exactly what she'd been afraid of.

THIRTY-NINE

'Okay, folks, let's get to it,' Kim said, trying to keep her voice even.

Her mood wasn't the best. She was unsure if that was due to spending barely any time with Barney or from what she'd seen on the Ring camera the night before. A discovery she'd chosen not to share with anyone.

Her mood wasn't helped by the fact she could still barely look at Stacey. Not something she was proud of, but it was what it was.

'Following on from yesterday, I think it's safe to assume that the Sentinel is our killer. He published Paul Brooks's name before it had been made public. He also seems to think that Brooks deserved no sympathy. We have on our hands either a modern-day vigilante who doesn't think the victims paid enough for their earlier crimes, or there's more to learn from their time at Welton; so I want an appointment with someone there as quickly as possible.'

She paused. 'Ryan West, the English teacher, gave me four additional names, which were Dean, Nathan, Leyton and Ian.

He doesn't have surnames so these may be hard to track until we've got more information from Welton.'

She sipped her coffee. 'It's also a safe assumption that the man who lives at the address the account is linked to, Don Beattie, is not our Sentinel. Get working on finding out how our guy is routing through the server. It's possible our killer got the details during a recent break-in where nothing was taken.'

'Got it, boss,' Penn said.

'I want to know where you can get fentanyl and what sort of knowledge you need to be able to inject it. Next, I want to know Paul Brooks's movements for the hours leading up to his murder. We think Eric was spiked outside the gym, and I want to know where it happened to Paul. Still want to know how he's moving them around as well.'

Penn nodded.

'Post-mortem is at 10 a.m. but I'll leave it to your discretion whether you attend or not. I've given you plenty to do here.'

She took another sip of her coffee. There was one more thing, but for this she did need to speak to Stacey.

On her late-night walk with Barney, it had occurred to her that she hadn't yet dealt with a killer like this. She'd never had a murderer who deliberately kept his victims alive so that emergency services trounced the scene, a murderer who was pretty much shouting from the rooftops on social media.

She really did need to know what they were dealing with.

'Stace, can you get Alison on the phone?'

'Err... no, boss.'

'Sorry?' Kim asked sharply. Now wasn't the time for the constable to be refusing her requests.

'I can't get her, boss. She's rock climbing in Shropshire. Phone is switched off.'

'Where exactly in Shropshire?'

Stacey hesitated.

Kim glared.

'Something called the Nesscliffe.'

Kim finished her coffee. 'Grab your coat, Bryant, and a map. Looks like we're going to start the day with a sight-seeing trip.'

FORTY

'You all right, Stace?' Penn asked once the boss and Bryant had left the room.

'Yeah, I'm good. Thanks for asking.'

From Penn's point of view, that had to have been one of the most uncomfortable briefings he'd ever experienced in his career. His old boss, Travis, at West Mercia, had been abrupt, dictatorial and non-inclusive. This morning, the boss hadn't been that bad, but her mood had welcomed no chat, no humour and responses only when asked for.

'It's only cos she cares, you know,' he told his colleague. The boss wasn't always easy to work out, but this was a no-brainer.

'I know,' Stacey said miserably.

Penn wished there was something he could do to help, but it had to come out in the wash as his mum used to say. They all knew that the boss was fiercely loyal to all of them, not to mention protective, especially towards Stacey. In his opinion, Stacey was the little sister the boss had never had. Unfortunately, her hurt normally manifested itself as anger, and his colleague just had to ride the storm until it had passed. There was little he could do to help.

'Okay, what jobs do you want?' he asked.

Stacey looked at her notes. 'Err... I'll take the victims' histories and movements of Paul.'

'Yeah, cos I definitely don't want to know about Paul's movements,' Penn said, raising an eyebrow.

Stacey laughed, and he realised it was a sound he hadn't heard for a very long time.

And that was how he knew he could help.

FORTY-ONE

It was almost nine when Bryant pulled into Oak car park. It was the closest they could get to the Nesscliffe Countryside Heritage Site, which Kim had learned on their hour-long journey up the A458 covered seventy acres. She had considered telling Bryant to turn back, knowing that finding Alison would be like finding a needle in a haystack. Further reading had told her that the acreage encompassed two wooded hills, a heather-covered ridge and an Iron Age hill fort. The former quarries that were now cliffs of soft red sandstone only accounted for a small portion of the site.

She spotted Alison's Citroën as she got out of the car.

The sun was just starting to peep out from behind the clouds, offering a pleasant temperature of nineteen degrees, with a gentle breeze. Perfect rock-climbing weather – or not, Kim thought as they headed towards a well-worn trail that she was hoping led them to the climb site.

'Why do people do this?' she asked, entering a wooded area.

'What? Take time off?' Bryant asked.

'Well, no, I get that, kind of, but why subject yourself to something like this?'

'Adrenaline? Doing something completely different?'

'Fine, go to Spain, get a tan, read a book.'

'It's an adventure, guv. A time to test the nerves, step outside your comfort zone,' Bryant offered with a smile in his voice. 'I mean, the woman is on leave.'

She wondered if this was Bryant's last-ditch attempt to stop her harassing Alison on her break.

'Cool, send our guy a message and ask him to take a pause until she's back at work.'

'There are other psychologists, guv,' Bryant said as the trees started to thin.

Yes, there were, and she trusted them all a lot less than Alison.

'Jesus, is she really gonna climb that?' Kim asked, looking up. The cliff face in front of them rose up almost fifty metres.

Kim couldn't get her head round the fact that nothing more than a piece of rope lay between you and instant death.

She spotted Alison at the foot of the rock, amongst a group of six or seven climbers, already geared up and ready to climb.

'Well, fancy seeing you here,' Kim called out. She definitely wanted to keep Alison on the ground.

The woman froze before turning. When she did, her face was a mask of pure horror.

'No way,' she said, shaking her head.

'Yes way,' Kim said, reaching her. 'We need your help.'

The instructors and climbers were watching with interest.

'Erm... I'm not at work,' Alison hissed. 'Did my out-of-office email and voicemail not give it away?'

'Yeah, but like I said, we need you.'

Kim looked around the group. 'Can you give us a moment, folks?'

They started to move away, but the instructor holding the rope attached to Alison stepped back just a couple of paces.

'We've got a killer on the loose,' Kim said, lowering her voice.

Alison looked at her as though she still couldn't believe what she was seeing. 'Do you have any idea how messed up this is?'

'How many times do I need to say we need your help?' Kim said, wondering why Alison wasn't already untangling herself from the complicated-looking harness.

'And how many more signs do you need that I'm not available?'

'The rock will still be here once we've caught him,' Kim said.

'Not really the point,' Alison replied, looking towards the instructor.

'He's leaving his victims on the edge of death, so we find them alive,' she said to whet Alison's appetite. She knew the woman loved an interesting case.

'There are no depths to which you won't plummet, are there?' Alison asked, shaking her head.

'Absolutely none.'

'You know, one day we should have a good chat about your sense of entitlement.'

'Great idea. Meet me back at the station and we can—'

'I'm ready, Pete,' Alison said to the instructor.

'Don't do it, Pete,' Kim said.

He got into position. 'No offence, but she's the one paying me.'

'She can't arrest you,' Kim threatened.

'Neither can you if I haven't done anything wrong,' he said with a confident smile.

'Wanna bet? I'm currently considering obstruction if you let her go up any further.'

'And I'm currently considering revealing that I work for the

CPS, so I know you're talking complete bollocks.' He paused. 'Alison, good to go.'

'Alison,' Kim said as the woman began to rise.

'Get someone else,' she called over her shoulder.

Bryant stepped forward. 'Guv, I think she's made herself clear.'

Kim turned to the other instructor, who was watching with amusement. 'Hey, buddy, hook me up, eh?'

'Oh Jesus,' Bryant said, standing back.

'The name's Nick. Have you ever done this before?'

'I'm a quick learner,' she said.

Alison wasn't going to escape her that easily.

'Here, put this on,' he said, passing her a helmet.

'What's that gonna do if I fall?'

'Not a lot if you're way up there,' he said, looking towards the top. 'It's more about protecting your head from falling rocks or safety equipment.'

'Yeah, I'm not planning on going that high. What the hell is that?' she asked as he produced a contraption with three hoops.

'It's a harness. This goes around your waist and these are the leg loops.'

'Bloody hell, there'd be less to put on if I was following her up there dressed as King Arthur. Hey, easy, tiger – watch where your hands are going.'

Nick kept a straight face as he fitted her into the harness, but Bryant burst out laughing.

'Come on, come on, come on,' she urged, watching Alison get away from her.

By the time he'd talked her through the carabiners, ascenders and descenders, Alison was a good forty feet ahead of her.

She dug her feet into the crevice and pulled on the ascenders to help her up. She didn't need to catch Alison, but she did need to be in shouting distance.

The behaviourist appeared to have hit a point that needed a

decision. While she debated her next action, Kim was able to gain a few feet. Again, she found herself wondering why the hell anyone would do this by choice.

'Hey, Alison,' she called out.

The woman looked down over her left shoulder. 'Jeez, Inspector. You really do have an issue with boundaries. Go away, I'm not coming.'

Kim pushed up the ascenders another two feet. 'He's vomiting verbally all over social media.'

'Good for him. I'm on holiday.'

One more foot.

'Looks like he's posing his victims to form letters, even breaking bones while they're still alive.'

'And I am still on holiday,' Alison hissed.

Kim was running out of temptations. 'Seems that both boys went to Welton, a youth offenders—'

'I know what Welton is. I don't know how many different ways I can tell you that I'm not giving up my holiday to work this case, no matter what you say.'

Really? Kim thought.

'Shame, cos your best buddy sure could use a friend right now.'

Kim hit the descender as she'd been shown and controlled her journey back to the ground.

'Hey, what's wrong with Stacey?' Alison called down.

Kim unclasped herself and stepped out of the harness.

'Oi, what's going on? Why does Stacey need—?'

'Thanks, guys,' Kim said, ignoring the voice from above.

She started heading back to the car.

Alison's cries got weaker and quieter.

'Bloody hell, guv. That was low.'

She shrugged as she walked.

Alison had called it right – there was no depth to which she wouldn't sink to get her to work this case.

FORTY-TWO

'Okay, Stace, I know you've got a lot on your mind, but I need your help and I'm running out of time,' Penn blurted out.

She looked up from her computer. 'Jeez, Penn, what's wrong?' she asked, obviously able to see the panic on his face.

'I'm meeting Lynne tonight for an early tea. We're doing a picnic at Clent before she goes on night shift.'

It had been difficult to fit something in around their work schedules, but it was important. Especially today.

'Okay,' she said as some of the concern fell from her face.

'It's our anniversary. Six months.'

'Oh, congratulations. But why is anything connected to that causing you the level of stress I can see on your face? Oh shit, you're not gonna break up with her, are you?'

He shook his head and groaned. Now he had to put the thoughts flying around his head into words.

'What am I supposed to do?'

'Penn, is that a trick question?'

'It's six months. How much fuss does that require? We're doing a picnic because of our shifts, but should I book a fancy restaurant for the weekend? Do I buy huge bouquets of flowers?

Do I get her a card? Do I book a blimp to do a flyover with a banner? Do I do some of the above or none of the above, and if I choose some, which ones—'

'Take a breath, man,' Stacey interrupted. 'What are you so worried about?'

'Doing the right thing. Doing the appropriate thing. I don't want to do too much in case I scare her off, and I don't want to do too little in case she thinks I don't care.'

'You know, Penn, you gotta stop thinking you're going to mess it up. I really think that Lynne knew how she felt for a long time and she was just waiting for you to catch up. You've got to loosen up.'

'I know. But what if I do something wrong?'

A strange look passed over his colleague's face before she spoke. 'We all make mistakes in our relationships. Some are small and some are big, but we just got to do what feels right at the time.'

For a minute Penn was unsure if Stacey was talking about herself or him.

'So, have you got any ideas?' she asked.

He reached into the bag at his feet. 'I got her two gifts,' he said, placing them on the desk. 'A book token and a gold bracelet.'

'Show me the bracelet,' Stacey said.

He opened the box to reveal what the sales assistant had called a 'delicate belcher' bracelet. They'd had chunkier chains, but Lynne didn't do bulky jewellery.

'That's really lovely,' Stacey said admiringly. She then widened her eyes. 'And a book token?'

'She likes to read,' he defended himself, feeling Stacey was mocking his choice. 'I just don't know which is the most appropriate for a six-month anniversary,' he said, looking from one to the other.

'Penn, answer me one thing. How does she make you feel?'

'Whole,' he said without thinking. 'I see her and the world is a brighter place. I wake up and she's the first thing I think about. When I know I'm going to see her, I wish the hours away and I never want her to leave. My heart is fit to burst when I see the relationship she's building with Jasper, and I literally cannot imagine my life without her.'

Stacey stared at him and he'd swear he could see tears in her eyes.

'So which should I give her, the book token or the bracelet?' he asked, still not sure of the right choice.

'The bracelet, Penn. Definitely the bracelet.'

FORTY-THREE

Welton was no less intimidating to adults as to kids, Kim thought as Bryant parked the car.

Built in the 1970s, it was a study in faceless, featureless concrete. There was nothing to soften the edges and appeared to be frightening from the minute you set eyes on it. There was no indication that any softness existed beyond the cold, unforgiving walls either.

Kim couldn't help the shudder that passed through her as they approached the double doors. She'd probably spent most of her teenage years just one fight away from ending up somewhere like this.

She'd seen facilities built in the decades since, and great care had been taken to make them appear less threatening. She'd seen photos of Hindley in Manchester, which was built of light brick and looked like an office block.

Stacey had managed to get them an appointment with the governor, who was running a few minutes late. After showing their IDs at the desk and following security protocols, they were directed to a waiting area.

'Pretty grim so far,' Bryant noted, sitting on one of the boxy chairs.

Kim stood at the small window which seemed to be the fashion throughout the building. 'I suppose that's the point,' she said.

He wasn't wrong, but it was important to remember that this wasn't a facility for unruly kids. The inmates at Welton had committed crimes, broken the law. It wasn't errant, rebellious behaviour but criminal activity. There had to be consequences. Another – smaller – voice in her mind insisted that they were still kids.

'Sorry to keep you,' said a female voice at the door.

Kim kicked herself for assuming the person they'd come to see was a man.

The woman was an inch or so taller than Bryant's six feet. She had the build of an athlete and long red hair, pulled back except for a few springy bits around her temple.

Bryant held up the ID he hadn't yet put away and introduced them both.

'I'm Josephine Kirk – please follow me.'

There was no offer of a handshake from the brusque woman, and she strode away at speed. Kim and Bryant shared a look before following her.

She opened a door and nodded for them to enter.

The office wasn't spacious; nor was it luxurious. As with the rest of the facility, everything was simple, square and without effort to soften the harshness.

Despite the brusqueness, Kim was prepared to offer the benefit of the doubt to any woman who had shoe-horned her way into a male-dominated environment.

'Your colleague mentioned a current case. How can I help?' Josephine Kirk asked, and Kim noticed there were no offers of refreshments or attempts at small talk. Kim didn't mind the absence of either.

'We have two victims, and we believe both of them spent time here.'

'Names?' she asked, tapping her computer screen into life.

'Eric Gould.'

'Age?'

'Thirty.'

'Yes, that inmate was here from 2008 to 2011. Next?' she said, her fingers poised to enter the next name.

'Paul Brooks.'

'Age?'

'Thirty-one.'

'Also here 2008 to 2011. Next?'

'That's it.'

'Well, in that case, I've answered your—'

'Is there anything more you can tell us about the two of them?' Kim asked. She appreciated brevity, but she'd been hoping for a little more than confirmation. She'd got that from the court records.

'Such as?'

'What they were like.'

Kirk shrugged. 'Very much before my time. We took over from the Youth Custody Service seven years ago. Personal knowledge of any prisoners before then is severely limited.'

'But the records?' Kim asked, pointing to the computer.

'Are the property of Acer Security Services and not accessible to you without a warrant.'

'But surely there's someone here who might recall these two boys?'

The woman took a long breath and folded her hands in front of her with an air of extreme patience. 'Inspector, when we took over Welton Hall, we were faced with, excuse my language, a shit show. The facility was built to house two hundred young offenders and at that time held almost double. Prisoners were sometimes confined to their cells for up to twenty-one hours a day, with access to very little support or education.'

'Never thought borstal was supposed to be fun,' Bryant observed.

'And I thought most of the dinosaurs in the police service had died out,' she said pointedly. 'No one calls it that any more. The first borstal opened in Kent in 1902. They were run by the prison services and were invented to reform young offenders. Luckily the system was abolished in 1982 and replaced with Youth Custody Centres.

'The old system was based on routine, discipline and authority. Because of course that will solve all of life's problems.'

'So why was this place still so far behind the times when you took over seven years ago?' Kim asked.

'The regime was the same as a prison but with a lower staff-to-offender ratio. It's much easier to keep inmates locked up when you haven't got enough staff.'

'I'm hearing a but in your voice.'

'It only delays the violence. Kids locked up with no hope are the same as kids wandering around with no hope, except they're angrier. Let them all out and it's like opening a bottle of cola after it's been in the washing machine. It's going to pop.'

'Don't three quarters of offenders re-offend within a year of being released?' Bryant asked.

'Or you could say that a quarter of them don't,' Kirk offered. The woman hadn't struck Kim as being a cup-half-full kind of person. 'Which is a statistic we are working continually to improve. Here at Welton, the inmates receive at least twenty-five hours of education per week, and there are opportunities for prisoners to undertake work in Community Service volunteer schemes.'

Kim wasn't interested in all the kids. Just two. 'But Eric and Paul...?'

'I can't discuss anything further about particular cases. The records were transferred to our care when we took over seven years ago, and we adhere to data protection diligently.'

'And there's not one member of staff here who might recall these boys?' Kim asked again, hoping she'd warmed up a little.

'All the old guards were given notice. We didn't want anything left of the former regime. New broom and all that.'

'Kitchen staff? Admin?'

She shook her head.

It wasn't the crime or conviction information she was concerned about. She had that from the PNC. Even juvenile records didn't disappear until the convicted reached the age of a hundred.

What she needed was intelligence. What had they been like? Had they known each other well? Who had they hung around with? Had they been remorseful for the crimes they'd committed?

The PNC wasn't going to tell her any of that.

'Is there no one?' Kim pleaded.

Kirk sighed heavily. 'Well, maybe the youth justice officer. He wasn't someone we could dispense with. Lenny Baldwin. Worked out of Wolverhampton, I think.'

'Thanks for all your help,' Kim said, standing.

'You're welcome. Happy to assist,' she said, not registering the sarcasm. 'So, are we done?' Kirk asked, seeing them to the door.

'Not even close,' Kim said. 'You'll definitely be seeing us again, and next time we'll be bringing a court order.'

FORTY-FOUR

'Little bastard,' Stacey said.

'Is that any way to talk to your bestie?' Alison asked from the doorway.

'Hey,' Penn said, looking up long enough to give the behaviourist a wave.

'What the hell?' Stacey asked. 'You're on holiday.'

'Not any more,' she said, putting her bag on the desk. 'Apparently I'm needed.'

Stacey couldn't believe the boss had managed to get Alison back there so quickly. 'What happened?'

'She found me, harassed me, bullied me and then followed me up a cliff face.'

'She did w-what?' Stacey spluttered.

'Yeah, wish I'd got photos now,' Alison said, removing her cardigan.

Despite the boss's anger with her, the image of it was funny, and that persistence was one of the reasons she'd always valued having the boss in her corner. She knew that was no longer the case.

'Jeez, Penn. I sure could use a drink,' Alison said, taking a seat.

Penn looked pointedly towards the almost-full coffee machine.

'Tea. I'm absolutely gasping for a cup of tea, and if you can make that happen, I'm going to owe you big time.'

Penn rolled his eyes as he pushed back his chair.

He looked from one to the other. 'I'm guessing you don't want me to rush back.'

'I swear to God, Penn. I might just be a little bit in love with you,' Alison said.

He laughed before leaving the office.

'So, wassup, buddy?'

Stacey groaned. 'She told you?'

Alison shook her head. 'She didn't tell me what was wrong, only that you could do with a friend.'

Stacey felt tears prick at her eyes. 'And that's why you left your holiday?'

'Err... obvs.'

She didn't mind if the boss had used her current situation as a tool to get Alison's help on the case. It was true that she really could do with a friend, even if it was a friend she'd already lied to.

She took a breath. 'Remember when I called you a couple of months ago for your advice on stalkers?'

'Sure do,' Alison said, taking a KitKat from her bag.

'Well, the advice was for me. I was being stalked by a man who I'd interviewed as a witness. I kept it secret from you, Devon and my colleagues – and the man concerned was killed in a hit and run on Monday night. Got it?'

Alison put the KitKat down. 'Not even close, matey. Do you wanna take it again, from the top?'

FORTY-FIVE

'Hey, Alison, what a surprise to see you here,' Kim said, entering the squad room.

'Oh yeah, shocker.'

Kim hid her smile as she removed her jacket and put it over the back of her chair.

By her reckoning, Alison would have arrived about forty minutes ago, giving Stacey plenty of time to explain the situation with Terence Birch.

'Okay, folks. Penn, stop whatever it is you're doing and get straight onto a warrant for the records at Welton. Ms Josephine Kirk is beyond unhelpful and refuses to co-operate one little bit.'

'Maybe you could use one of her friends' well-being against her to get what you want,' Alison suggested.

'Good idea. Wish I'd thought of that. And while I've got your attention, did you hear everything I told you at the rock face or do I have to repeat myself?'

'Leaves his victims barely alive, likes to pose them, even breaking bones to do it. He's vocal on social media, and both victims spent time at a young offenders institution. Did I miss anything?'

'Nope, that's about it. What do you think?'

Alison hesitated for a minute before looking to her left. 'Penn did it. I reckon he's the one. Actually, no, I did it. Shit, I was in Shropshire. Okay, definitely Penn.'

Kim folded her arms and waited.

'I've been here less than an hour. I haven't opened my laptop, I haven't read a single report, witness statement or seen a photo of either body. So if you want a quick answer, your guy is Penn.'

Kim held her inner smile in check. She'd forgotten how easy it was to get a rise out of Alison. Suitable punishment for making her climb up the side of a bloody rock.

'Ooh, someone's tense. You could probably do with a holiday. Moving on, anything on Paul's movements before our guy got him?'

Stacey shook her head. 'Struggling to find anyone who cared at all what Paul was doing any day of the week, but I'll keep digging.'

'Okay, well—'

'Just one more thing, boss,' Stacey said, almost apologetically.

Kim nodded for her to continue, half wishing she could do her work from the archive room. The anger hadn't diminished anywhere near enough for her to interact with Stacey on any kind of normal level.

'I've been keeping an eye on the Sentinel account. No more tweets, but there's an interesting account that retweets everything he says. They're sharing his posts all over the place and making sure he reaches a wider audience.'

'Go on.'

'It's the BCA.'

'Who's the—? Oh no,' Kim said as the penny dropped.

The Black Country Angels were a vigilante group that operated out of a small shopfront on the edge of Wrens Nest.

She'd had a couple of run-ins with them over the years. Not so much recently, as they seemed to be keeping a lower profile. In the early days of their formation, it had been an almost weekly occurrence that they'd frogmarch someone to the station and try to force them into confessing to some perceived crime.

'Any comments from the Angels?'

'Only thumbs-up emojis.'

'Great. Our local vigilante group approves of our killer. Warms my bloody heart.'

'What if it's more than that though, boss?' Penn offered. 'What if our guy is an actual vigilante and is using the platform to further his own audience?'

'Possible,' Alison added. 'There's definitely a vigilante tone to the tweets Stacey showed me. He clearly feels these people need punishing, so there's every chance he could have links to a vigilante group.'

'Okay, great pit-stop, guys. Carry on while Bryant and I go talk to some Angels.'

Kim tapped the two addresses of Paul Brooks's and Eric Gould's historic victims on Stacey's desk as she passed. 'Find out what they're up to. We'll visit them if we think it's necessary, but I think the link we're looking for is at Welton. The number six is coming up a lot, and so far prison is the only place their paths appear to have crossed.'

Stacey re-tacked the notes to her notepad as Kim headed for the door.

Not once had she looked the girl in the eye, and it was for more reasons than the one Stacey knew about.

FORTY-SIX

'Jeez, she is pissed, isn't she?' Alison asked once the inspector and Bryant had left the squad room.

'Oh yeah,' Stacey said, looking miserable.

In truth, Alison was still trying to process what Stacey had told her. She remembered their conversation well. She also remembered sending Stacey links to articles about women who had been killed by their stalkers, which she could absolutely kick herself in the head for now. Stacey must have been terrified.

A small part of her identified with how the inspector was feeling, even though she understood that many stalking victims kept it to themselves for years. Sometimes they felt they were exaggerating and blowing things out of proportion.

When nothing physical had happened, it was easy to dismiss someone walking past your house or sending you messages. It was simple for onlookers to minimise the impact on someone's life.

Victims always hoped that if they were patient enough, the whole thing would just stop and their life could return to normal.

Even knowing everything she did about victimology and self-blame, she couldn't help but feel a little hurt that Stacey hadn't trusted her enough to confide what she'd been going through.

But her friend would never know that. She would keep in the forefront of her mind that Stacey had been the victim, and she would give her nothing but support.

'She just needs time,' Alison observed. 'Her feelings are complicated when it comes to you.'

'She hates me,' Stacey said, turning away.

Alison kept quiet as she opened her laptop, because she knew that couldn't have been further from the truth.

Initially she'd felt her anger rise at the inspector for her treatment of her best friend. The tension when they were in the same room was palpable. There had been a set expression on Kim Stone's face every time Stacey had spoken. Alison had wanted to shake some sense into her, but as she'd listened, she'd realised one very important thing. Her expertise wasn't needed on this case. In her own twisted way, the boss had made sure Stacey had someone to offer the support that she herself couldn't give her.

FORTY-SEVEN

'Guv, can I ask...?'

'No,' she said as he turned the engine off.

She looked out at the property she'd directed Bryant to. 'Sometimes I have to just ask you to trust me, okay?'

'Got it,' he said as she got out the car.

She hadn't told a soul about what she'd seen on the Ring camera the night before. There was only one person she was prepared to discuss that with. And it was the person who drove the small blue car.

She pressed the call button, and Devon's voice reached her through the speaker.

'It's me, Stone. Can I come up?'

Kim wasn't sure how to introduce herself. She wasn't here as a friend and nor was she here as an investigating officer. She was somewhere in between.

Devon was waiting in the open doorway, already dressed for her late shift as an immigration officer.

'Not sure why you're here, but come in.'

Despite the edge she heard in the woman's voice, Kim walked past her into the home she shared with Stacey.

'I hear you're not taking the news of Stacey's deceit well,' Devon said, closing the front door.

'When did she tell you about Birch?' Kim asked, turning to face her.

Stacey's wife or not, Kim wasn't going to discuss her own feelings on the matter.

'About twelve hours before she told you from what I understand.'

'And you were angry?'

Devon had the grace to look shamed. 'I'm not proud of the way I took the news. I'm her wife. I realised my mistake and got that Stacey had been terrorised. I apologised and offered my full support, and it's a shame her boss and colleagues can't—'

'So what did you do?' Kim asked, fighting down the anger. She wanted so badly to respond, but then she'd just be thrown out of the house without the answers she needed.

'What do you mean?'

'Immediately after she told you. What did you do?'

'I stormed out, cooled off, cleared my head, came to my senses and came home.'

Shit, she was lying.

'Do you want to think about that and then answer again?' Kim asked.

Devon folded her arms. 'Excuse me?'

'I'm just asking if you'd like to refresh your memory.'

'You know, I thought you were here to talk about how best we could jointly support Stacey. That's why I let you in, but your hostility is—'

'Because I don't like being lied to, Devon.'

'How dare you come into my home and call me a liar!'

'I'll ask you one last time: what did you do when you left this flat on Monday night?'

'I've told you. I—'

'Fuck it, Devon. I saw you. One of your neighbours has a

camera that captured you giving Terence Birch a good old right hook.'

'Wh-what?'

'I don't blame you for doing that for one minute, but I don't understand why you've just blatantly lied about it.'

'I have nothing to say,' Devon said, turning away.

'And then you got in your car and followed him,' Kim pushed.

'I need you to leave.'

'A witness has identified a small blue car at the scene. We know that car didn't hit Terence Birch, but the behaviour of the driver caused the accident – and I need you to give me a damn good reason why I shouldn't go to the person running the case and give him your address and phone number right now.'

'P-please leave.'

'Devon, someone is going to pick up this trail. If you have something to say, it's best you say it sooner—'

'You think I did it?' she shouted, eyes blazing. 'You think I was responsible for a man's death?'

'If you won't tell me where—'

'Get out of my home now. You're not welcome here. You can't even support your own team member, and now you accuse me of this?'

'I'm going,' Kim spat, allowing the rage to spill out of her. 'But don't you dare fucking say that Stacey's colleagues aren't supporting her. You have no idea of the lengths her team is going to to keep her safe. How fucking dare you!'

'Get out.'

Kim growled as the door was slammed behind her.

Damn it. That hadn't gone quite as she'd planned.

FORTY-EIGHT

The Black Country Angels didn't advertise their presence at the edge of the Wrens Nest housing estate. In fact, the premises still bore the name of the Chinese takeaway that had closed more than two years earlier.

The frosting of the windows prevented her seeing anything other than shadows moving around within the space.

She tried the door. It was locked.

She knocked hard and continuously until the door opened and her knuckles almost met the chest of a stringy male.

He rolled his eyes dramatically and called over his shoulder, 'Feds are here.'

'Why did you say that? This isn't America and we don't have Feds. How does it even work?' Kim asked.

'What do you want?' he asked. 'Is this another attempted raid for our intel?'

'Oh please, enough with the dramatics. Just let us in already. And if you'd let us see any authentic intel before posting it on social media, we might not be too late to seize evidence.'

That was the problem with vigilante groups. Most of them wanted to be useful but often ended up being a nuisance.

This particular group had formed in the late nineties, following a spate of local burglaries where elderly people were targeted and beaten for purse change. A group of twenty had formed immediately and grown to more than fifty volunteers who patrolled target areas in pairs.

The attacks hadn't stopped straight away, but the presence of the volunteers had restricted the culprit to a smaller area, where he'd eventually been caught.

In the years since, those concerned citizens had faded away and been replaced by a younger core with a more proactive approach. Another word for it was entrapment. She remembered a case around six years ago where one of the Black Country Angels had posed as a fourteen-year-old and had lured a man from Walsall to Cradley Heath train station. They'd filmed the encounter, complete with accusations, and uploaded it to YouTube before the day was out. When officers searched the man's home, it was clear that he, having seen his face all over the internet, had taken the precaution of destroying every piece of evidence. They hadn't been able to charge him with a thing.

The man stepped aside for them to enter, and Bryant introduced himself and Kim.

'I'm Reedy, and this is Banksy,' the man replied, pointing to another man sitting at the second desk in the room. Beyond was a kitchen that had probably been left behind by the previous occupants as well.

'You the one doing all the graffiti?' Kim asked the guy, sullen looking beneath a heavy beard and a baseball cap.

'He ain't that Banksy,' Reedy said, sitting down.

'No shit,' Kim replied as she took the last chair and Bryant perched behind on one of the window seats.

'Full names please,' Kim said as her colleague took out his notebook.

'I'm Elliot Reed and this is Gordon Banks.'

Bryant snapped his notebook shut.

'How's business?' Kim asked.

'The usual. We follow tips. We do stuff you lot can't be bothered to do.'

'Yeah, I checked out your social media. Still bugging that guy from Stourbridge.'

'He's a paedophile. His neighbours should know.'

'It's a bit more than that when you picket his place of work and lose the guy his job.'

Reedy shrugged. 'He's a danger to kids.'

'He served his time seventeen years ago, and there ain't many unaccompanied kids going to the tip to my knowledge.'

Kim didn't have a great deal of sympathy for the man concerned. But the methods of the group went far beyond monitoring.

She also knew that sometimes overeager individuals accused the wrong person of horrific crimes, which resulted in assault and even murder.

For vigilantes, the burden of proof was much lower than that required by the police. They operated on little more than rumour and hearsay.

She remembered the case of a man named Bijan Ebrahimi, forty-four, who'd taken a series of photos of youths attacking his hanging baskets for evidence. Someone saw him with the camera and told the police. He was quizzed, rumours started and two days later his neighbours beat him unconscious, dragged him into the street, doused him with white spirit and set him on fire. The man had done nothing wrong.

'So, you're enjoying the exploits of the Sentinel?' Kim asked.

'Looks like he gets stuff done.'

'Someone you know?' she asked, hoping for a miracle.

'Doubt it, but I like his methods. He's got the courage to act decisively to stop bad people.'

'And you're sure they're bad people?'

'I don't have to be. I ain't the one killing them.'

Reedy's smug attitude was starting to wear on her nerves.

'So, you work off tips that come in from the public?'

'Sometimes.'

'And how does that work?' Kim asked. There was a possibility that someone within this group was acting on information being fed to them, carrying out the murders based on the tip-offs they received. The BCA didn't normally exact this type of vengeance, but their list of members was changing all the time.

'We get an email or a message, and we begin surveillance.'

'Which you're trained in?'

'It's just people watching. No training required.'

'Of course not,' Bryant said, rolling his eyes.

'And then?' Kim pushed.

'We build a file. If there's nothing to report, we close the file. If there is something, we pass it on to you guys and then nothing gets done.'

Kim had never seen one of these files, but she was willing to bet that hard evidence was thin on the ground.

'That must be frustrating. You do all that work, and it goes nowhere.'

'Of course it's bloody frustrating. We have a team of nineteen volunteers who all have real jobs aside from doing their public duty. They give up hours and hours of their time to help rid the streets of paedophiles, abusers, rapists. They feel passionately about public safety, and they get no support from you lot.'

'Passionate enough to kill?' she asked.

'None of our members would go that far.'

'You don't know that, so I'm gonna need to take those seventeen names, Reedy, and don't get me started on your morals and values. What was that fuck-up a couple of weeks ago?'

He had the grace to colour slightly. 'It wasn't me.'

'So you weren't the one pretending to be a sixteen-year-old, except that you never told him you were sixteen, so the guy actually thought he was meeting an eighteen-year-old?'

'He was married and cheating on his wife.'

'Which isn't illegal. And he's certainly no paedophile, but of course your lot posted the video of him being confronted for grooming and now he's lost everything. He's had to move house, and his wife tried to take her own life following the abuse and death threats. Great result. So if you can let me have that little angel's real name first, I'd really appreciate it.'

He shook his head. 'Not happening. Data protection. You can't make me.'

Those last few words were spoken like a petulant child.

'Where's your civic duty now? People are being murdered. Don't they need protection too?'

'Not if they've done bad things.'

'Okay, enough games. Hand over the names.'

'No chance. You're thinking that one of our volunteers would take matters into their own hands.'

'And your refusal to give me their names makes me think I might be right.'

'No, no. I've already told you that none of our people would do that.'

'Give me their names and we can check 'em out for ourselves,' Kim insisted.

Reedy crossed his arms. 'Not happening, Inspector. Come back with a warrant.'

'Count on it,' she said, getting up from her seat.

Bryant opened the door for them to leave.

It wasn't until she got to the car that Kim realised Banksy hadn't spoken once.

FORTY-NINE

'Okay, that's another warrant and two more names to check,' Penn said after ending the call from the boss. She sure wasn't leaving any stone unturned on this one.

'We following the prison lead or the vigilante lead?' Stacey asked.

Penn wasn't sure, but he was growing more and more uncomfortable with the boss's refusal to speak to his colleague.

This wasn't the natural order of things. He beavered away under his own steam, and Stacey maintained contact. If he was feeling the change in dynamics, then she had to be too.

'Follow the lead with the biggest dicks,' Alison said.

'What was that now?' he asked.

'Look at it,' she continued. 'We've got a guy taunting you with nearly dead bodies. He doesn't know for sure that they aren't going to manage to communicate something. He takes the time to pose them to send a message and then he's shouting about it on social media. He's waving his dick about all over this. Now that's either because he really does have a big dick and he wants to flaunt it, or he's trying to compensate for something,' she said, wiggling her little finger.

Stacey chuckled but Penn turned towards the behaviourist. Just like he valued a good post-mortem, he liked it when Alison came to play. It was just as riveting to learn about the workings of the mind as the mechanics of the body.

'Are you saying this is all to do with the actual size of his penis?'

'I'm speaking metaphorically, Penn. What I'm saying is that this killer is filled with arrogance. That he has an oversize ego that makes him think he can leave whatever tracks he likes and still get away with it. The killings are important, but he could be doing them with a lot less fuss. Why bother with the posing? Why bother to leave them alive? If he didn't piss about so much with the bodies, he wouldn't need to contaminate the crime scene. Again, why post on social media? The job is done, the target is dead. Mission complete. Why the sideshow?'

'Are you going to answer any of those questions? Cos I'm totally invested now,' Penn said.

'He wants something. He's keeping himself attached in too many ways, so he's definitely after something. But I'm just not sure yet what it is.'

'Don't leave me hanging too long.'

Alison chuckled and returned to her screen.

'What do you want, Stace – warrant or names?'

'Penn, you don't have to treat me with kid gloves. I can pull my weight.'

'I know that, but I'm on a roll with the court orders. I'll stick with that, and you take the names.'

By far the most interesting, distracting part of the task.

'Penn, I honestly—'

'Don't make me pull rank, Stace,' he warned.

He groaned internally as his phone signalled another call from the boss. He sure hoped life was going to return to normal soon, he thought as he pressed to answer.

FIFTY

'Bryant, save me from doing something I know I'm going to regret,' Kim said, tapping her phone on her knee as Bryant drove them towards the home of Lenny Baldwin. It seemed that the youth custody officer was the only person who could answer their questions.

'Not sure I can do that, guv. Basis for a warrant for the Angels' membership is a bit slim. We might not get it.'

She hadn't told him what she was planning to do, but he knew her well enough to understand how much she wanted the information. And the lengths she was prepared to go to in getting it.

'You don't always have to tell me the truth, you know,' she said, bringing her phone to life.

She scrolled to the number and jabbed it harshly, knowing that she had no other choice but that this was going to be painful.

'What the hell have I done this time?' Frost answered icily.

Kim closed her eyes as she said the words that were going to cause her physical pain. 'Frost, I need your help.'

She opened her eyes again during the silence that followed.

'What do you want now?' Frost asked wearily.

Kim smiled at the response. Such was the nature of their relationship. Whether the reporter had disregarded their earlier spat out of curiosity about her imminent request she didn't know, but the harsh words that occurred between them rarely left a lasting scar.

'Black Country Angels. I need the names of their members.'

'Go to their website and Facebook page. You'll find them shouting loud and proud about their achievements. They're not exactly shy.'

'Most of them are aliases, and those aren't the names I want. Anyone I'm interested in probably isn't going to be screaming their vigilante ties from the rooftops.'

'You think the killer is a vigilante?' Frost asked.

Kim said nothing. Frost had the ability to search through any article written about the group past and present and dig out contacts and likely members. She probably had other sources beyond that too, but the less Kim knew about that the better.

Realising Kim wasn't going to divulge anything further, Frost sighed heavily. 'Okay, leave it with me.'

Kim ended the call, and Bryant chuckled.

'What?'

'Weird dynamic you two have. You're like... I don't know... fristers.'

'What the bloody hell is a frister?' Kim asked, aware that she hadn't been made to sell her soul, eat shit or even sacrifice a body part for her earlier outburst. Oh, it could have been so much harder.

'Well, neither one of you is ever going to admit to being friends. Normally only blood relatives, like siblings, can get away with what you two do to each other and then continue as though nothing ever happened.'

She grunted at him dismissively, but she supposed in a way he was right. She and Frost had had their moments over the years. There was a time when they'd saved each other's lives while in the clutches of a madman hellbent on revenge. There was also a time that Frost had been in possession of a file containing every detail of Kim's early life. Instead of reading and publishing it, she'd simply handed it back. On another occasion, she'd invited Frost to spend the night, just the one, in her guest bedroom, when she'd been injured while researching a story. But there was one time she remembered above all else. Frost had come to her home to offer support and advice on dealing with her complicated feelings after being beaten half to death by Symes.

Despite all this, the woman was still a raging pain in her ass, she thought as Bryant pulled the car into the kerb.

Lenny Baldwin lived in the Kingswinford end of Wall Heath. The street was lined with trees and small front gardens with driveways on every property.

The houses were semi-detached with adjoining single car garages. It wasn't an area of great affluence, but there were far worse places to find yourself living in the Black Country.

She understood from Penn that Baldwin had recently retired from his role in the Youth Custody Service.

The man who answered the door looked every one of his sixty-seven years. The lines around his eyes were deep, and his skin tone was on the pasty side. He had a full head of completely white hair.

Bryant introduced them, and he stood aside for them to enter.

'I thought you might get to me at some stage,' he said, closing the door behind them. 'I watch the local news.'

'You recognised the names of the recent victims?' Kim asked, noting a male and female set of everything she passed – wellington boots, jackets, scarves – and yet the house sounded deathly quiet beyond them. There was no distant hum of activity.

'I hope we're not disturbing you or your wife from anything.'

'You'd be hard pushed to disturb Lizzie – she's been dead for three months.'

'Sorry for your loss,' Bryant offered automatically.

And yet she was still everywhere, Kim thought, now seeing sadness in the pairs of items around the house.

'Did you consider coming to see us and mentioning you'd known them both when you recognised their names?' Kim asked as she took a seat on a well-worn sofa.

'And tell you what? That I knew both boys fifteen years ago? That would hardly help you now.'

'We had a visit from Ryan West, who also remembered them and was able to give us the link back to Welton.'

Baldwin sniffed. 'Not sure what he can tell you. He barely knew them.'

Ryan had admitted he hadn't been there very long.

'We understand that you were the only staff member to continue at Welton after Acer Security took over the contract.'

'Only because they couldn't get rid of me. I was pretty smug back then, but in hindsight, I wish they had thrown me out with the rest.'

'Why's that?' Kim asked.

'Bloody soulless place. You start off with the best intentions, you really see yourself making a difference, but you never do. You try and take your victories where you can find them, so you don't give up. Your ambitions change from helping a kid to turn his life around to just being grateful he doesn't stab you. Your hope dies and your passion fades.'

'When did your views change?' Kim asked.

He shrugged. 'I don't know. At first the job was as advertised. I was supervising young offenders on court orders and community sentences, and supporting them after release, trying to get them into education, work or training. But gradually it was all about spending time with them in secure institutions, offering one-to-one support, managing day-to-day activities and helping them build routines through education and social inter-actions. At first you'd see a kid through from beginning to end, but then they had some of us doing all the prison work and others doing the aftercare support. There was no way to build a bond before handing them over to the next person, and the kids knew that. Made them feel like they were in a system so they didn't give a shit.'

'There's no hope then?' Kim asked, trying to keep the sharp edges out of her tone. She understood Welton was for young offenders, but they were still only kids. There had to be hope.

'How many cases have you worked in your career so far?'

Kim shook her head, indicating that she had no idea.

'Hundreds?'

'Definitely.'

'Charge rate percentage mid-eighties?' he asked.

'A little higher.'

'Conviction rate low eighties?'

'Thereabouts.'

'Okay, now consider it was zero. How long do you think your enthusiasm would last if you had a success rate of exactly zero?'

'You don't think you had any successes?' Kim asked doubt-fully. His career had spanned more than thirty years.

'No. People need to want to be helped, and if that means breaking habits or putting in effort to change, then forget it.' His right hand clenched into a fist. 'I gave it my best years. Taking them on, trying to improve their lives. Every ounce of energy I had, I put into those kids. Every week of every year, and some weekends I was too exhausted to haul myself out of bed. Physically and mentally. Even when I wasn't at work, I was thinking about some of them, thinking of ways to help them turn their lives around. And all the time Lizzie supported me, comforted me and let me dedicate myself to the job.'

Kim knew what was coming. She could do the sums in her head and could see the root of the bitterness.

'I finally retired. It was our time. They were someone else's problem, and I could leave with a clear conscience. Literally one week later, Lizzie was diagnosed with terminal lung cancer. Palliative care only. She lasted six weeks, and she struggled through every one of them.'

Kim heard the catch in his voice and waited a short minute for him to recover.

'I'm so sorry for your loss, Mr Baldwin.'

'Thank you. But I'm sure you can understand why I don't wish to give Welton any more of my energy.'

'I get it, but you literally are the only person we can ask. Perhaps just a few questions and then we'll leave you in peace.'

His face tightened, but he nodded.

'We understand that Eric Gould and Paul Brooks were at Welton at the same time. Would their paths have crossed?'

She deliberately left out the names offered to her by Ryan West, to see if she got the same story from this man.

He spluttered. 'Paths crossed? Are you kidding? They were best friends. Thick as thieves. They shared a room and were always together. I mean, it wasn't just them. There was a core group, six of them if I remember correctly.' He tapped his head. 'Of course. They used to call themselves the Superior Six. It was their little gang name. We had a nickname for them as well, but it wasn't quite that pleasant.'

'What was it?'

'The Psycho Six.'

'And why was that?' Kim asked.

'Because they were a bunch of nasty little bastards.'

FIFTY-ONE

'To be fair, neither of these two seem to be geniuses,' Stacey said, prompting both Penn and Alison to look up.

'Which two?' Alison asked.

'Elliot Reed and Gordon Banks from the Black Country Angels. Elliot is the son of a surgeon and has spent most of his thirty-two years being completely average. His father is revered for his skills in orthopaedics, and yet junior was a C-plus-average student right up until his last two years when a private tutor was engaged to get his grades up for college, which he dropped out of halfway through his first year. He's worked as a barista, a car wash attendant, a hotel porter in Birmingham and he still lives at home with mummy and daddy. I'm surprised he feels passionate about anything. Strikes me as a bit lazy to be honest.'

'Or dyslexic,' Alison offered. 'He works low-skill jobs that don't require much mastery of the written word. Many people have been mislabelled as lazy or stupid but really do have a prohibitive learning difficulty.'

'Fair point,' Stacey admitted. Perhaps she had assumed that because he was from a wealthy family, he was an entitled good-for-nothing layabout. Not the same for Gordon Banks, who appeared to have fought his way through school with his fists and disappeared from the education system in his mid-teens. Now in his late twenties, his socials consisted of lewd jokes and funny videos. Both seemed to lack passion, vocation and direction.

'I can't quite work out what possessed them to volunteer with the Black Country Angels. Neither of them appear to be political activists or vocal about social injustice.'

'Maybe they've been victims of crime,' Alison offered. 'Our first reaction to crime isn't fear, it's anger. Anger often requires action to neutralise it.'

'But to join a group of interfering, obstructive—'

'Hey, some people appreciate the work of vigilantes,' Alison argued. 'In 1981 in Missouri, a resident of Skidmore shot and killed the town bully in broad daylight after years of crimes without any punishment. He'd basically raped, looted and pillaged his way around town for years. Forty-five people witnessed the shooting and not one would identify the shooter.'

'But that's still murder,' Penn protested.

'Forty-five people say otherwise. As did the two hundred women in Kasturba Nagar, India, who lynched a man who'd raped them repeatedly for more than a decade. They cut off his penis, and he died from seventy stab wounds. It's not just the recent trend of paedophile hunting and entrapment. Vigilante groups have been around for decades. There's a group in El Salvador called the Sombra Negra or Black Shadow, and they're mostly retired police officers and military personnel whose sole duty is to cleanse the country of impure social elements by killing criminals and gang members.'

'Not on the level of El Salvador, but wasn't there a guy in Hampshire some years back that went around slashing tyres because he'd seen the drivers using mobiles?' Stacey asked.

'Yeah, I remember that. He clearly felt strongly about folks and their phones,' Penn added.

'But people do feel strongly, Penn,' Alison said. 'And as I said before, it tends to come from anger at some kind of injustice. I read somewhere that in some US cities, people have created real-life superhero personas, donning masks and costumes to patrol their neighbourhoods.'

'So are these people doing it for the feeling of power?' Stacey asked.

'Some are, yes, but there are also groups with a genuine wish to protect. The Gulabi Gang in Uttar Pradesh is a female vigilante group dedicated to protecting women of all castes from domestic abuse, sexual violence and oppression.'

'Now that's a group I'd volunteer for,' Stacey said as she saw Penn steal a glance at his watch. He looked her way and saw that she'd clocked it.

'I'm not going to get out in time, am I?'

It was already five and there was no chance they were leaving on time tonight.

'I can cover, matey. It's your anniversary. Just take an hour and come back. I'm sure the boss won't mind if—'

'We're swamped, Stace.'

He wasn't wrong, but the offer was genuine. She knew he'd do the same for her. Still, knowing Penn as she did, he'd never expect anyone to take up his slack.

'Back in a sec,' he said, taking his phone out into the hall.

His hunched demeanour told her he really didn't want to make the call, but the job often required changing plans and short-notice cancellations.

She just hoped that six months in the relationship could wear it.

FIFTY-TWO

'I can't remember everything about all of them,' Baldwin said, 'but they were a nasty little bunch. Top dog was definitely Ian Perkins. He was the oldest and had been in the longest. Also guilty of the most serious crime.'

'Which was?' Bryant asked.

'Murder. His brother.'

'Jesus,' Kim said. 'For what?'

'Sexual abuse. His brother abused him from the age of seven. Finally told his parents when he was twelve. They didn't believe him so Ian killed his brother a week later.'

'No self-defence or extenuating circumstances?' Bryant asked.

'Luke was fast asleep in bed when Ian knifed him seven times.'

'Bloody hell.'

'He showed no remorse for the act, and his parents disowned him; they didn't go to his trial and never visited him at Welton. Completely cut off from the family.'

So many different points of view on that one. The abuse must have been horrific to endure. No doubt it scarred the boy, but he'd had the courage to speak. His parents had ignored him. Were his extreme actions understandable? She wasn't sure. In any case, his family had picked a side and it hadn't been his.

'That's rough.'

'Trust me, you wouldn't have felt sorry for him for long. He transferred out of Welton and into the adult prison system when he was twenty-one.'

'Isn't that late?'

'It's the highest age to transfer. He could have gone earlier, but he was under appeal, so they kept him until the maximum.'

'And both Eric and Paul were in this gang?' Kim asked, bringing his attention back to her victims.

'Yeah, along with another three. Let me think. Nathan Yates, Dean Newton and a quieter kid, Leyton something. I can't remember.'

Bryant didn't need telling to write down the names they were missing.

'So, Eric and Paul...?'

'They really were awful. I'm not sure how they would have been singly, but as part of that group they bullied every new kid, smacked around the younger ones, stole stuff, intimidated every-one. The guards had trouble controlling them all. They spat, threw things and possibly worse.'

'Go on,' Kim urged.

'I wasn't there at the time, but I heard about an incident where they cornered one of the female guards and dragged her into the boys' showers. Went as far as pulling down her trousers before someone got to wondering where they all were.'

The intent had been clear.

'She left. Didn't press charges and wanted nothing more to do with the place. I also remember hearing talk of them being in the area when a particularly strict officer fell down the stairs and died. That's just a couple of incidents. There were many. This wasn't kids acting up. It was mean, nasty, vicious. It's as though being part of that group brought out the worst in all of them.'

'Anything you can remember where just Eric and Paul were involved?'

He thought for a moment.

'There was one kid. I can't remember his name – he was only thirteen, I think. He was put in with the two of them, and they weren't happy. They tied his wrists and ankles together, put him on the top bunk and pushed him off repeatedly. Stuffed his mouth with a pair of his pants and just kept doing it. He couldn't even break his own fall because of how they'd tied him up. He was discovered the next morning by the guards, unconscious and covered in blood. He was in the hospital for a week and then transferred to another wing.'

'Charges filed?' she asked hopefully.

Baldwin shook his head. 'The boy was promised an early release for his silence.'

'Seriously?'

He frowned at her. 'Inspector, how do you think these places work?'

'By the book and, hopefully, best practice guidelines.'

'Oh dear. I hate to be the one to disillusion you, but I visited probably seven or more institutions in my career, and I can assure you that very few of them are run to any book I've ever read. A book or a process is a rigid instrument. Human beings are not. We adapt, we learn, we barter, we bargain. We do what we need to get the job done.'

'Mr Baldwin, you are destroying my illusion of—'

'You have a book, don't you – your PACE regulations?'

She nodded.

'It's very black and white, isn't it? Tells you everything you need to do in any situation.'

'Yes.'

'And you're telling me that in a major investigation, you don't deviate from the script to get the desired result?'

Kim saw the list form in her mind's eye.

Breaking into the home of a dead man.

Tampering with evidence once inside said home.

Secretly questioning a colleague's wife about a man's death.

Yeah, nothing to see here, she decided, pushing the thoughts aside.

'There are grey areas, Inspector. The management team at Welton didn't want certain incidents travelling up the food chain and so deals were made.'

'What about you – did you make any deals?'

He shook his head. 'Absolutely not. I would never do such a thing.'

'Did this Psycho Six ever target you?'

'No, I got off very lightly. They left me alone.'

One had to wonder why, Kim thought, but she said nothing.

None of the questions running around her head could be answered without access to the historic records at Welton. Who was the boy bullied mercilessly by Eric and Paul? What happened to him? Where was the woman they attacked? How had it affected her life? Had that prison officer's fall been a tragic accident?

'Just one last thing, Mr Baldwin. Is there any way you can give us a list of the people that Eric and Paul really pissed off?'

He shook his head in the negative.

'Why's that?' she asked.

'Because quite honestly, the list would be far too long.'

FIFTY-THREE

The trip to the canteen had done little to lighten Stacey's mood.

She was trying to force herself to be interested in the things she'd enjoyed before, and food had been a good one. Her failure to find anything appealing was no reflection on Betty's efforts but more the fact that her body wasn't yet returning to normal.

She dropped the requested jacket potato with beans on Alison's desk as she passed.

'Cheers, big ears. What you got?'

Stacey shook her head as she retook her seat. 'I'm not hungry, so don't even try forcing something on me.'

'I'm your friend not your keeper,' Alison said as Stacey turned back to her computer. 'But as your friend I'm saying you could at least give yourself a short break from the screen.'

Penn was having a fifteen-minute walk around the outside of the building to get away from the desk. He'd cancelled his date with Lynne, who had completely understood.

'Yeah, I will,' Stacey said, still miffed at the conversation she'd overheard in the canteen between two male officers chowing down on cottage pie.

She logged into the daily reports and found the incident they'd been discussing.

She knew there'd been a sexual assault reported yesterday when the boss had been interviewing the two men downstairs, but what she'd just heard had piqued her interest. The two officers had flippantly been saying that the sarge was on her way to tell the victim there was little more they could do given that her best description of her attacker was that he was a fat bastard.

'Wouldn't really get to court anyway,' the shorter officer had said while chewing a mouthful of mashed potato. 'Seeing as he barely touched her.'

'Yeah, makes no sense. He traps her in the alleyway, pushes her to the ground and then just stops cos he thinks he's killed her. When she came to, he was gone. Really?' his mate had asked disbelievingly. 'Nah, it's a case of buyer's remorse there. She fancied it and changed her mind and had to explain the head injury to her fella.'

Unfortunately for the man who'd made that little speech, her stumble behind him had brought his fork into contact with his nostril.

Her mumbled apology had been lost beneath his loud exclamation of pain and shock.

She read through the details of the assault until she reached the description of the attacker. Although not overly detailed, it did say a little more than 'fat bastard'.

And those extra few details were what interested her.

Stacey pulled up her files and sent a document to print. As it whirred slowly out the top of the machine, she grabbed her jacket and satchel.

'What's up?' Alison asked, wiping bean juice from her mouth.

'Gotta go out. If the boss comes back, just tell her you don't know where I am.'

'Not a lie, seeing as you haven't told me.'

'Exactly. Won't be long,' she said, rushing out the door.

As she headed down the stairs, Stacey felt the butterflies fluttering in her stomach.

But these weren't the dark, cloying, carnivorous, life-sapping moths that had been with her for weeks.

These were the good ones.

FIFTY-FOUR

'Hang on, isn't this guy a timewaster?' Bryant asked as they neared the address in Dudley Wood. 'You've spoken to him already.'

'You know, if you listened to everything I say instead of half of it, you'd know what I said.'

'Yes, but then I wouldn't get to hear that note of barely concealed contempt in your voice that I so enjoy.'

'I thought he was a timewaster, but he actually taught the boys English at Welton.'

She chose not to add that it was only for a few short months.

'That one,' she said, spying the number of the address he'd left her.

Bryant pulled into the small driveway of a three-storey townhouse as her phone began to ring. It was a number she didn't recognise, but as she was dealing with Traffic as well as her own case, she had no choice but to answer it.

'Stone.'

'Inspector, it's Lynne... Penn's girlfriend. We met back—'

'I know who you are, Lynne. We worked a major case together. What's up?'

'Penn just called. He's cancelled our picnic. It's our anniversary and I know he feels shit. I get it, honest, but is there any way I could drop by the station and grab him for an hour later, surprise him before I go on shift, so he knows it's not a problem and that I'm not angry?'

Kim understood the pressures the job put on personal relationships. For every marriage that made it, there were probably two that didn't. And the ruination of this love story wasn't going to be on her conscience.

'No problem at all – enjoy,' Kim said before ending the call.

Bryant smiled at her as they got out of the car.

'What?' she asked.

'You really are a nice person when you want to be.'

'Yeah, just watch how nice I can be if you start spreading that rumour,' she said, approaching the front door.

Ryan West answered on the first knock. 'Hey, Inspector, good to see you again,' he said, stepping aside and nodding towards Bryant.

Kim introduced him as she took in the teacher's attire.

The open-neck shirt and loose tie were the same, but the smart black trousers had been replaced with grey joggers.

'Skype class,' he explained, leading them into the kitchen, where his laptop was open. 'Just finished an online lesson with a group of Afghan refugees. Already grasped the concept of a dangling participle quicker than many of my students.'

Kim regarded him blankly.

'Not important,' he said, closing the laptop and pointing to the chairs. 'How can I help?'

'We've been talking to Lenny Baldwin about the Psycho Six.'

Ryan shook his head. 'Bloody hell, I'd forgotten that's what some people used to call them. To be fair, they were pretty horrific. Some more than others.'

'Would you happen to have remembered their full names?'

'Um, hang on,' he said, tapping the table and searching his memory. 'You already know of two,' he went on, counting them off on his fingers. 'There was Ian Perkins.' He shuddered.

'The ringleader?'

'Definitely. Then there was Nathan Yates, Dean Newton and Leyton... ooh Leyton Parks – yes, I think that's it. I've been trying to remember since we last spoke.'

Bryant added the missing details into his notebook.

'Strange that's the name I'd have most trouble remembering.'

'Why strange?'

He shrugged. 'He wasn't so much like the others. We got on okay. He fell into the group by accident, I suppose, due to being cellmates with one of the others, but he was quieter, gentler than his friends. He liked to read. He enjoyed the written word.'

Kim could understand why the English teacher might have formed a bond with that one.

'Lenny told us about a couple of incidents involving the boys. An attempted sexual assault?'

'Before my time, I'm afraid, but I did hear the rumours.'

'And of a boy that was terrorised quite badly by Eric and Paul?'

Ryan shook his head. 'Not during the time I was there, but I could easily believe it.'

'Did they try anything with you?'

'Err... besides the human excrement in my briefcase and the ejaculate in my coat pocket, nothing to write home about.'

'No such problems with your Afghan refugees?' Bryant observed.

'Quite,' Ryan answered with a smile.

'Nothing violent?' Kim pushed.

Ryan shook his head.

'Nor with Lenny Baldwin?'

'No.' He frowned. 'Actually, I don't think he even got the turds in his bag. Then again, there was gossip.'

'About what?'

'Look, I wasn't there long enough to judge, and we're talking about a man's career.'

'He's retired, and we're not going to broadcast it on social media,' Kim said.

'Well, his reports held a lot of weight. In some cases, they made the difference between a kid being released early or not. I'm not saying he did anything untoward by promising early release or anything like that, but there was talk,' he said, opening his hands expressively.

Kim tried to fight down the ball of suspicion in her gut, but it was hard when the man himself had already admitted to operating in the grey area of his job description.

She thanked Ryan for his insight before leaving.

She put in a call to Penn to chase the court order for Welton. She needed to know which boys Lenny Baldwin had recommended for early release.

FIFTY-FIVE

Stacey knocked gently on the door of the house in Lye. She wasn't sure why, because she had to knock loud enough for the woman to hear her, but she supposed it was an unconscious move aimed at sensitivity and care after what the woman had been through.

The door opened slowly. Behind it was a figure in an oversized woollen jumper with a neck that came up to her chin and a hem that reached down to her knees. Damp brown hair was pulled back into a tight ponytail. Her face was pale, make-up free and wearing a suspicious expression.

Stacey held up her ID and introduced herself.

'What is this? A second visit to tell me there's fuck all you can do?'

Stacey shook her head. 'I'm CID. I understand a sergeant was here.'

'Yeah, to tell me they weren't gonna be able to catch the bastard who—'

'Is that what she said?' Stacey asked doubtfully.

'Not exactly, but I got the idea. I suppose you'd say she came to manage my expectations.'

'May I come in?'

Karen Boyd let go of the door in a 'do what you like' manner.

Stacey closed the door behind her and followed Karen to the lounge.

The woman sat on the single chair and pulled her legs and feet inside the jumper like a security blanket. She leaned forward, took a cigarette from the box and lit it.

'Sorry, used to smoke outside, but not any more. Don't even feel safe in my own back garden.'

Stacey's heart went out to her. Her own recent experiences had taught her a lot about how the fear of what might happen had the power to affect things you'd done before without a minute of consideration.

'May I call you Karen?' Stacey asked.

She shrugged. It clearly made no difference to her.

'Do you mind telling me what happened the other night?'

'For what reason? So you can choose not to believe me as well?'

'Please, Karen, I'm hoping I can help.'

She took one long draw on her cigarette and then ground it out forcefully. Her arms then disappeared into the jumper with the rest of her, leaving only her head exposed.

'I was on my way back from the pub. Birthday drinks for my boss. It's a short walk, half a mile. I refused the next drink so I wouldn't be leaving in the dark.'

So many considerations just to get home from a night out.

'I mean, who gets an Uber for half a mile?' she said in a tone that hinted she really wished she had. 'I didn't even realise there was anyone behind me. I heard no footsteps, sensed nothing. I was about halfway. I was distracted messing in my handbag for my k-keys.'

She paused and took a few breaths.

'Take your time. There's no rush,' Stacey said gently.

'Next thing I knew, I was knocked so forcefully I thought a car had hit me. I was on my side, on the ground, in the alley. I'd hit my head. I was dazed. Before I opened my eyes, I could feel something pulling at my clothing. There were hands on my thighs, pulling up my skirt. I realised that the figure above me wasn't helping me. He was going to rape me.'

The tears were rolling over her cheeks.

'His hands were all over me, pulling, pushing, searching, grabbing. I started to kick and punch, but it's like my struggling was helping him to get me into the position he wanted. He managed to get himself between my legs. It was only then that I started to scream. He smacked me here,' she said, removing her hand from the cocoon briefly and pointing to her forehead. 'My head went back and hit the ground. I was trying not to pass out cos then I wouldn't be able to scream, and then it stopped. Suddenly the weight was gone, and I could breathe.'

The memory prompted her to take a few deep breaths before continuing. 'My clothes were all around my waist. Every intimate part of me was exposed.'

'So there was no—'

'No,' Karen said, cutting off the word she didn't want to hear.

'And you saw no one else?'

'It was a couple of minutes before someone found me. I was just sobbing against the wall, too scared to come out of the alley. It was a man and he took care not to touch me. He stood in front of me and called the police. He just kept telling me he wasn't going to leave me and that no one was going to hurt me.'

The sad smile on her face told Stacey this had helped her to feel safe while waiting for the police to arrive.

'Do you think your attacker just changed his mind?' Stacey asked, understanding the ridiculousness of the question. Rapists stopping midway wasn't a common occurrence.

Karen frowned. 'At first I thought so. I thought my

screaming had attracted attention, but there are things that don't make sense. No one came to my aid immediately.'

The words ended but the frown remained. There was more. 'Go on.'

'It's hard to explain, but he didn't get up off me. There was no gradual easing of the weight on top of me. I can't explain it. It was like he was there one second and gone the next.'

'Like someone else kind of hauled him off you?' Stacey asked.

Karen nodded slowly. 'Yes, exactly like that, but that can't be right, can it? Cos if someone had pulled him off me, they would surely have checked on me?'

Not if they wanted him more than they wanted to be seen by the police, Stacey thought.

'And you got a good look at him, the man that attacked you?'

Karen allowed her hands out of the cocoon again long enough to wipe her eyes. 'I did.'

'But he wasn't amongst the photos you were shown.'

She shook her head as a fresh wave of tears sprang from her eyes.

'I wish to God he had been. Much as I didn't want to see his face again, I now know that the odds of him being caught are slim to none. The sergeant hinted at that half an hour ago. But how do I ever feel safe again? How do I know he's not gonna come for me a second time? If he tried it once, he could try it again. It happened just down the road for God's sake. I can't step outside on my own, and even if someone is with me, I'm looking everywhere for him while just wanting to throw up.'

The last sentence brought emotion to Stacey's throat. It was a fear she could easily identify with.

'Hey, give yourself time,' she reassured Karen. 'It's barely been a couple of days.'

'But when will it end? How will I ever feel safe again knowing he's still out there?'

Stacey took out her phone as Karen lit another cigarette with trembling hands. She scrolled to the least horrific photo she'd received from Keats of the body of Paul Brooks.

'Karen, is this the man that tried to rape you?'

The sharp intake of breath was the answer she'd been after.

FIFTY-SIX

'Thanks for joining us,' Kim said as Stacey entered the room.

'Sorry, boss, just something I wanted to follow up,' she answered, throwing her satchel under the desk.

'And given recent events, it might have been appropriate to let someone know where you were going,' Kim snapped.

She'd been less than thrilled to arrive back at the office to be told that Stacey had disappeared without telling anyone where she was. It had been that kind of stupidity that had caused the trouble in the first place.

Kim knew she wasn't being fair and that Stacey had only been doing her job, but now wasn't the time to test her patience.

'I took a car,' Stacey offered quietly.

Kim grunted in response.

She'd returned to the office expecting Stacey to request a private word. Didn't she want to know why her boss had spoken to her wife? Was she not pissed off that they'd had quite the hostile conversation? Unless Devon hadn't told her. That possibility prompted all kinds of questions in her mind.

'Paul Brooks is the person who attacked Karen Boyd,' Stacey said, pulling her chair into her desk.

Kim frowned. Karen Boyd wasn't a name she recognised.

'The attempted sexual assault the other night,' Stacey clarified.

Kim recalled the activity in the station when she'd been interviewing Philip Drury and Ryan West.

'You're sure?' Kim asked as movement in the car park caught her attention. Lynne's VW Polo had just driven in and parked by the wall. Kim opened her mouth to say something to Penn but paused as Lynne reached into the passenger seat to retrieve something.

'She identified him from the photo, boss. Definitely him,' Stacey answered.

'Bloody hell. Why attempted? Something scared him off?' she asked, taking another look outside. She hid her smile as she saw Lynne laying out a blanket in a three-car-wide space. On the blanket was a picnic basket which she was emptying and arranging in the centre of the throw.

She knew there was a reason she'd liked Lynne when they'd worked together a few years back, and this was it. She cared nothing for what anyone thought.

Stacey opened her mouth, and Kim put up a hand to stop her.

'Penn, do me a favour, eh? Someone's having a bit of trouble changing a tyre in the car park. Wanna go lend a hand?'

'Sure, boss.'

'And don't rush back.'

He frowned, but she waved him out of the room. He'd understand when he got down there.

Three pairs of eyes regarded her curiously. She pointed to the window.

Stacey turned in her chair, and Alison and Bryant approached.

'Oh my God,' Alison said, placing her hand over her mouth.

'That is soooooo romantic,' Stacey offered.

'And he is absolutely floored,' Bryant noted as Penn rushed out of the building and came to a complete standstill when he saw Lynne standing by a picnic blanket complete with glasses and sandwiches and little plates.

He looked up to their window and his expression was enough.

'Okay, guys, leave them in peace for a bit,' Kim said, moving them away.

Once the oohs and ahhs had subsided, Kim continued the discussion about the sexual-assault victim.

'You were saying something stopped the attacker, Stace?'

'Ah, well, that's where it gets a bit strange. Karen thinks someone grabbed him before he could actually do it.'

Kim caught up quickly. 'You think our guy stopped him?' she asked, wondering if the real Stacey was starting to turn up for work again. It was going to take a bit more than one or two useful insights to undo the damage that had been done though. And there was still Devon to think of.

Stacey nodded. 'It's possible. We've not been able to trace Paul Brooks's movements prior to his murder, and Karen feels that he was forcibly removed from her.'

'But he wasn't on our system as an adult?' Kim asked, realising what had bothered her about his clothing. He'd left the house intending to commit rape, and he'd worn his oldest, shabbiest clothes, fully intending to destroy them, along with any physical evidence, once the crime had been committed.

Bile rose in her throat at the thought.

'No, boss, and neither was Eric Gould,' Stacey answered.

Kim was thinking of an answer when her phone rang.

'Stone,' she answered, seeing that it was the front desk.

'Lady down here wants to see you, Inspector.'

'A bit busy at the minute, Jack.'

'Okay, she'll wait, but she's not leaving until she's had a word.'

Jesus, she hated the persistent ones.
'What's her name?'
'Charlotte Danks.'
'Tell her I'm on my way down.'

FIFTY-SEVEN

On Kim's instruction, Jack had placed Charlotte in interview room one. For some reason, the woman wasn't what she'd been expecting. Everything about her was average. Her hair was mid-brown and cut into a bob with a blunt fringe that rested above hazel eyes. Her features were attractive but not striking. In her mind, Birch had been attracted to Charlotte because of her stunning appearance, but as pretty as she was, she wouldn't have stood out in a crowd.

Kim introduced herself as she sat.

'Is it true?' Charlotte asked, clenching her hands together on the table.

Kim needed no explanation of the question. 'Yes, he's dead.'

'I want to see him,' she said, pushing out her chin in readiness for the battle.

'I can confirm without question that Terence Birch is dead. I met him on a previous case, and I attended the crime scene. It was him.'

'Not good enough. I need to see it for myself.'

Kim reached for her phone. 'I have photos of—'

'No, I need to see him. There's no other way.'

'You're not related or—'

'I'm his victim, Inspector. I can assure you that no one has given that man more thought than I have.'

'Ms Danks, I can't—'

'Yes, you can, Inspector,' she said as her chin began to wobble with emotion. 'You, as a police officer, can do what you all failed to do for ten years, which is to give me peace of mind.'

Kim briefly considered arguing the point that the force had done everything they could, but it would make no difference. Nothing they'd done had altered the way Charlotte had been forced to leave her life and her family behind for her own safety and sanity.

People often thought that once confronted by the law, individuals stopped their aberrant behaviour, but some criminals wouldn't be deterred regardless of the consequences. Terence Birch had been one of them.

Kim opened her mouth to argue again. This wasn't normal practice.

'If you're going to offer anything other than a date and time, please save your breath. Even if I have to camp outside the closest entrance I can find to the morgue with a tent and camping stove, I'm going to do it. I have lost years of my life to that man,' she said, whispering those last few words.

Kim finally got the reason for the woman's attitude. It was bravado. Beneath the hostility and the aggression, she needed to know if she could live again.

No amount of assurances from anyone else would give her that peace.

'Let me take your number and I'll see what I can do.'

Charlotte quickly rattled off her number, and Kim put it into her phone.

'If I can swing it, I'd rather you didn't do it alone.'

'I'll be fine. I don't want my family to know what I'm doing – they'll just try and talk me out of it.'

And still the secrets couldn't be left behind.

'Leave it with me. I'll be in touch,' Kim said, standing and opening the door.

'Thank you, Inspector. I really appreciate your help, and I'm sorry if I came off a bit...'

'It's okay,' Kim said, showing her back through to the reception.

She continued watching the woman, contemplating how she was going to ask Keats for a favour without owing him something in return.

She was still deep in thought when Charlotte pulled out the station car park in a light-blue Fiat Panda.

FIFTY-EIGHT

'Okay, Alison, talk to me,' Kim said, once back in the office. It was getting late and her team was tired, but she wanted any insights that Alison had gained.

'Nice bit of weather we're having.'

'I'd prefer you talk to me about the Psycho Six, and who might want to hurt them.'

'Well, to begin with, that's an unfair label seeing as they were all under eighteen when they committed their crimes. None of them were psychotic and, at worse, they would have been diagnosed with conduct disorder, a mix of aggressive, deceitful, destructive and rebellious behaviour.'

'What are the later signs of psychopathy?' Bryant asked.

'Behaviour that conflicts with social norms. Disregarding the rights of others. Unable to distinguish right from wrong, no empathy, lying often, manipulating or hurting others, disregard for safety and responsibility, anger on a regular basis. Three or more of the above.'

'What about conduct disorder?' Kim asked.

'Bullying, aggression, forcing sexual activity, using a weapon. Lying, breaking and entering, stealing, forgery, arson or other destructive acts, truanting, running away, drugs and alcohol.'

'Forgive my stupidity, but list two sounds an awful lot like list one,' Bryant noted.

'Oh, you caught that, eh? Can't get anything past you, Bryant. Detecting psychopathy in young people is no different to detecting it in adults. The label you apply when you find it is just different, and that depends on the age.'

'But aren't there early signs?' Bryant asked. 'I've seen stuff on Discovery.'

'Someone needs to take that channel away from you,' Alison joked. 'Are you talking about the Macdonald Triad?'

'Burger, fries and a milkshake?' Penn asked with a smile.

His mood had been decidedly chipper since his impromptu date with Lynne on a blanket in the car park.

Alison offered him a tolerant eye roll. 'It's a triad of sociopathy detailing three factors: cruelty to animals, obsession with fire-setting and persistent bedwetting past the age of five. Allegedly, having two of three present is linked with later predatory behaviour. Although I'm guessing that the term "Psycho Six" was just a nickname and not a psychological evaluation.'

'Okay, but should we be considering this triad while trying to find the actual psycho who's targeting our six?' Kim asked, wondering if searching the records at Welton for fellow inmates meeting the requirement of the triad and cross-referencing with names of people the six had bullied might throw up a few worthwhile names.

'Not so fast,' Alison cautioned, destroying Kim's hopes of whittling down people at Welton using that criterion. Alison's 'not so fasts' were like a sharp pin in her balloons of hope. 'Further studies have shown that both arson and animal cruelty are linked to extensive periods of humiliation. Repeated animal cruelty has more of a link to violence against humans. It can be viewed as a rehearsal for killing people and the same methods might be used. Bedwetting can be an indicator of possible childhood abuse. So all of these contributors can also be indicators of sustained physical or emotional abuse.'

'You're saying that all inmates of Welton Hall are innocent victims of family or social trauma, abuse or neglect?' Kim asked, watching her potential line of enquiry fading into the distance.

'I'm not saying that at all,' Alison defended herself. 'And I especially love coming here so that you can argue with everything I say.'

'Happy to oblige, but crack on cos we're all running on fumes right now,' Kim advised.

'There are many reasons why kids get into trouble. There are genetic causes like brain damage. In some kids, anger and violence is connected to fear and anxiety, medication side effects, sleep disorders, chronic pain. Young people are increasingly being referred to child or adolescent mental health teams for assessment due to violent acts. Depression in adolescence can manifest as anger and aggression.

'Hyperactivity and attention disorders predispose children to both antisocial behaviour in adolescence and antisocial personality disorder in adult life.'

'Okay, great,' Kim said. 'How is that narrowing our list of potential suspects?'

There had been many times over the years when Alison had offered great insight and clarity as to what they were looking for. This wasn't one of those times.

'I can't pick a name out of a hat,' Alison said.

Kim sighed. 'Okay, for now, we're still going to assume that our killer has some kind of connection to Welton. We already know that our delightful group of six didn't win any popularity prizes with other inmates or staff. We desperately need the records from Welton, and tomorrow the focus is on tracking down and warning the others. Someone has it in for that group.'

She was pleased to see the names of Ian Perkins, Nathan Yates, Leyton Parks and Dean Newton already on the board.

'I already know where Ian Perkins isn't,' Penn offered.

Kim waited. From what she understood, he was the oldest, the ringleader and the only one who'd taken a life.

'He's no longer incarcerated. He left Welton aged twenty-one, when his appeal failed, and entered the prison system. He was released four years later.'

'Shouldn't be too hard to track—'

'New identity.'

Kim groaned. 'Witness protection?'

'Yep. A month before he was released, he testified against a Turkish drug runner who'd revealed secrets of his operation to Perkins, allowing the Met to aim further up the food chain. Got himself a new name and everything.'

'Anyone got any good news for me?' Kim asked, noting that Stacey in particular seemed to have something on her mind.

'Boss, I know we're going down the line that these are some kind of revenge attacks for what the Psycho Six did to people, but maybe there's something else.'

'Like what?'

'Eric Gould was in Welton for violence against his girl-friend. His relationship with Teresa Fox was heading in that direction. Paul Brooks was in Welton for sexual assault; he was on track to repeat the offence, but he was murdered before he could do it. Is there any chance these people are being murdered not for what they've done but for what they're about to do? Maybe they're being watched by someone, or by the Black Country Angels, and they know stuff we don't know.'

'You do know *Minority Report* was just a film, eh?' Penn asked with a wink.

Stacey responded with a raised eyebrow.

'Interesting theory,' Alison volunteered.

'And one we'll study in more depth tomorrow,' Kim said, pushing herself away from the desk.

There was a great deal to explore, but her team had been at it for over fourteen hours, and she had something else on her mind.

'Back at seven,' she called, heading into the Bowl.

Without further prompting, the four of them got busy closing down computers and stacking paperwork.

Stacey cast her a sidelong glance as she passed by the glass partition. Kim looked away. There would be a conversation, but she wasn't there yet.

There was no doubt that Stacey disliked her right now, but at the moment, she was focussed on making contact with someone who disliked her even more.

FIFTY-NINE

As Stacey opened the door to her home, she was thinking less about Terence Birch and more about the state of her relationship with her wife.

It had been months since she'd viewed the flat as her safe space. She knew there had been a time when she would have kicked off her shoes and settled in for a night of takeaway pizza and rubbish TV after a long hard day at work. Normality, the small things. She missed them. And she missed the storm-free sanctuary she'd shared with Devon. It was as though their blow-up the other night had allowed the rain clouds into their idyllic haven. Yes, Devon had apologised, and of course she'd accepted it, but forgiveness didn't come with an eraser.

'Hey, Dee,' she said, walking into the kitchen.

Devon turned from the boiling kettle to offer a one-armed embrace and a quick peck on the lips.

A wave of sadness washed over her. What the hell had been lost and would they ever find it again?

Devon handed her a glass of white wine while cradling a mug of coffee. 'How was your day, babe?'

Stacey considered offering a glib one-liner that would mean

she didn't have to give her time at work any more attention, but she didn't know how they would ever find each other if she closed up again.

'Pretty shit. My boss still hates me,' she said, taking a seat.

'Yeah, pretty sure she hates me too,' Devon said, taking the opposite seat.

Stacey now saw that Devon wasn't distant or cold as she'd thought, but pensive and tense. Her relief was short lived as she digested Devon's words.

'Why would she hate you?'

'She was here, earlier today.'

'Whoa, what?'

'Yeah, that's probably not gonna be the most surprising thing you're going to hear tonight, but I did let her have it, babe.'

'Oh Jesus,' Stacey said, taking a huge gulp of wine. Like she didn't have enough problems with the boss right now.

'Sorry, but her treatment of you is appalling, and I told her so.'

'Hon, she's my boss,' Stacey groaned.

'Then she should bloody well start acting like it, not least by offering you some support for what you've been through and an apology for exposing you to a man like Birch.'

'She couldn't have known what he was. I interview witnesses alone all the time.'

Devon shook her head. 'I knew you'd defend her. I wish I understood what she'd done to deserve such blind loyalty.'

Stacey felt sick. The thought of her boss and her wife at loggerheads was just too much.

'We're a unit,' Stacey explained. 'We work together day in and day out. There are bonds. It's tough to explain.'

Devon's own workplace differed since they had a high turnover of staff and the team she worked with changed on a weekly basis.

'I get it, babes, but those same bonds run both ways.

However angry she is with you, she should have your back right now.'

'She's not like normal people, Dee. She shows her emotions in different ways, but...' Stacey stopped speaking, aware the conversation was diverting from something that was way more important. 'Hang on. Why was she even here?'

'Ah, well, she wanted to talk to me about the night Birch was killed.'

Stacey felt a rush of emotion: anger, injustice, fear. Her boss had talked to her wife in connection with a man's death, as a police officer, and hadn't even mentioned it. What right did she have and, more importantly, what cause?

She reached for her satchel. This was too much. She wanted to be back on good terms with her boss, but what right did she have talking to Devon behind her back? 'This is not on. I'm gonna call—'

'Hang on. Let me tell you the rest. Take a good chug of wine,' Devon advised.

Stacey did so, wondering what the hell more there could be.

'She came to talk to me because she saw some footage.'

'Of what?' Stacey asked as a finger of fear travelled up her spine.

'Of me punching Birch.'

'Wh-what? How? When?'

Stacey wondered whether, if she stepped outside and entered the flat again, this would all make sense.

'When I stormed out on Monday night, I caught him up. I shouted at him. I punched him. It was caught on someone's door camera.'

'But you went out in the car,' Stacey said.

'After I'd confronted Birch, I did. And your boss wants to know where I went. The camera also showed my car driving off in Birch's direction.'

'Oh Jesus,' Stacey said, burying her head in her hands. She

knew little of the details surrounding her tormentor's death, but she did know a second car had been involved.

The sickness in her stomach was overwhelming. There was a surrealness to sitting at the kitchen table with a glass of wine while trying to digest all that she'd been told.

Devon reached for her hand. 'Babe, I know I shouldn't have confronted him. There are many things I shouldn't have done that night, and I know my actions have only made things worse for you. But when I saw him outside knowing what he'd put you through, I just saw red.'

But how deep a shade of red was the question that shot into Stacey's mind.

'If I could take back—'

'Did you do it, Dee?' Stacey asked before she could stop the words coming out of her mouth.

Devon froze. The hurt was written all over her face.

'You really think I could do something like that?' she asked, snatching her hand away.

'Right now, I don't know what I think.'

'Okay,' Devon said, pushing her chair away from the table. 'I'm gonna go and have a shower and try to forget you ever asked me that question.'

'Dee, listen...'

It was too late. Devon had already left the room.

Stacey swiped the wine glass from the table onto the floor and just stared at the mess of broken glass and liquid.

Ironically, even in death, Terence Birch was still managing to ruin her life.

SIXTY

'Okay, boy, so how are we going to do this?' Kim asked as Barney took a good drink of water.

Since coming home, she'd fed him and spent half an hour throwing his favourite tennis ball around the garden. The May sun was setting, bringing a chill that bothered Barney a lot less than her, but he'd now be satisfied until their late walk around midnight.

'Really?' she asked him as he left a trail of drool from the bowl to the rug.

He swished his tail in response. She realised he probably wasn't going to be too helpful with her current predicament as she wiped up his slobber and threw the kitchen roll in the bin.

She washed her hands and poured a coffee while still mulling over the question that had formed in her mind since learning of the release of Ian Perkins.

How did you make contact with someone who didn't want to be found? And she wasn't talking about the child murderer who'd changed his name when leaving prison. She was talking about the woman who probably knew where he was.

She took a seat on the sofa, cradling and tapping her coffee mug.

How was it even possible that this woman had been in and out of her life twice now and she had no way to make contact?

She understood that Leanne King's chosen profession dictated that her life was shrouded in secrecy, that she moved amongst the shadows protecting people Kim wasn't sure deserved protecting. The secrecy around witness protection had always been necessary, but before meeting Leanne, Kim had never understood or appreciated the sacrifice or commitment given by the officers involved.

Not that any of that had made the woman any more likeable, as she'd found out when Leanne had become her personal protection officer when Symes was threatening her life.

Jesus, the woman had spent three nights under her roof. She'd spent under five minutes with some of the contacts listed in her phone. But Leanne had made sure Kim could never trouble her again. She knew virtually nothing about Leanne, yet the woman knew pretty much everything about her. Kim glanced at the toaster, a permanent reminder of Leanne in her home. It was while dismantling her old one that Kim had shared intimate details about her then dying mother. In return, Leanne had revealed that she was adopted, which had done nothing to solve the mystery of whether she'd been born naturally or manufactured on a production line.

Kim had considered asking Woody for a method of contact. He'd achieved it himself when he'd felt she'd needed a minder. Whatever strings he'd pulled were probably a one-time offer though, and she would be advised that the protection officer was not their inroad to everything related to witness protection.

Kim had little time for such sensibilities. Leanne most likely had access to information she needed. Being able to warn Ian Perkins might well save his life.

She growled as she put down her coffee cup. Everything in

her home had been changed to accommodate the woman's instructions. Every area of her private life had been invaded. Leanne had been aware of Kim's every move thanks to a tracker device in her boot. Her home had been turned into a fortress with locks, cameras and a monitoring company. Much of which she'd done away with once the threat of Symes had been neutralised.

'Hang on a minute,' Kim said as Barney poised himself to join her on the sofa. He paused.

'No, not you,' she said, patting the space beside her.

The monitoring company. The service was still in place – she just chose never to set the alarm in case she activated it by mistake and had to explain to the despatched patrol officers that her life wasn't being threatened, she was just shit with technology.

She scrolled to the number on her phone Leanne had put in when she'd set up the account.

The phone was answered on the second ring. She listened as the male operator stated the name of the company and an offer to help.

'Hi, I wonder if I might check the details on my account to make sure they're up to date.'

'Of course,' said the friendly voice. 'Let me just ask you some security questions to verify your account.'

After answering a few questions, as well as giving her password, the operator was happy to help.

'I'm sure my own details are correct as the first keyholder, but I think the second keyholder may be out of date.'

All monitoring companies insisted on at least two contact numbers in case the first couldn't be reached.

'No problem. I can update that for you now.'

'If you just read off the existing number, I'll know if it's right.'

He was happy to do so, and she quickly wrote it down. She

smiled. It wasn't a number she recognised, meaning there was a good chance, given what had been going on at the time, that Leanne had listed herself as second contact.

'Oh no, I was wrong,' she said to the waiting operator. 'That is the correct number. Please leave it as it is.'

She thanked him and ended the call. Maybe one night for shits and giggles she'd set off her alarm and then not answer the safety-check call so Leanne would get a nasty surprise.

She keyed in the number and prepared herself for a barrage of anger and indignation. It wasn't a number that Leanne had offered for general use.

The call rang out until it clicked over to a generic voicemail.

Damn it.

She tried again.

Same response.

Kim hoped Leanne wasn't under the impression she was ringing for a leisurely catch-up. She guessed the other woman was as fond of those conversations as she was. This was business and she needed answers.

She growled at her phone and wondered if it was possible to have any interaction with her that wasn't fraught with frustration.

'Okay then,' Kim said, hitting the message icon. One way or another, she was going to tell Leanne what she wanted.

She typed and read her text three times.

Ian Perkins, mid-thirties, released from prison eight years ago under assumed identity. Need his details. Life and death situation.

There, short and to the point, she noted before pressing the send button.

She watched the message as it was delivered. Within a minute, it had been read.

She waited patiently for any sign of a response.

She took her phone back to the kitchen while she poured another drink.

Nothing.

She sat back down beside Barney, who hadn't even bothered to follow her.

'Come on,' she snapped at her phone. Even if it was a call or text full of abuse, it would be something.

With her limited patience already running low, she hit the call button again. If Leanne thought she was going to give up so easily, she could think again.

The call went straight to voicemail.

Damn it, the woman had blocked her number.

SIXTY-ONE

It was 3.15 a.m. when Kim's phone rang.

Oh yeah, it would be just like Leanne to call at such a time, she thought, reaching for the sudden light source.

'Hell no,' she said, seeing the caller's name.

'Get to the hospital,' he said breathlessly.

'Jesus, Keats, for what?' she asked, hauling herself out of bed.

'We've got another one.'

'Why aren't you with him?' she asked, switching the phone to speaker. She grabbed a pair of black canvas jeans from the wardrobe.

'I didn't get the call. Paramedics attended the report. There was some small movement so they knew he wasn't dead. Initially thought he was passed out on drink or drugs, so no forensics, no photos. I only know because Jimmy was working late. He grabbed a coffee and heard the paramedics talking about it while they were having a bite to eat.'

'Shit, how far into this are we?'

'About three hours I think. So do you want to get off the phone and get to the hospital as quick as you can?'

'What about you?'

'About five minutes away from leaving the house.'

'Why are you coming?' Kim asked, grabbing her jacket.

'Because if he's anywhere near the same state as the others, it's only going to be a matter of time.'

'Okay, don't suppose you got a name for me?'

'Yep, Jimmy clearly had his thinking head on. The man's name is Nathan Yates.'

'Damn it,' she growled, heading out the door.

SIXTY-TWO

At 3.45 a.m., Kim was parking her Ninja on the pavement outside the doors to A&E at Russells Hall Hospital.

Despite there already being a few hours on the clock, this was where Nathan would have started his journey after being brought in. It was quicker than running from ward to ward explaining herself every time.

Kim wasn't surprised to see the waiting room three quarters full, though she often wondered what people were doing at this time in the morning to injure themselves.

'Nathan Yates,' she said to the receptionist as she held up her ID. 'Brought in a few hours ago.'

The woman tapped the name into her computer. 'What do you need...?'

'Where's he been sent?'

'Nowhere,' she said, shaking her head. 'He's still under assessment.'

'Oh Jesus,' Kim said, heading straight for the door that led through to the medical assessment area, ignoring the protests from the receptionist.

The security guard stepped into her path.

She held up her ID. 'Seriously, mate, get out of my way.'

He stepped aside and reached for his radio.

Crack on, buddy, she thought, sure that he was summoning assistance.

She approached the nurses' station and showed the ID that was still in her hand.

'I need to speak to whoever is taking care of Nathan Yates.'

'The drunk guy?' asked a doctor leaning on the desk completing paperwork.

'He's not drunk. Where is he?' she asked, noting his badge, which labelled him as Doctor Samuel. She had no clue if that was his first name or last.

'I think you'd better—'

'Oh, that one,' she said, following the direction of the quick flick of his gaze when she'd asked the question.

She turned and headed to the curtained cubicle in the corner.

'You can't go in there,' Doctor Samuel said from behind.

'Wanna bet?' she said, pulling back the curtain.

The man lying on the bed was average build, dressed in jeans and a sweatshirt. Kim could instantly see that he wore good-quality clothes and had a decent haircut. His skin was smooth, and his body showed no signs of trauma.

She turned to the doctor. 'How long has he been here?'

'I'd have to check the—'

'Jesus, even I know he's been here for a few hours. Has he moved one muscle in that time?'

'Well, no, but a good session can—'

'A session this good and he'd have pissed himself or vomited by now. It's drug poisoning, fentanyl to be exact, and this man didn't get this way by himself. Weren't you informed by Jimmy Keene?'

'The morgue assistant?' Doctor Samuel asked with a derisive look. 'He did say something, but do you think I'm going to trust a morgue assistant over my own judgement? I'm a doctor. I deal with the living and—'

'And he's already seen two exact same cases this week.'

'The guy is next on my list to—'

'Boy, are you going to be in some serious shit if you're too damn lazy and pig-headed to—'

'Excuse me, Inspector,' he said, colouring. 'It's the middle of the night, I'm the only doctor here and so far I've dealt with five broken bones, a motorcycle collision and a severed finger.'

'And you're going to have a dead body if you don't pull your head out your ass and start treating my attempted murder victim.'

'You mean someone tried to kill him?'

Kim watched the disbelief in his face as his least-troublesome patient suddenly became his highest priority.

'He needs naloxone, and if you want to know how the two victims before him are doing, give the morgue assistant a call and I'm sure he'd be happy to show you.'

He swallowed deeply as his disbelief turned to panic.

'So you go and see what you need to do medically while I stay with him so he knows he's not alone. And make sure no one without police ID gets anywhere near this cubicle.'

Without speaking, he headed back towards the nurses' station.

Kim took a seat on the man's right-hand side. She had no clue if he was going to be able to hear her or not.

'Nathan, I'm a police officer and we know what's happened to you. The doctor is getting advice so they're probably going to move you soon.'

She looked to his face, but there was no indication from his features that he knew she'd spoken.

Her gaze was drawn down to the fingers on his right hand.

There was the smallest of movements where his thumb was touching his middle finger.

She pulled her chair closer and touched his arm. She didn't know if this was an intentional movement or some kind of involuntary reflex in response to whatever was going on in his body.

'Nathan, are you able to stop that movement with your fingers?' she asked, holding her breath.

The movement stopped.

She had a rush of both euphoria and sadness. The first because he was alive and she could communicate with him; the second because it was incredibly sad that his mind was working perfectly fine inside a body that wouldn't follow any of his commands.

She pushed the emotions aside, trying not to think about how terrified he must be.

'Touch once for yes and no touch for no. Do you understand?'

One touch.

'Are you in pain?'

Like anyone else, her first priority was his immediate welfare. Given he'd been lying on this gurney for more than three hours, she was guessing he might be in all sorts of agony.

Even so, there was no touch of the fingers.

'Nathan, we need to try and find out who did this to you. I know you're frightened, but I'm going to ask you some questions. Is that okay?'

One touch.

'Do you know the person that did this to you?'

One touch.

'Was it a family member?'

No touch.

'Is it someone from your past?'

One touch.

'Is it linked to Welton?'

One touch.

'Was it a...?'

'Excuse me, Officer,' Doctor Samuel said, opening up the curtain. 'You need to leave. We're taking the patient to intensive care.'

Two porters entered and headed for the bed.

'Five more minutes,' she tried, but the porters were already positioned at the foot and head of the bed.

'Not possible. He needs urgent medical assistance.'

'Which you wouldn't have known if I hadn't arrived.'

'And we're very grateful,' he said, stepping out of the way so the patient could be moved.

She couldn't argue. The earlier delay had been beyond her control, but she would do nothing to prevent the man getting medical care now, no matter how much she wanted to ask more questions.

'Damn it,' she said. She was surprised to see that Nathan's thumb was still hitting against his middle finger even though she'd stopped talking to him.

The trolley disappeared from view and she sighed heavily.

Now that Nathan was no longer his problem, Doctor Samuel allowed the relief to show on his face. Any mortality statistics wouldn't be added to his department.

'Give them half an hour to get him started and then maybe they'll let you see him.'

She nodded her thanks and headed back to the entrance, where Bryant was just coming in. Even more people were waiting to be seen, as they appeared to have shifted from middle of the night mode to early morning.

'What took you?' she asked, sitting down.

'Bloody hell, guv, it's only been thirty minutes since you called.'

It felt a whole lot longer.

'So, what's the story?'

Kim caught him up with events, ending with the fact they now knew it was all linked to the victims' time at Welton.

'Do you think he's got any chance?'

Kim shrugged. If only hoping made it so.

She stood. 'Come on, Bryant, for once the coffees are on me.'

SIXTY-THREE

'You got everything?' Kim asked when Bryant finished his call. The coffee she'd bought from the hospital cafeteria was now cold, and her attention was still fixed firmly on her watch.

'Yep, the names and addresses of both paramedics, who finished their shifts two hours ago and are probably tucked up in bed with the sandman.'

Without photographs, they'd need to interview the first responders to understand exactly where and how Nathan Yates had been found. And in the absence of any more conversations with the victim, she didn't care who they were in bed with, they were still going to get a knock on the door.

'You let Keats know?'

She nodded. 'Yeah, he's going to stay in the morgue and wait for the call.'

'I should hope so,' Bryant said, widening his eyes. 'Who wants the pathologist walking round the wards. It's a bit Grim Reaperish.' He sipped his drink and then pushed it away. 'He's not hopeful for a recovery then?'

'After seeing the first two victims, he's probably tapping his fingers on his gurney right now.'

'And that's not a macabre thought at all,' he said.

She looked at her watch. 'Three more minutes.'

'Just about long enough for me to tell you I called Laura when I got home from work. I apologised for not showing the correct amount of enthusiasm, and I assured her that Josh was a welcome addition to our family.'

'Hallelujah. About bloody time. Did she roast you for throwing your teddy out the pram?'

He coloured slightly. 'She said she hadn't noticed anything but appreciated the call.'

'She's lying, but she's letting you off because she loves you. Jeez, she's a good kid.'

'Thanks for talking some sense into me the other—'

'Time to go. It's been half an hour,' she said, getting to her feet.

Bryant fell into step beside her as she headed towards the ITU. It was almost 5 a.m. and the corridors were filling with people about to start their day. The middle-of-the-night intimacy was gone.

'Can you imagine anything worse though?' Bryant asked.

'What, than having Keats waiting to cut me open with his selection of serial-killer tools?'

'Not what I meant, but that's a tough act to follow. I was talking about being unable to move but your brain still being active. A fertile, conscious mind suffocated by a useless sack of flesh.'

'Retirement won't be that bad, I swear.'

Bryant laughed, catching the stern attention of a nurse just entering the ITU.

Her colleague sobered as they reached the door, but the nurse had ensured it had closed behind her.

'And anyway, I'm not retiring until they throw me out. Jenny said so.'

Kim smiled at the thought of Bryant's wife. Nope, there was

no way she was going to allow him to vegetate in his favourite armchair.

She pressed the intercom button and introduced herself.

The door buzzed open, and Kim allowed herself to hope that she would be able to continue her conversation with Nathan.

However long it took, she could base many informative questions on yes and no answers.

'May I speak with Nathan Yates?' she asked.

The kindly looking nurse shook her head with regret, and Kim knew instantly before she spoke.

'Unfortunately, we lost him about ten minutes ago.'

SIXTY-FOUR

Kim's mood had improved little as she readied herself for the 7 a.m. briefing.

With a heavy heart, she'd left the hospital feeling as though there was more she could have done. She'd extracted little information, and the guy had died anyway.

The need to sleep had long since left her so she'd walked Barney and showered before heading into work.

Unusually, the first person to walk in was Stacey, who didn't head for her own desk but tapped on the open door of the Bowl.

Kim nodded for her to enter. Even though she'd been expecting this conversation, her back stiffened in anticipation, and she felt no satisfaction from the misery she saw on the constable's face.

'You spoke to Devon yesterday?'

'I did indeed.'

'And you didn't tell me?'

'I figured you'd find out soon enough, and if we're talking about keeping secrets, you're still way ahead on that score.'

If Stacey was waiting for any kind of apology, she was going to be waiting a long time.

'Can I at least have an explanation?'

Yes, she could have that.

'I followed where the investigation took me.'

'But it's not our investigation,' Stacey argued.

'You're right. I wouldn't have had to touch it with a ten-foot bargepole if one of my team wasn't attached to it. I mean, do you have any idea what it could do to your career if your name came anywhere near this? Your irresponsibility in prioritising your own well-being defies logic, not to mention your training as a police officer.'

'But no one would ever have linked me to him,' Stacey protested.

Kim thought of the bedroom wall in Birch's house. 'Oh, trust me, they would have.'

Stacey frowned. 'What do you mean?'

'Nothing,' Kim said, gathering paperwork for the briefing.

She wasn't stupid. The only way Vik hadn't found the photos was because they were no longer there. She hadn't removed them – and Bryant had made sure he was protecting more than Stacey when he'd refused to tell her what he'd done.

'Let's just say Birch made no secret of the fact that you were his target.'

Stacey looked stunned.

'And there'd have been no conversation with Devon if I hadn't watched footage of her punching him and then following his direction of travel in a car that bears a striking resemblance to the one that reportedly caused the accident that killed him.'

'But there's no way Devon could ever do something like that.'

'She told you where she went on Monday night?' Kim asked. 'Please share – I'll check it out and that'll be the end of it.'

'She just wouldn't do anything like that,' Stacey said, giving her no answer to her question. 'She wouldn't jeopardise her career for someone like Birch.'

'That's a statement, not an alibi, Stace,' Kim said, folding her arms. 'We don't always think clearly when we're angry. You'd just told her what had been going on. She felt side-lined, useless, unable to protect you. She was full of rage when she stormed out of your flat. You didn't even know she'd punched him, so do you really know what she might have been capable of?'

'Yes, I do. I know she isn't capable of such a thing even in anger. How could you even question it?' Stacey asked.

'I'll tell you why I question it, Stacey. The minute you told me what you'd been going through, I could quite easily have torn Terence Birch apart limb by limb. Knowing that he'd caused you so much suffering would have prompted me to run my car at him then reverse and maybe even do a few donuts on his ass if he'd been right in front of me. That's how I felt as your boss. I can only imagine how Devon felt. So unless you can tell me where she was with a time stamp or witnesses, Devon's name stays firmly on the list.'

Stacey was almost as shocked as she was at the outburst she hadn't known was coming.

Kim nodded towards the squad room, which was filling up fast. 'Briefing in two minutes.'

Stacey turned and left the Bowl to a room of curious glances.

Bryant looked Kim's way and raised an eyebrow.

She nodded that she was fine and took a moment to compose herself before officially starting the day. She hadn't meant to share the depth of her own rage, and it still coursed through her when she thought of the power that insignificant little man had managed to wield.

She pushed down her feelings and headed into the squad room.

'Okay, folks, that's now three of our Psycho Six dead, so let's see if we can get our arses in gear before we lose any more.' She turned to the behaviourist. 'Thoughts, Alison?'

'It definitely seems like a vengeance campaign. This group pissed off a lot of people.'

'We won't know exactly how many until we get the court order into Welton's records,' Kim responded, looking at Penn.

'First job after briefing, boss.'

'There's something else though,' Alison said, frowning.

'Go on.'

'The social-media posts. With our last victim, he didn't incite any confusion or disruption. Almost like he knows you're miles away, or he's cocky enough to know you're not going to get anything forensically. But the post he's put up this morning is a bit odd.'

Alison grabbed her phone and read aloud. '"Don't waste your tears on poor little Nathan Yates. He's been a very bad boy and he needed to be punished. He'll cause no more harm 3/6."'

Yes, Kim had seen it when she'd been walking Barney.

She held up her hand to Alison and turned again to Penn. 'Get onto Lloyd House. If they've had no luck in tracing this guy through the IP address, get round to Don Beattie's house and switch off his router. Tell him his daughter sent you.'

'Boss, I'm not sure—'

'Close him down, Penn,' she said, turning back to Alison.

'You're making a mistake,' Alison offered, folding her arms and sitting back.

'He's causing chaos. He's running the show,' Kim protested.

'He's not doing either of those things. The crime scenes are already ruined. His plea to generate false leads went nowhere. By tweeting, he's satisfying some kind of need, but with each tweet, we learn something else.'

'Like what?'

'I think he feels as though he's entitled.'

Kim waited.

'It's like he feels he has the absolute right to be taking the action he is.'

'Doesn't every vengeful person feel that way?' Bryant asked.

'Absolutely... but it's some of the terminology, like *waste your tears, poor little Nathan, very bad boy.*'

'You're thinking someone older?' Kim asked.

'It's strange language to use for contemporaries.'

'Unless it's a deliberate misdirection,' Bryant suggested.

'Okay, I want everyone on the board: names, photos, connecting lines. I want more background on the vigilantes, and I want the current locations of Leyton Parks, Dean Newton and Ian Perkins. The last one might be harder, but that's no excuse not to try.'

'Okay, boss,' Penn and Stacey said together.

'Ha, you wish that was it,' Kim said, rubbing her hands. 'Penn, I need you to go see the paramedics that responded to the call for Nathan Yates. I know there won't be photos, but we do need to know his positioning and anything else useful they can offer.'

'Boss, I might be able to help with that,' Stacey offered.

Kim waited.

'If we're right about the letters he's been forming with the victims, I'm guessing Nathan Yates might have been shaped as a P. He was convicted of sexually assaulting an eight-year-old girl when he was fifteen.'

'Jesus,' Kim said as the nausea rose in her stomach.

Just hours ago, she'd been holding his hand, offering comfort to a convicted paedophile.

The sickness didn't abate when her phone rang and she saw the name of the caller.

She stepped into the Bowl. 'What?'

'Err... you asked me for a favour, but I could always spend my time doing my own bloody job.'

'Yeah, yeah, yeah. You got some names for me?'

'Yep, found a few less-visible members of the Black Country Angels.'

'Any background on any of these names?'

'Jesus, Stone. You don't just look a gift horse in the mouth, you actually kick it in the teeth.'

'I'm assuming that's a no.'

'Correct. I am not your bloody gimp. Ready?'

'You never heard of email?'

'Not putting this in writing, Stone. I shouldn't even know about some of these names.'

Kim took the phone into the squad room, put it on speaker and placed it on Bryant's desk. 'Someone write these names down.'

Both Stacey and Penn reached for notepads.

'Go ahead, Frost,' Kim instructed.

'Okay, I've got around twenty names. Gerald Foster, Ray Wilkins, Darren Skelton, Curtis Jones...'

Every pair of eyes in the room went to the phone. Kim put her finger over her mouth for them to stay silent. The last thing they needed was for Frost to understand the significance of one of the names she'd given them.

Stacey went back to her notepad to continue writing the names Frost was offering.

'That it?' Kim asked when she'd finished.

'Yep, anything of any use?'

'Don't think so, but you were ahead of the warrant, so thanks for that,' she said before ending the call.

Curtis Jones, ex-boyfriend of Teresa Fox, fiancé of their first victim, Eric Gould. What the hell was his name doing on there?

SIXTY-FIVE

'Did we disturb something earlier?' Alison asked as Stacey took her pile of paperwork over to the whiteboard.

Penn had exited just moments after the boss and Bryant, leaving her and the behaviourist alone.

'Only me asking why my wife is a suspect in the death of Terence Birch.'

'Devon?' Alison asked with wide eyes.

'No, one of my other wives,' Stacey said with a shake of the head.

'Come on. Even the boss knows that's ridiculous.'

'Not when there's footage of her punching him shortly before his death.'

Stacey didn't bother to add the detail of the car. The first fact was bad enough.

'Why is the boss even involved? It's not like it's a murder investigation... and even as I'm speaking, I realise she's involved in case your name comes up.'

'Yep.'

'Remember what I said about her wanting to protect—'

'I get it, but right now all I can picture is the two of them going at it. My wife and my boss going toe to toe and saying things that cannot be unsaid. There's hostility between them, and it's all because of me. I don't even know how this can ever be right again. At the minute, neither one of them can stand to look at me.'

'Hang on, I thought you said things with Devon were okay.'

'They are... they were... I mean...'

'What did you say when she told you about the boss's suspicions?' Alison asked, narrowing her gaze.

'Nothing, we just talked and—'

'You asked her if she did it, didn't you?'

Stacey nodded.

'Oh shit, Stace. Talk about opening your mouth to change feet. Are you really on a mission to see how many of your closest people you can piss off in one week?'

Stacey couldn't argue. She'd known the minute the words were out of her mouth that she'd overstepped the line. Devon had showered and left for work before any more words could pass between them. A curt text this morning had informed her that she'd gone to her mum's for some kip between night shifts.

'You gotta put it right, girl,' Alison said. 'There are some things said in arguments that don't wear away with time.'

'Alison, with all due respect, shut up. Jeez, it's annoying having a profiler for a best mate.'

'Yeah, true. I once dated a nutritionist who detailed every harmful ingredient in a bag of smoky bacon crisps. No fun.'

Stacey smiled, turning back to the board.

She loved Alison to bits, but right now she just wanted time in her own head while she completed the first task of the day.

She'd expected the conversation with the boss to get heated. Stacey was caught between the woman she loved with every ounce of her being and a woman who had her loyalty, trust and respect.

Despite their words the night before, Stacey knew Devon

hadn't been involved in Terence Birch's death. She knew the boss would discover that soon enough. Any other option just wasn't possible.

What had shaken her during their conversation was the depth of rage the boss had shown.

She was beginning to understand just how poorly she'd judged the people around her. She knew her work performance had suffered the last couple of months and yet the boss had had her back, checking on her, covering for her.

She was sick to death of this feeling inside – powerlessness, weakness, a lack of control. He was dead. He was gone. He didn't have the power to hurt her any more.

She wanted her life back. She wanted herself back. She wanted to feel joy again when she walked in her own front door. She wanted to earn back the boss's respect. She wanted to be the person that the boss always called.

It was time to remove and burn the victim tee shirt she'd been wearing for way too long.

And her first move was to show the boss that she was able to do her job.

SIXTY-SIX

Kim was still trying to wrap her head around Curtis Jones's involvement with the Black Country Angels when Bryant pulled up at the address of their most recent victim.

She suddenly remembered Rufus saying something about Curtis not having had it easy as a child. A fact that hadn't mattered much at the time but mattered a whole lot more now. It was something she'd be asking him to explain once they'd spoken to the woman widowed in the last few hours.

The door was answered by a woman dressed in jogging bottoms, trainers and a tee shirt.

Her eyes were red but not deadened or numb. This wasn't Mrs Yates.

Both Kim and Bryant held up their IDs.

'Come in. I'm Amy Petracek, Katie's sister.'

Amy pointed to the hallway, indicating her sibling was at the rear of the house.

Kim found Katie Yates sitting at a picnic bench table that was too big for the small kitchen.

She was dressed in plain yellow pyjamas and staring down into a coffee mug.

'Mrs Yates, we're so sorry for your loss,' Bryant said before Kim had a chance to open her mouth. Never knowing if she was going to remember that bit, he sometimes liked to make sure.

Katie raised her gaze from the cup and nodded her acceptance of the platitude.

'I've not been told anything,' she said as her eyes filled with tears.

Kim took a seat at the edge of the bench, choosing not to do the manoeuvre that would place her legs beneath the table.

Amy did it as though it was second nature and placed her arm around her sister's shoulders.

'Katie, there's no easy way to tell you this, but your husband was murdered.'

'What?' the sisters said together.

Kim waited a few seconds for it to sink in.

'He was found barely conscious and in a state of paralysis. He'd been poisoned with a drug called fentanyl.'

'But he was at the hospital. The officer told me he'd been taken in by the paramedics.'

'There was nothing they could do to save him.'

Kim didn't think explaining the effects of the drug would do her any favours.

'But why?' Katie asked.

Amy tried to pull her sister closer, as though trying to use her own body as a shield, but Katie pulled away. She wanted answers.

'That's what we're trying to find out,' Kim said. 'Can you tell us a bit more about him?'

'Of course, but there's nothing that's going to help you. There must be some kind of mistake. Nathan gets on with everyone. He's a gentle, sweet man. He never raises his voice, doesn't get angry. He's wonderful. No one would want to hurt him.'

Kim didn't doubt the sincerity of her words. The speed at which they came out of her mouth was like she was trying to stop an error from happening. Like if she acted quickly enough, the mistake could be undone and Nathan would walk back through the door.

'May I ask how you met?'

'Through me,' Amy offered as a flash of discomfort passed over Katie's face. 'He was my boyfriend first. I'm three years older than Katie. I met Nathan at college. We fizzled out, and then Katie bumped into him again a while later.'

'I was sixteen,' Katie offered for no reason Kim could fathom. It only served to throw doubt on the truthfulness of the statement, alongside the fact that Katie's discomfort had returned. Given what she knew, Kim couldn't help wondering if Nathan had preferred the younger model.

'And you didn't mind?' Kim asked the older sister.

Amy waved her hand. 'We were well over by the time they met up again.'

She had to be blind not to see the unease in her sister's face. This was a subject she wanted to move away from. Kim was happy to oblige. She got the picture, and it sickened her.

'And you got married?'

'When I was nineteen. Three years ago.'

Jesus, the girl was twenty-two and already a widow.

'Can you tell us where he worked?'

Happy to be away from that subject, the relief flooded her face. 'He was a night manager at Asda in Great Bridge. He'd not long been promoted. He loved his job, and they think the world of him there.'

'Had he had any trouble?'

'No. None at all. They love him. He's really popular. He's always laughing and joking.'

'Had he mentioned anything odd? Strange phone calls, maybe friends from his past turning up?'

She shook her head. 'I don't think he kept in touch with anyone from school.'

'His teen years?' Kim pushed, but Katie's face remained blank, confirming that she didn't know about his time spent at Welton or the reason for him being there.

It was likely to come out in the press and that was soon enough. The woman had had enough shocks for one day.

Right now, there was nothing to suggest he'd done anything further. His job didn't put him around children, and he was happily married, albeit to a much younger woman that he'd been seeing since her teens.

'Had anything at all changed in his life recently?' Kim asked, briefly considering Stacey's theory of the victims being murdered before they committed a crime. She prided herself on always taking her team's theories seriously, however outlandish.

'Nothing at all. He was just happy and going about his life.'

As she'd thought.

'Okay, Mrs Yates, thank you for talking to us at such a difficult—'

'Oh, there was one small thing, but I don't think it helps in any way, just Nathan being his normal generous self.'

'Go on,' Kim said, feeling the smallest of pits forming in her stomach.

'He'd applied to be a volunteer at the local youth club.'

SIXTY-SEVEN

It was almost lunchtime when Bryant pulled into the car park of the West Midlands Hospital on Colman Hill. They were saved the bother of requesting the presence of Curtis Jones when he came striding out of the front door. A simple sports jacket did little to hide the nurse's uniform beneath.

'Just the man,' Kim said, stepping into his path. 'May we have a word?'

His smile faltered. 'A quick one. I'm meeting a friend for lunch.'

'We'll try not to keep you. We understand you're a member of the Black Country Angels vigilante group?'

The promise of a frown materialised. 'How do you know that?'

'We just do. Would you care to tell us why?' she asked.

'Why what? I haven't done anything wrong, have I?'

'Not that we know of, but there has to be a reason why you joined them. What prompted you?'

He shrugged. 'My sense of community service.'

'I'm gonna call bullshit on that,' she said, raising an eyebrow.

'People normally join up with vigilante groups because they feel a sense of injustice, that they're trying to right a wrong.'

'That's them, not me,' he said, looking over her shoulder and shifting from one foot to the other.

Her experience with Alison and her own powers of observation told her that this man wasn't telling them the truth.

'What happened to you, Curtis?' Kim asked.

'Nothing happened to me, Inspector.'

'So, why are you...?'

'If you really want the truth, I joined because of you. I joined because I don't trust you lot to do your fucking jobs.'

Kim was stunned as his pleasant, affable expression turned dark. There was a rage simmering here below the constructed calm exterior.

Bryant stepped forward. 'Easy, buddy.'

'She asked. She kept asking, so now I've told you. You lot are shit. I lost my dad. He was murdered, and you lot did fuck all about it. Murderers are walking the streets free as birds because the police can't do their job. At least the Black Country Angels are proactive and trying to get the scum off the streets.'

'What happened to your—?'

'No. We're not going there,' he said, stepping around her. 'You lot had your chance back then, and you blew it. I'm not going there now.'

Kim turned to watch him walk away as a small van marked with the livery of 'Fox's Veterinary Services' pulled up at the edge of the kerb. Teresa Fox's father, Rufus, lowered the window and nodded in their direction as Curtis headed to the passenger side.

The two of them drove away, and Kim realised there was a lot more going on here than she'd expected.

SIXTY-EIGHT

Stacey put down the phone with a smile. The boss had called her directly for the first time since she'd found out about Birch. Okay, maybe it was because she knew Penn was out talking to the paramedics, but it was a start. Equally gratifying had been the boss's admission that she might be on to something about the killer aiming to prevent the victims' crimes.

'Nathan Yates was trying to volunteer at a local youth club,' she said, speaking to Alison for the first time.

'No way. Wonder how that was going to work out for him. Did he not think they would do vetting checks?'

'Maybe he thought that his juvenile record wouldn't show up.'

'How's it going with tracking down the others?' Alison asked.

'Dean Newton wasn't too hard to find,' Stacey said.

Knowing she'd have little luck tracking down the ringleader, Ian Perkins, she'd looked at Dean Newton and Leyton Parks first.

Dean Newton was well known to them and had a hefty record on the PNC. Having been sent to Welton aged fifteen for minor involvement in the armed robbery of a petrol station in Coseley, he'd done nothing to change his ways since. After being released, he'd wound up in adult prison for robbery-related crimes. From his record, there were no episodes of violence, mistreatment of women or sex-related offences, and his crimes hadn't escalated in the years since his first offence. He simply couldn't keep his hands off other people's stuff. He was a career burglar, and his time inside was treated like an occupational hazard. A brief calculation told her that since his first spell inside, the days he'd spent incarcerated by far outnumbered the days spent free.

She'd searched social media, and his only real presence was on Facebook, where his favourite activity was posting photos of every pub he liked to frequent. She counted almost thirty separate photos of a pint.

There was no doubt that the man wasn't hard to find. Trail the pubs around Hollytree for long enough and you were bound to trip over him.

His last photo had been posted just the night before in The Tenth Lock in Brierley Hill.

Dean Newton was definitely still alive and kicking. For now.

SIXTY-NINE

'Colourful,' Bryant noted as they knocked on the front door of Dean Newton's address.

'A bit like his record,' Kim said above the shouting she could hear within. Apparently all the occupants wanted someone else to answer the door that had been battered in so many times she could see three different colours of paint.

Eventually, the door was pulled open by an emaciated male in his forties, dressed only in boxer shorts.

Kim fought the stench of the flat to produce her ID. 'Dean Newton?'

He glowered and shook his head, calling behind. 'Newt, pigs are 'ere.'

Oh, it had been a while since they'd been called that.

'Yeah, mate, the nineties called. They want their insults back,' Bryant offered.

'Fuck you,' the man said, walking away from the door.

The history books recorded a time when there had been a natural respect for police officers. Kim couldn't quite imagine it now, as a lad no older than nineteen passed by the door wearing a pair of pyjama bottoms and holding a can of Stella.

Dean Newton had yet to appear, but it didn't take a genius to work out that this was a doss house. Dean Newton was the legal occupier on the council tenancy, but it appeared that he opened up his home to any degenerate.

To prove her point, the guy who'd answered the door plonked himself down onto a mattress in the front room and took out his drug paraphernalia.

Kim looked to Bryant.

'On it,' he said, stepping away to call it in.

The second the door opened, she'd known the place was awash with drugs, but to actively start using in front of a police officer was a bit of a piss-take. She couldn't help but wonder at the guy's complete lack of self-preservation in not getting himself nicked. How devoid of hope would you have to be to basically not give a shit if you were arrested or not, knowing that life was equally as appealing being locked up or free?

'Dean Newton?' she asked again as another male stepped in front of the doorway.

This one was in a dressing gown. His short brown hair was tousled, and a scar ran two inches across the skin of his left cheek.

Did no one in this place wear proper clothes?

'What?' he asked with the attitude of someone used to visits from the police.

'CID. We need to talk to you about your time at Welton.'

His scrunched-up face told her that was the last thing he'd been expecting.

'Wanna come in?' he asked, stepping aside.

'Not even if my life depended on it. You wanna put on some clothes and step outside?'

He grunted and disappeared from view.

She stepped away from the stench of grease, vomit, body odour and, God help her, urine.

'Logged, guv,' Bryant said, rejoining her.

She could imagine the long sigh of whichever officers caught this call. Uniforms would be no strangers to this address.

By the time Kim had moved a safe distance away, Dean Newton was striding towards them dressed in plain trackie bottoms and a body-builder vest top that was way too big for him.

A lit cigarette dangled from his fingertips.

'Be quick,' he said, looking around.

Oh yeah, any credibility he had on Hollytree was going to be decimated if he was seen talking to her.

'I'm assuming you know about your old mates?' she asked.

His blank expression said no. Kim had to marvel that in this day and age, you could miss three murders of people you once knew.

'You don't watch the news?' Bryant asked.

He shrugged. 'Doesn't affect me.'

'Three of your old buddies from Welton are dead.'

He shrugged again and took a draw on his cigarette. 'Don't give a shit about folks I know now, never mind back then.'

Kim felt the Hollytree shadow of despair creep towards her. The man in front of her represented the very ethos of this estate. No one gave a shit about anyone else. Maybe if they had, Mikey, her twin, would still be alive.

She shook away the thoughts, eager to get this done and dusted so she could get away from this soul-sucking environment.

'You were part of the group known as the Psycho Six?' she asked.

He smiled widely. 'Yeah, that was a cool name. We had a laugh. Who's carked it?'

'Eric, Paul and Nathan.'

'Jeeesus. How come?'

'All murdered.'

He didn't look the slightest bit troubled.

'You do realise there's a chance you might be next?'

He shrugged yet again and drew on his cigarette beyond the filter, giving off a foul sulphuric smell. 'Come get me. I ain't going nowhere.'

'You're not concerned?'

'Pfft... I been in and out of clink since I was fifteen. You think I ain't had death threats before?'

'And yet you keep going back?'

'A way of life, I suppose. I've got no complaints. I ain't looking for sympathy. I take my chances.'

'None of your buddies re-offended,' she told him.

'And how's that working out for 'em?' he asked, lighting another cigarette.

'Any idea who might have wanted them dead?' Bryant asked.

He laughed. 'You want a list? We were a bunch of little fuckers.'

'Little fuckers who broke the rules or little fuckers that hurt people?'

'Probably both,' he said without remorse.

'Nice.'

'Ah, wake up,' he said, showing annoyance. 'You do what you gotta do to survive. You gravitate towards similar people. Safety in numbers and all that.'

'Was there safety in numbers when you tried attacking that female guard?'

He laughed, and Kim fought the urge to slap him.

'Fucking hell, I forgot how much fun we used to have.'

'That's your idea of fun?' Bryant growled, stepping forward.

Newton held up his hand. 'Simmer down, big boy. No one got hurt. We barely got her knickers down. No harm done.'

Only because they got disturbed, Kim thought but gave Bryant a sideways glance.

This lump of flesh had been in and out of prison for fifteen years. He'd made no effort to move away from a life of crime. They weren't going to instil a moral compass in the man in one meeting, but they still had questions to ask.

'You know you're a piece of shit, right?'

He didn't bat an eyelid at her insult. Kim would now try to communicate in a language he understood.

'It was attempted rape, mate, and you're lucky someone came along when they did. Whose idea was it?'

'I'm not sure, but we all took part in it. It was no great—'

'And what about the kid who was beaten up in the cell?' Bryant asked.

'What about him? You think this is some kind of revenge shit?'

It was her turn to shrug.

'He wouldn't have the guts. I don't care how many years have passed, that kid didn't grow balls big enough to stand up for himself.'

'People change.'

'Not that much. He was a pathetic little shite. Just someone to punch around when you were having a bad day.'

'Did he have a name?' Kim asked.

'Yeah, but I don't know it. Not sure I even knew it back then. He wasn't important. Just a punchbag.'

'So it wasn't just the cell incident?'

'Ha, he wishes. Nah, he was our little gimp. No serious harm done though. It's not like we killed him.'

Dean Newton wasn't the most despicable person she'd ever met, but he was heading towards her top five. He hadn't experienced one minute of meaningful reflection in his life.

She found herself having to check her own thoughts because, right now, if their killer wasn't yet done, she hoped this guy was going to be next.

'You lot pretty much terrorised the whole of Welton, other

inmates and staff alike. Was there anyone who was out of bounds?'

'Maybe Baldy.'

'Lenny Baldwin?' she clarified.

'I mean, we still gave him shit, but not too bad.'

'Why not?'

'Cos he'd got the power, innit?'

'And how did he use that power?'

'Can't remember now – it's been a while,' he said, moving from one foot to the other.

'What are you not telling me?' she asked.

'If I told you, I wouldn't be not telling you, would I?' he asked with a cocky grin.

'Did something happen with Lenny Baldwin?'

'Next,' he said, waving his hand, making it clear he was saying no more on that subject. But there was obviously something he didn't want to admit.

'And Ryan West?' she asked, moving on.

'What, the teacher? Nah, he was okay. He listened to us, and Parky liked him. He liked books and shit.'

'Parky. You mean Leyton Parks?' she asked.

'Yeah, I forgot his real name. Him and the prof got on, so we let him be.'

'And where is Leyton now?' Kim asked as a squad car pulled up beside them.

Newton didn't bat an eyelid. He either knew they weren't here for him or he didn't care.

Bryant headed towards the driver.

'For your buddy who decided to shoot up right in front of us,' Kim explained.

'Dickhead,' he said as the officers entered the flat.

'Leyton?' she reminded him.

'Fuck knows. The kid didn't like people all that much. He was pretty quiet. All he did was throw some rocks off a bridge. How was he to know the driver couldn't control the car?'

Not exactly the story she'd got from Stacey. The driver had died, and his girlfriend had been left with life-altering injuries.

'I did look for him once,' Newton admitted.

'I didn't think you cared about any of them.'

'I don't, but I was one short for a project I was working on.'

He was talking about a robbery.

'Couldn't find the git anywhere. Disappeared into thin air.'

Kim paused as the officer brought out the addict. Judging by his hooded eyes, he'd managed to get a good dose into his veins.

Newton didn't give him a second look.

'What about Ian Perkins? Got any idea where he is?'

'Nope and I couldn't care less. These folks mean nothing to me, and if you're scared for Ian's safety, save your energy – he can take care of himself. He murdered his own fucking brother for no reason.'

'I think there was more to it than a random act of violence,' she said, more than happy to end this conversation now. The man had been warned, and he had nothing useful to offer on the whereabouts of his old friends.

'You know, for just a minute, I thought you had an ounce more grey matter than your sty mates,' he said, tapping his temple. 'But you're all bloody useless.'

'Go on,' she urged, sensing that he was bursting to enlighten her.

'I can tell you think Ian was justified in what he did to his brother. The police officers thought it, the judge thought it and the parole board thought it, but not one of you knows the fucking truth.'

Kim waited.

'He was pissed off cos his brother beat him on the PlayStation. There was no sexual assault. He murdered his brother because of a game.'

SEVENTY

'Say that again,' Penn said, taking the bandana from his drawer.

'The boss called...'

'Hallelujah,' he cried, throwing his arms in the air.

Although Stacey laughed, his body was flooded with relief. The cosmos was once more falling into line.

'She wants to know if there's any way we can verify Ian Perkins's accusation of abuse against his brother.'

'A bit tricky seeing as his brother is dead,' Penn offered. 'Why the doubt?'

'Dean Newton claims Ian Perkins played the system, told lies to get a lighter sentence. That it was all to do with who got the high score on *Sonic*.'

Penn thought for a minute. 'Does it matter? I mean, surely we still want to warn the guy his life might be in danger, so what's the difference?'

'It's the difference between a psychopath with no remorse or empathy and a damaged individual who could take no more abuse,' Alison said without looking away from her computer screen.

'Fair enough,' he said, choosing not to argue with the expert.

'Hey, how'd it go with the paramedics?' Stacey asked, reminding him of what was in his pocket.

He took out the piece of paper and held it up.

'That's how he was positioned when they found him?' Stacey asked.

'Yep,' Penn said, pressing some Blu-Tack onto the back of the paper and putting it on the board.

'Rolled onto his side with arms stretched out to make a circle.'

'Definitely a letter P,' Alison observed.

'And he'd just volunteered at the local youth club,' Stacey added.

'How the hell does our guy know all this?' Penn asked.

'Not that hard,' Alison said. 'Follow someone around for a few days, follow their socials, see who they're friends with, things they like, links they share.'

The woman knew too much about finding out someone's movements.

'Alison, you got something to tell us?' Penn asked, raising an eyebrow.

She laughed but was saved from answering when his phone rang.

'Hey, Jack,' Penn said.

'Delivery down here for you. If you're going to want it upstairs, I'd bring some help.'

Penn frowned. He wasn't expecting anything, but his curiosity got the better of him.

'Back in a sec,' he said, sure that he'd be able to handle whatever it was.

He whistled his way down the stairs and into Jack's office.

'Oh, what the hell is this?' he asked, stopping dead.

'The note is on the top,' Jack called over his shoulder.

Penn reached for the slip of paper on top of the fourth archive box.

'Are you kidding?' he asked once he saw the name of the sender.

Yes, he'd been expecting Welton to produce their records, following the issue of the court order, but he'd anticipated they'd arrive electronically.

He took down the first box, opened it and sighed heavily.

If he didn't know better, he'd think that Josephine Kirk was trying to make his job as hard as possible.

SEVENTY-ONE

Kim left Bryant gobbling a sandwich for lunch as she headed towards the main entrance at Russells Hall Hospital, the place they'd last visited in the early hours of that morning.

Interruption to his sleep tended to hit her colleague in his stomach, as though his body was seeking the lost sleep through additional calories. It manifested in her as an unquenchable thirst for caffeine.

Bryant hadn't minded being told to stay in the car with his lunch while she escorted Charlotte to the morgue.

She wasn't surprised to see the woman already waiting inside, looking around and wringing her hands.

'Hey, you still sure you want to do this?' Kim asked, gently touching Charlotte on the arm.

'Of course. I have to know for sure.'

Kim opened her mouth but realised that no amount of reassurance was going to trump the proof of her own eyes.

She started walking, and Charlotte fell into step beside her.

'Have you seen a dead person before?'

She nodded. 'My grandpa. He died of the same thing my mum has now.'

'Ella told me. I'm sorry.'

'It's coming on fast. She struggles to tie her shoelaces, but she can do the daily newspaper crossword in ten minutes. I've lost so much time with her.'

Kim had no words of comfort to offer. The actions of one man had torn this family apart, and precious time had been lost. There was nothing she could do about that, but she could offer some comfort and resolution to this woman now.

'Through here,' Kim said, opening the service doors into a corridor that would eventually lead them to the morgue.

Keats's initial response had been a flat no, until she'd explained the circumstances. He'd relented and given her a time so he could cover the viewing himself on his lunchbreak.

She pressed the call point, and Jimmy appeared from nowhere to let them in.

He nodded to them both as they passed.

'Anteroom,' Jimmy said as a visible shudder passed through Charlotte.

Her gaze darted around the cold, sterile space. Seeing it through her eyes as though for the first time, Kim could understand the involuntary physical reaction. There was no balance. Everything was about death.

Again, Kim wondered if this had been such a good idea.

'I... I'm fine,' Charlotte said, as though reading her thoughts.

Kim pushed open the doors to Keats's preparation room. The space was no warmer or more welcoming than the actual morgue, but there were fewer terrifying tools of his trade on show.

The body of Terence Birch lay on a gurney, covered with a simple white sheet.

Charlotte faltered for a second, and Kim had to remind herself that although this wasn't a grieving relative or spouse, there was a great deal of emotion attached to this moment.

'Ready?' she asked, touching Charlotte lightly on the elbow.

She nodded.

Keats peeled back the sheet down to the neck.

Charlotte gasped and then wobbled. Kim steadied her but said nothing as a multitude of emotions passed over her face.

The room was silent as Charlotte stared at the body as though waiting for movement or answers.

'Okay, please get me out of here,' she whispered.

Kim nodded her thanks to Keats as she guided Charlotte through the door and out of the morgue.

Neither of them spoke until they were back in the main section of the hospital.

'Can I sit?' Charlotte asked with a voice full of tears.

Kim guided her to a bench next to the lift.

She sat and began to tremble with sobs.

'I know it's a tough—'

'Thank you,' Charlotte said through the tears. 'I needed this. I needed to see him dead, but I wasn't expecting this.'

'What?'

'The tears are coming from anger. There's a rage burning inside me. He's so small. I thought he was taller, bigger, more powerful.'

A trick of the mind, Kim thought. Her perception of his physicality was directly linked to the power he'd wielded over her.

She wiped her nose with a tissue. 'It's myself I'm angry with. How the hell did I allow him to take away so much of my life? Lying in there, he was so small, so pathetic, but he's been in my head for over ten years.'

She buried her head in her hands. It seemed to Kim that there was a decade's worth of release seeping out of her, which was healthy. The self-blame was not.

'I've missed so many years with my mum, and now she's sick. She's progressing quicker than my grandpa did, and I've missed vital time with her.'

She punched her own leg. Hard.

'You're not the only one he terrorised,' Kim said, grabbing her fist.

'Huh?'

'He turned his attention on to one of my officers.'

The crying stopped as Charlotte's eyes widened in a mixture of shock and horror.

'He was a witness to a murder. She interviewed him. She did nothing wrong. He'd been stalking her for two months before his death.'

'Oh God, no.'

'I'm telling you because it wasn't your fault. None of it. She's a police officer. She knew what to do, but she didn't do anything. She kept it to herself and suffered in silence. Like you, she thought she'd invited it, she thought she could handle it on her own. She thought if she ignored it for long enough it would go away.'

Charlotte was nodding in complete agreement.

'She's had to put up with it for a couple of months, and I can see the toll it's taken on her. So give yourself a break. You didn't cause this. He caused it and now he's dead. Your only responsibility going forward is to live your best life and make as many memories with your mum as you can.'

Charlotte took in a deep breath and stood.

They walked to the main entrance in silence. When they reached the doors, Charlotte paused.

'Will you give her my number, your colleague?'

'Of course.'

'If she wants to talk or wants to just sound off, I'm available any time... and oh my goodness, that's the first time I've voluntarily offered my number to anyone in years.'

'Thanks for that. I'm sure she'll appreciate it.'

'I know she's got all the support she needs between her family and her colleagues, but I'm here if she needs me.'

'Appreciated,' Kim said again as Charlotte thanked her before heading across the road.

Kim stood still for a moment, fighting the nausea burning the back of her throat. Yes, Stacey had support from people that cared about her.

But not all of them.

She watched Charlotte disappear from sight.

There were questions she'd have liked to ask, but she hadn't bargained on how emotional this identification was going to be. She needed answers that could help clear up what had happened to Terence Birch on Monday night. But the chat about the small blue car would have to wait for another day.

SEVENTY-TWO

It was no secret to anyone that Penn loved a puzzle. He'd always been the same, even as a kid. Sometimes the harder it was the better. When he was a child, he'd loved doing jigsaws, but he'd never seen the end result of one of them. He'd never done them with the picture facing up. He hadn't wanted the help of the image. Instead he'd focussed on shapes, edges and holes. In any puzzle there was a moment, a lightbulb second where you knew you were on the right track and the puzzle would be solved.

As yet he had no such feeling with the records that had been sent from Welton Hall.

Four boxes were full to the brim with single-leaf pages, as though every file and folder had been deliberately emptied and spread between all the boxes.

He'd taken over the meeting room on the third floor and had paced the space many times to work out how to sort the documents in order to find anything. His logic was to go big pile, little pile.

By grouping everything into big piles, he could then do sub

files for each big pile. The only alternative was to read every single piece of paper as he came to it.

So far, he had a pile for inmates, staff, medical records, court information, incident reports and miscellaneous.

He took the pile dedicated to inmates and quickly made two piles, one for the Psycho Six and another pile for anyone else.

He then divided the pile so that each of the six had their own stack.

He knew that the boss was keen to learn about Lenny Baldwin's involvement with their release dates, so he went through each pile looking for the recommendation report from the youth service officer and grabbed a piece of scrap paper.

Eric Gould – Yes

Paul Brooks – Yes

Nathan Yates – Yes

Leyton Parks – Yes

Dean Newton – Yes

Ian Perkins – Yes

Okay, perhaps he was just a lenient kind of guy. Maybe he thought every kid deserved a second chance.

He pushed the piles aside and reached for the stack containing the records of other inmates during the same period of time.

He found a total of twenty-seven names,

Not one of them had been recommended for early release.

SEVENTY-THREE

Kim hadn't expected to be knocking on Lenny Baldwin's door again so soon. He appeared equally surprised to see her.

'May we come in?' she asked as he stood in the doorway.

'I don't see how I can help you any further.'

'Just follow-up,' she said, taking a step forward. It was either move or she'd just walk straight into him. 'We've received the files from Welton. They make for interesting reading.'

He stood aside, and she pushed past him, heading into the lounge.

'I should imagine so. It wasn't a place to house choirboys.'

Kim sat where she had on the previous visit. 'Judging by your early release recommendations, you had a lot of faith in those six boys to turn their lives around.'

'You don't think they deserved an opportunity?' he asked.

'Quite the backtrack from what you were saying earlier. You gave us the impression that they were all beyond hope and that they'd sucked the blood from your body and ruined your life.'

'I only recommended early release to the boys I felt genuinely deserved it,' he said, shifting in his seat.

'Okay, let's play along with the bullshit you're trying to feed me. You're saying you felt that Eric had learned his lesson about hitting girls who didn't do what they were told?'

'I felt he'd made progress.'

'And you believed that Paul Brooks deserved special treatment after a sexual assault?'

'He was genuinely remorseful.'

'Was Nathan Yates equally as remorseful about sexually assaulting a minor?'

'He really thought she was older.'

'She was eight. Did he think she was ten?'

His lips thinned.

'And Dean Newton...'

'Inspector, you can ask me about all of them if you want to waste your time, but I can tell you that I had valid reasons for recommending leniency for every boy I put my name behind.'

'Even Ian Perkins, who killed his brother either because of sexual abuse or a PlayStation game. Who knows?'

His face crumpled in confusion. He was obviously one of the many plebs Dean Newton had been referring to when saying everyone had swallowed Ian's story.

'I don't know anything about a PlayStation game, but I did feel that Ian's violence was a one-time thing. I didn't feel he was a danger to anyone.'

'Even though he was the ringleader of that band of merry little men?'

He opened his hands. 'My job was to form an opinion after spending time with them. Mine wasn't the only judgement considered when making final decisions on early release dates.'

'So you took each case on its own merit?'

'Of course.'

'And you stand by that?'

'I do.'

'So why, in the five years from the start to the end of your time assessing these boys, did no other prisoner receive a positive recommendation from you?'

Colour began to drain from his face. 'I don't think that's correct.'

'It is. We checked. Not one other boy had an early release recommended.'

He shook his head.

She stood. 'Okay, we'll show the records to your old supervisor, see if they can explain.'

'Wait, wait, let me think,' he said, motioning for her to retake her seat.

As she'd suspected, he'd retired with his good name intact. He wouldn't want that tarnished now.

'Why were no other boys granted leniency?' she asked, sitting back down. 'Just give us the truth, Mr Baldwin, or I guarantee there's going to be a leak and you're going to be reading about this in the press.'

It was an empty threat, but he didn't need to know that.

'Because they didn't deserve it. I judged each one individually and, if you want the honest truth, they were all scumbags who were never going to change. Most of them liked being that way, and the rest knew no better. Either way, they didn't deserve to be released one minute earlier than their mandated sentence.'

'And yet the only six you recommended were from the same group? Give us a break, Mr Baldwin.'

'Purely coincidence.'

'Purely bullshit,' she said, caring nothing for his sensibilities. 'You promised them all a positive recommendation if they agreed to leave you alone.'

'I don't think you'll find any proof of that anywhere. It's a suspicion on your part and nothing that will be confirmed by me.'

'Were you that scared of them? Did you really sacrifice your professional integrity so cheaply?'

'What did they have on you?' Bryant asked after watching the man's reactions closely.

His index finger was tapping furiously on the arm of the chair, and Kim could see a bead of sweat forming at his temple.

'Nothing,' he insisted.

Bryant stood. 'Okay, there's one member of the Psycho Six that's being really helpful to our investigation. We'll just go ask him and hope there are no reporters around when—'

'No, don't do that,' Baldwin said, holding up his hand.

Kim appreciated Bryant's little bluff as he sat back down. She nodded in his direction to take the lead.

'Were they blackmailing you?' her colleague asked.

Baldwin paused for a good five seconds before nodding.

'For what?'

'I'd rather not say.'

'And we'd rather you did,' Bryant said.

He sighed heavily. 'They found certain videos on my computer. Ones I wouldn't have wanted to share with my wife.'

'We're talking pornographic videos?' Bryant clarified.

He nodded, wringing his hands.

'Children?' Bryant asked sternly.

'God no. Not at all. Never. No, they were videos of gay sex.'

'Are you gay? Bisexual?'

He shook his head. 'I've never been physically attracted to a man, but after watching one video, I found I couldn't stop.'

'And one of the boys found these videos?' Bryant asked, needing no more details.

He nodded. 'Two of the other boys caused a diversion and Ian got hold of my computer. He was smart, found them in no more than a couple of minutes. He told me that if they weren't all recommended for early release, he'd tell my wife.'

'He didn't threaten your job?' Kim asked.

'Where would be the gain in that? They wanted me there so I could give them all recommendations when their dates came up. Getting me fired would have served them no purpose.'

'So you agreed to do as they asked in return for their silence?' Bryant asked.

'I did. And a lot of good it did me because they told my wife anyway. Once I retired, she received an anonymous letter. It was just days after her diagnosis.'

Kim felt a rush of sympathy for the woman whose life had totally collapsed around her in a very short period of time.

'What did you do?' Kim asked.

'I denied it, strenuously, but there was a look in her eye that never left her until the day she died.'

'Why would they do that?' Bryant asked.

'You're just not getting it, are you? They were a despicable group of boys. There wasn't one good one amongst them. At one point, there were even rumours they pushed a prison guard down the stairs to his death. They were a bunch of ruthless little psychopaths, and to answer your question, they told my wife because they could. They destroyed a thirty-year marriage because they had that power. Although we didn't separate, I knew that she would never look at me the same way again after reading that letter, and I'll never forgive them for that.'

'As you've lied to us consistently, Mr Baldwin, I do feel compelled to ask if there are any more little secrets you'd like to unburden during this confession?'

Lenny Baldwin stood. 'Please leave my home now.'

'Happy to,' she said, heading for the door, finding his presence sickening. The man had foregone all professionalism and integrity to cover up his own little secret, which had been revealed to his wife in the end anyway. She could feel no sympathy on behalf of Lenny Baldwin; her only sympathy was with his wife.

'I know you think you've gained some great knowledge in what you've learned today, but if you want some really juicy secrets, you might want to take a closer look at the current Welton staff,' he said before slamming the door behind them.

SEVENTY-FOUR

It was almost 4 p.m. when Kim poured her first coffee in the squad room.

Penn had been summoned from the third floor and she was awaiting his arrival before voicing her plan.

After speaking with Lenny Baldwin, she'd realised their leads were going nowhere. They were getting nothing from forensics, the court orders were coming through slowly and, when they did, the paperwork was slow to decipher. Throw in the fact that the group had made so many enemies during their time at Welton that the suspect pool could fill a football stadium.

Three of the Psycho Six were already dead. Of the three survivors, one had a protected identity, another had dropped off the face of the earth, but Dean Newton was living loud and proud with no intention of taking steps to protect himself.

'I'm back,' Penn said, sliding into his seat.

'All locked up and secure?' she asked.

'Yep, office locked and out of bounds until tomorrow.'

Kim had explained to Penn he wouldn't be going back to it tonight.

'Just to update, Curtis Jones admitted to becoming a Black Country Angel because we're shit at our jobs. He doesn't trust that we take the bad guys off the streets and prefers the vigilante method of justice.'

'You can kind of understand how people feel though. Confidence in the police service is at an all-time low,' Alison offered.

'You really think that justifies people taking the law into their own hands?' Kim asked, crossing her arms.

'If I was in trouble alone, late at night, and someone came to help, I wouldn't care if they were a Black Country Angel. I'd just be grateful.'

'But it's no longer about keeping the streets safe, is it?' Kim challenged her. 'This isn't Batman protecting the poor and needy folks of Gotham City. We're talking groups proactively seeking out wrongdoers and meting out their own form of punishment.'

'And they don't always get it right,' Penn added. 'I read about a sixty-year-old guy, shot dead for kidnapping a one-year-old who was found an hour later safe and well. He'd had nothing to do with her disappearance.'

'But some people do get it right,' Bryant said.

'You support these actions?' Kim asked, shocked.

'Not always, but sometimes even the court system is in agreement with a vigilante's actions. In America, a father shot dead the karate instructor who'd repeatedly raped his eleven-year-old son. The judge gave him a suspended sentence, probation and community service. How are you not gonna want to pat that guy on the back?'

'And no one here cares that the majority of vigilante acts can't be committed without breaking laws?'

'Eggs and omelettes,' Alison said.

For some reason, Kim was surprised at the response of her team. Stacey had offered no thoughts on the subject, and Kim could guess why. Given her recent experiences, Stacey's views towards vigilantism might have undergone a drastic change and, most likely, she didn't want to voice obvious disagreement in the current climate between them.

'Well, anyway, Curtis's dad was murdered and we didn't catch the killers. I know there's little we can do now, but we should dig a bit more into the circumstances surrounding his dad's death. I'd like to know the exact reason for Curtis's hatred of the police.'

'Unsolved murders involving the surname Jones. Shouldn't take long,' Penn quipped.

'Next, we had a good chat with Dean Newton who seemingly couldn't give two shits that three of his old mates are dead. Strange given how close they were when they were at Welton.'

'Not really,' Alison said, screwing up a Twix packet.

'Go on,' Kim said. She'd been troubled by Newton's coldness about the murders.

'Is there any evidence they kept in touch after Welton?' Alison asked.

Kim thought of all the conversations she'd had with the victims' loved ones and shook her head.

'In situations that are unfamiliar, we find safety in numbers. We form groups, gangs. It's a protective barrier against a threat. But group dynamics demand a structure, a hierarchy, in order to function. Normally it mimics family dynamics, i.e. parents make the rules for children to follow. Almost forty per cent of children in custody come from a care environment. One in three have mental-health issues. The hierarchy provides order, safety. There are leaders and followers, which prevents chaos, and everyone in the group is happy.'

'But the closeness doesn't last?' Kim asked.

'Have you ever spent a night or two in hospital, on a ward?'

Kim shrugged. She had but she'd never bonded with other patients.

'I have,' Bryant offered, raising his hand as though it was a school test.

'Did you become close to the other patients?' Alison asked.

He thought for a moment and then nodded.

'You're cut off from the world in a cloistered environment, seeing the exact same people hour after hour. The rest of the world is carrying on without you. That moment in your life only exists with those few people. It creates a bond, a closeness, almost an intimacy with people you might never have met in normal life.'

'Yeah, I see that,' Bryant agreed.

'Still doesn't answer my question,' Kim said.

'It's not real,' Alison continued. 'It's a substitute for what you have in real life. You've seen all those reality shows where people couple up or form close groups very quickly when cut off from the outside world. They're substituting the relation-ships they have in real life for temporary ones to get them through their current situation.' Alison turned to Bryant. 'How many of those people in hospital did you stay in touch with?'

'None.'

'So you're saying the Psycho Six weren't close?' Kim asked.

'Not once they left Welton. The group had served its purpose and was no longer needed.'

Sometimes Alison made perfect sense and actually offered useful background information but nothing that would help them right now.

'Okay, who fancies a bit of surveillance?' Kim asked, rubbing her hands.

Penn and Bryant groaned, and Stacey's face fell. As a non-driver, it was an aspect of the role she couldn't be involved in.

'Come on, guys, think about it. Dean Newton could be next on the list. Our killer has to be after him soon, and he's got no intention of hiding. We can look at it two ways: we're covering him to offer him protection from a credible threat, or we're keeping the live bait on a short line to see what bites.'

Despite the groans, she could tell they all agreed with her logic. It was rare they had such a clear indication of where the killer might strike next.

Setting up an official surveillance operation would be subject to protocols, meetings and risk assessments, and certainly wouldn't be taking place that night. It was something they were going to have to cover between themselves.

'It's a colourful place, and there'll be a lot of comings and goings, but the only thing we're interested in is Dean Newton. If he steps outside, we follow him. Got it?'

Kim noted that Stacey was still looking pretty miserable. She hated not being able to pull her weight and share the load alongside the rest of her team.

'I'll take the first shift and cover him until ten,' Kim said. She'd already sent a text message to Charlie asking him to take Barney back a bit later and to give him his tea.

'Bryant, get some rest and take me off at ten until two.'

'Got it, guv.'

'Penn, you relieve Bryant at two and pick up Stace en route. You can take it in turns to nap before coming in for the 7 a.m. briefing.'

Stacey's face lit up as Kim had known it would.

Kim looked around the room. 'What are you all still doing here?'

They scrambled to get their stuff together to fit in some rest before their shift.

Stacey paused. 'Boss, thanks for—'

'And you text me the minute you see anything suspicious, got it?' Kim asked before heading back into the Bowl.

SEVENTY-FIVE

Being given an early release from work to fit in some rest before the stakeout couldn't have come at a better moment for Stacey. It had given her time to hatch a plan that had nothing at all to do with resting.

And that was why she found herself sitting on a bench at Sedgley Hall Farm park at six o'clock in the evening.

Devon tried to jog at least three times a week to clear her head and this was her favourite spot, with its hilly contours and views across the Shropshire countryside. The place was alive with families and couples enjoying the evening sunshine.

Right on cue, Devon appeared in the distance, her short, dyed-blonde hair a beacon above her navy shorts and tee shirt. Stacey knew her earbuds would be blaring rock music into her ears as she moved.

Devon spied her and instantly stopped running. She slowed to a walk, her face a picture of mixed emotions: surprise, anger, sadness, regret.

Stacey was filled with a surge of love. She'd never valued anything more in her life than this woman who'd managed to reach every part of her. She wasn't going to let their marriage get away from her. While there was breath in her body, she would fight for what they had built.

'What are you doing here?' Devon asked, stopping in front of her and removing the buds from her ears.

'We need to talk, Dee.'

'What's left to say? I don't even recognise us any more,' Devon said.

'We knew each other less than a week ago. We can't have destroyed what we had in that time. We just can't.'

Devon frowned as she took in Stacey's appearance. 'Are you wearing running gear?'

Stacey nodded.

'You hate this type of exercise.'

'I'll chase you around the park all night if I have to. I'm not leaving your side until you've listened to what I have to say.'

Devon wavered but still didn't sit.

Stacey reached into her back pocket. 'See this? Superglue. Strongest and most durable type of glue on the market. Either listen to me or so help me God I'll stick myself to you until they have to surgically separate us.'

'Okay, okay,' Devon said, taking a seat beside her.

A small smile had played on her face at the sight of the glue, which was what Stacey had intended. The real glue would come in what she was about to say. Without the whole truth, she knew her marriage was over.

'We don't have enough fingers and toes to count the ways in which I've been stupid recently,' she said, just allowing the truth to fall from her lips. 'I've let down everyone around me in not trusting them to help me. I've avoided, I've lied, I've ignored, I've deceived, but most importantly I accused you of doing something so out of character that it's caused you to doubt whether we even know each other at all.'

Devon turned the earbuds in her hand, staring down at them with great concentration. Stacey could feel the sadness, the hopelessness, emanating from her. No, she wasn't too late. She couldn't be.

'I shouldn't have asked you that question, Dee. It was unforgiveable. But it has nothing to do with me thinking you're capable of such an act.' She took a breath. 'I asked you because if the situation was reversed, I'm not sure I wouldn't have done it myself.'

The tears spilled from Devon's eyes, and instinctively Stacey reached out to pull her closer. Relief surged through her when Devon didn't object.

'I just don't know where we go from here,' Devon said into her shoulder.

Stacey tipped up her head. 'You still love me?'

'Always,' Devon breathed.

'Then that's a damn good place to start.'

SEVENTY-SIX

Kim sighed heavily as she pulled away from the park-up spot on Hollytree at 10.05 p.m., after briefing Bryant on the activity in and out of the target property.

Whereas the other occupants had been in and out, Dean Newton had left only once to visit the row of shops at the edge of the estate. She'd trailed him on foot and watched as he'd bought four beers and a pack of cigarettes. He hadn't noticed her presence and had re-entered his home untroubled fifteen minutes after leaving it. He'd been there ever since.

Much as she'd attempted to keep her mind occupied during the five-hour stint, her brain had constantly tried to take her back to when she was six years old.

She'd remembered the feelings of fear and dread as she held Mikey's hand walking the short distance back from school. Always trying to think of a way she could make them escape, wondering if all the kids in their class were going home to a mother who wanted to kill them. As she'd watched Newton buy his beer, her mind had travelled back to when the boarded-up space next door had been a fish-and-chip shop.

She'd taken Mikey in most nights to ask for a bag of bits; the burned, crispy, fat-soaked crumbs fished out at the end of a frying and put to the side. They were free but somehow, just now and again, a stray scallop had found its way into the bag from the kindly owner.

Mikey would whoop with delight as he peeled back the batter to reveal the potato disc inside. He would offer it to her to share and she'd scrunch up her face in disgust so that he could eat the whole thing guilt-free. He would savour every bite, closing his eyes tight in ecstasy. And those were the moments that Kim had tried to prolong, to capture for him, a happy memory before they went home.

She felt the weight of her past lifting as she travelled further away from the estate. It was as though being there geographically transported her back in time.

She'd shaken off the feelings of helpless rage by the time she pulled onto the drive.

This was her safe place. Hollytree and all its evils had no place here. She let out a contented sigh, picturing Barney on the other side of the door, eagerly awaiting her return. They were going to have a good few hours of quality time together.

She unlocked the door and stepped inside as she always did. Barney appeared by her legs, but something wasn't right. He was just a second or two late.

Her senses moved into hyper alertness. Something in her home had changed.

She switched on the light and jumped out of her skin.

'Fucking hell,' she cried as her heartbeat pounded in her ears.

Leanne King was sitting on her sofa with an unreadable expression.

'Really? I mean, what the fuck do you think you're doing in my house?'

'What the hell do you think you're doing calling me on a number you shouldn't even have?'

'You shouldn't leave it lying around then, although I think mine was the lesser offence,' Kim said, waiting for the blood to stop pumping in her ears.

'I don't believe in proportional response, and what I have to say is best done in person.'

'Splendid. You want coffee?' Kim asked, adjusting to the situation. Annoying as it was, the witness protection officer never did things conventionally. She wanted to speak in person, so she'd broken in and sat in the dark, waiting.

Kim appraised the woman quickly as she stood and headed for the kitchen. She wore light-blue jeans that hugged her long legs without stifling them. Her ankle boots added another two inches to her already impressive height. Her plain black tee shirt was covered by a navy-and-white baseball jacket. She remembered those exact same clothes. Just like her, Leanne had found a style that she was comfortable with and stuck to it.

In the short time Leanne had been forced to live with her as a protection officer, she'd learned some of Kim's habits. Not least that the first job on coming home was to head for the kitchen and fire up the coffee pot. Second job was to let Barney out into the back garden, but he was still quite enamoured with their guest.

'Stay away from the bad lady, boy – she told me to get rid of you.'

Leanne rolled her eyes. 'Still with the dramatics, eh, Stone? I only advised you that he was your biggest weakness. Which he is. Ooh, nice toaster.'

'Yeah, it was a gift from an insufferable colleague of sorts who broke my old one.'

'Well, technically, you dismantled—'

'Coffee or not?' Kim asked, urging Barney out the back door.

Leanne shook her head.

'Ian Perkins?' Kim asked, hoping Leanne had brought

details of his whereabouts.

'Is living a perfectly respectable life and hasn't been in any trouble since his release. He's doing well.'

'I need to warn him,' Kim said, wondering if Leanne understood the gravity of the situation. 'He was part of a specific group of six at Welton Hall. Three of the six have been murdered this week.'

'Shucks, anyone would think I don't have access to newspapers, or a TV or a smartphone.'

'I don't know what amenities your cave has, and I don't care. I need to know where he is and warn him of—'

'Already done. He's seen the articles your buddy has been writing. He's seen the names of the victims and he's not stupid. He'll take extra precautions.'

'Just tell me where he is,' Kim demanded.

'No.'

'I know, why don't you just hand over his details then?'

'Due to his court testimony, he has a new identity. That gives him rights.'

'For fuck's sake, Leanne. Is there any chance you might trip up and accidentally be a police officer one day?'

One thing that never changed was Leanne's stubborn wish to stick to the rules.

'You know what my job entails, and if you think I haven't bent the rules to come here and tell you this, then you understand nothing.'

'Grrr...'

Leanne tipped her head. 'Did you really just growl at me?'

'You frustrate the shit out of me.'

'Aww... sorry I don't jump when you tell me to, but guess what? You're not my boss, and I don't even like you.'

Kim gave up. 'Thanks for coming. You can leave the same way you came. You've delivered your message.'

It was one she could have texted. And then Kim realised

why she hadn't done exactly that.

'Ah, you've already changed your number, haven't you?'

'I'm not your inside person at witness protection. You can't just call me up and badger me for info. I'm not your direct line. You know I shouldn't have got you an answer to your questions about Ian Perkins.'

'So why did you?'

Silence rested between them for a full minute.

Barney barked at the back door to be let back in.

'I chose a way of life, Stone. I knew what I was doing and what I was giving up. I adapted and I hardened. I live in the shadows because I have to. My work demands it. I love my job, and I'm damn good at it. But the only way I can do it is to live apart. I can't have friends, connections, expectations. You can't just fucking call me.'

'Got it,' Kim said, striding to the front door.

Leanne approached the door slowly, meeting Kim's gaze and holding it. 'It's just the way it has to be.'

'So we're done?' Kim asked.

Leanne nodded, taking a step closer.

'You've changed your number?'

'Yes,' she said, taking another step.

'You've made sure I can never reach you?'

Leanne shook her head. Only a foot separated them.

Kim held out her hand. 'Then give me my fucking house key back.'

There was no evidence of any break-in. Leanne must have had a copy made when she was her protection officer.

Leanne placed the key into her palm and gave her a half-smile before stepping out of the door.

Kim slammed it shut behind her and stood against it.

Her mind was whizzing with an unfamiliar sensation. She felt as though she'd just lost something she'd never had in the first place.

SEVENTY-SEVEN

It was 7.05 a.m. when Kim stepped out of the Bowl into the squad room. Both Penn and Stacey had rolled in at 6.45 a.m. and taken quick showers in the locker rooms to freshen up. They'd had a long night which was probably going to run into a long day while they tried to make some progress on finding the killer.

Her own night had been less than restful. The presence of Leanne in her home again had been unsettling and yet familiar. Her initial shock had been replaced with an acceptance that, like her, Leanne would never do anything conventional like knock on the door. Leanne didn't play by anyone else's rules, which Kim could only respect.

She knew she'd used her one opportunity to make contact with Leanne and that there'd be no other chances. She'd made it clear they wouldn't meet again and, much as Kim despised the woman, for some reason, the thought saddened her.

It hadn't been the only thing troubling her during the night as her mind had processed the events of the day, but she'd worry more about that later.

'Okay, folks, someone explain to me why Dean Newton isn't dead,' Kim said.

'Cos we were watching him?' Penn asked.

'He went out to get a paper at what time?' she pushed.

'Six oh three,' Penn answered.

'Anyone around?'

'On Hollytree?' he asked with a raised eyebrow. It was hardly awash with the gainfully employed.

'Exactly. The man has a habit of going out for a newspaper when there's no one else around. Our killer seems to know the movements of his victims. So why is he not dead already?'

'Maybe he's done,' Penn suggested.

'But why?' she insisted. 'We know of no incident that involved just the three of them.'

'He's not done,' Alison offered.

'Jesus, I forgot you were here,' Kim said. 'Feel free to tell us why not.'

'Because he told you from the outset what he was going for. His first tweet stated his intended number of victims. He didn't say one of three. He clearly wants all members of the Psycho Six dead.'

'Bloody hell, Alison, I could work that out myself. Give me something I don't know,' Kim begged. 'You gotta be up to speed by now.'

Alison waved a piece of paper in the air. 'I was about to offer my thoughts. I think the man you're looking for is both devious and clever. He's also a show-off. He likes to perform. He's not a random vigilante, but he may well have links to vigilante groups. There's no question that he's arrogant but also intelligent.'

'Age?' Kim asked.

Alison shook her head. 'I've deliberately omitted my thoughts on that. He's definitely a risk taker, which often comes with youth, but there are signs that it's a mature person exerting parental authority. The normal reason for that is experience and age, but it can also come from an assumed authority. For example, there may only be a couple of years difference between siblings, but the older one will often adopt a parental tone with a younger one. It can even come from colleagues, like with bosses and subordinates, so that doesn't help us narrow his age.

'He's physically able and patient. He's planned and waited to get his victims without witnesses and without giving anything away on CCTV. He abducts his victims, transports them and stages them without being seen. That tells us he has nerve. He also has focus. He's using a lethal drug and he knows just how much to inject to get his victim pliable but not enough to kill immediately. He's prepared to break bones just to get his message across. He's acting like a vigilante, and in some ways I think he wants you to think he's a vigilante, but there's definitely more to it than that.'

'Dean Newton?' Kim asked, still wanting to know why the man wasn't yet dead.

'I can only assume there has to be a certain order to his process,' Alison said.

'Maybe he changed his mind. Maybe three is enough,' Penn offered.

'He's not done,' Stacey said.

'That's what I'm saying,' Alison repeated.

'So is he. He's just posted on Twitter. "Busy day 4/6."'

'Shit,' Kim said. 'He has to be talking about Dean Newton or Leyton Parks; I can't imagine he's found Ian Perkins. We've tried our best to warn Newton.'

'What if he's found Leyton Parks, boss?' Penn asked.

'Stace, do nothing else until you can tell me where he lives. Penn, call Dean Newton and tell him to stay home and not answer the door to anyone.'

'Think he'll listen?'

'That's his choice. We can't babysit him any longer and try to find our killer at the same time.'

'Got it, boss. Oh, the warrant is in for the Black Country Angels. I amended it yesterday to add Curtis Jones as a link, which seems to have pushed it through.'

'Great. Penn, I want you back on the records from Welton. I want the name of the boy who was terrorised and also pay particular attention to the staff. Lenny Baldwin hinted at something going on there. I'm not— What the hell are you doing here?' she asked as Bryant strolled into the office. 'I told you to come in late.'

'I did,' he said, removing his jacket.

'Fifteen minutes?'

'Serious case of FOMO.'

'Quit using acronyms way below your age range, partner,' she said, mentally checking off the list in her head.

'Okay, guys, let's get to it. Stace, a word,' she said, heading into the Bowl.

She stood by the door and waited for the constable to enter. 'Feel free to keep your seats this time, folks,' she called, closing the door.

'Have a seat,' she said, taking her own.

Stacey did so but said nothing. Kim couldn't blame her for not knowing how this was going to go.

'How are you doing?'

'I'm okay.'

'How are you doing, Stace?' Kim asked again.

'Not great. I'm trying, but the anxiety won't go away.'

'Your body didn't get into this state overnight. It'll take time, and I think you might need help.'

'No, boss, no, I don't need—'

'Hang on,' Kim said, holding up her hand. 'I didn't mean on the record.' Great efforts had been made to keep this whole thing off the damn record and she wasn't yet totally sure they'd succeeded.

'I was with Charlotte Danks at the morgue yesterday. She wants you to call her.'

'No, I couldn't. No.'

'Why not?'

'She suffered him for ten years. My ordeal was a couple of months. I couldn't ask her to relive—'

'From what I saw yesterday, she's still reliving it every day. Only you two get it. Only you two understand what that man was capable of. Do you not think you could support each other?'

Stacey looked doubtful. Kim knew she was comparing what each of them had been through and was minimising her own suffering compared to Charlotte's ordeal.

Kim slid a piece of paper across the desk. 'Call her or I'll make it official, but one way or another, you will get the help you need.'

It was an empty threat, but she had to know Stacey was talking to someone.

'And then there's me. Any time, day or night. You wanna talk, call me.'

'I shoulda told you, boss.'

'Yep, you should, and I should have been a bit more support-ive. Well, maybe more than a bit, but let's just go forward, eh?'

'Happy to, boss,' Stacey said with a genuine smile.

'Okay, get to work.'

Stacey walked back to her desk with a lighter step, and much as she'd wanted to ask how she and Devon were doing, she couldn't. Not yet.

She took out her phone and scrolled down her contact list.

'Hey, Vik,' she said when the traffic officer answered.

'Jesus, if you're going to keep badgering me until I agree, fine, you can take me out for a drink.'

'Smashing. Bring your wife and kids. My shout.'

He laughed. 'What now?'

'Just wondering if there was any progress on that small blue car.'

'Just so you know, my suspicions about your interest rise every time you call me about this case.'

'Just curious cos he was known to us. And I'm a bit bored on a surveillance right now.'

The best lies always stayed close to the truth. 'Last call, I promise.'

'Nothing more since our last conversation. I've got a witness who was coming out of the chippie says the vehicle was white, and my two witnesses who agree on the colour disagree on the make and model.'

'Damn it,' Kim said, feeling that was the appropriate response.

'Yeah, sorry about that, Stone. We're doing our best, but if I'm being completely honest, our chances of tracing that driver have got no better odds than you and I having a secret love child.'

Kim laughed. 'Thanks for being honest, Vik. Now I know that I'll put it to bed.'

She ended the call and allowed a small smile to tug at her lips.

And she would indeed be putting it to bed.

SEVENTY-EIGHT

Kim could see from the upstairs window that someone in the household was up. Being such an early riser herself, she wasn't sure what time constituted an early morning call.

'Guv, do you mind telling me why we're here again?' Bryant asked.

'Mind telling me why you can't follow a simple instruction on your start time?'

He didn't answer as she unbuckled her seat belt.

He went to do the same.

'I won't be long,' she said, leaping out of the car.

Charlotte answered the door wearing cropped trousers and a tee shirt. 'Hi?'

'Just wanted to make sure you were okay after yesterday.'

'Please come in. I'm just fixing Mum's breakfast. She's in there,' Charlotte said, pointing to the lounge. 'Can I get you a coffee?'

'Yes, please. Is Ella here?'

'She's getting a well-deserved lie-in.'

'And how's your mum?' Kim asked.

Charlotte beamed. 'It's a good day today.'

Kim stepped into the lounge and smiled at Mrs Danks. 'Hello again. How are you?' she asked, taking a seat on the sofa.

'Who are you? What are you doing here? I'll call the police.'

'It's okay, Mrs Danks. I am the police. I'm not going to hurt you.'

The woman grunted and looked away.

Kim sighed. 'So sorry to learn you're unwell, Mrs Danks. It must have been terrible for you when you first noticed the symptoms of your dementia, especially after caring for someone with the exact same disease. You must have known exactly what was coming and how it was going to progress.'

Mrs Danks said nothing.

'I bet you were terrified you'd never see Charlotte again, or if you'd recognise her when you did.'

A tear formed in the woman's eye.

'I can only imagine how you must have felt, knowing what was coming and yet still having normal capacity most of the time. Still able to wash and dress yourself, cook, clean. Drive.'

The DVLA records listed Mrs Danks as the registered owner of the small blue Fiat Panda.

The woman's gaze met hers and what Kim saw was pure, heartbreaking fear.

Kim touched her hand lightly, not envying the future that she faced. It didn't need to be any worse. She'd suffered enough. They all had.

'Unfortunately, Mrs Danks, I fear they'll never find the person responsible for Terence Birch's accident, so I'm not able to offer any update on that. The investigation into the other driver is about to be closed.'

The fear was ebbing, but her gaze remained guarded.

'I understand that you have good days and bad, but it's okay to enjoy the good days to their fullest. Do you understand, Mrs Danks?'

She nodded slowly. The exaggeration of her symptoms was no longer required. The actuality would arrive soon enough.

Kim stood. 'Take care, Mrs Danks.'

She was heading for the door when she heard a voice barely louder than a whisper.

'Thank you, Inspector Stone.'

She continued towards the kitchen.

'Charlotte, so sorry, urgent call, can't stop for coffee.'

'Oh, okay,' she said, putting down the mug.

'But I've just had a lovely chat with your mum and you're right, she does seem to be having a good day. I've got a feeling there'll be plenty more of those to come.'

Charlotte gave her a quizzical smile.

'Get on with your life and enjoy her for as long as you can.'

'I will. I promise.'

Kim closed the front door behind her.

The case of Terence Birch had now well and truly been put to bed.

SEVENTY-NINE

Penn looked up as the door to the meeting room opened.

'Thought you might need one of these,' Stacey said, placing a cup of coffee on the table.

'Thanks, Stace. I swear to God the authorities really didn't want anyone finding out about this incident with the kid who was bullied.'

'Medical records?' Stacey asked.

He'd already considered that. 'As with every other piece of paper sent over from Welton, there's no order to the medical records, and even if there was, I'm looking for a kid injured during a three-to-four-year period in a boy's prison.'

'Didn't he require hospitalisation?'

'Not according to what's in these boxes. Only seven inmates were referred for hospital treatment in the years our boys were there. A broken arm, a rib fracture, two viruses, a perforated eardrum, an appendectomy and an in-grown toenail.'

'Are you joking?' Stacey asked. 'In more than three years?'

'And not one of the reasons for hospital attendance was given as violence. The two broken bones were both supposedly accidental.'

'No warning on the files of any of our six?'

'Not for that. Plenty of notes for minor stuff, but there isn't any mention of the big stuff.'

'We've obviously got them all wrong. Proper little group of angels,' Stacey offered, heading back towards the door.

'Either that or someone has defied the court order and been pretty choosy with the documentation they've turned over to us.'

And, of course, proving that would be another matter entirely.

He sighed heavily, realising that he might well be looking for something that just wasn't there.

There was no question in his mind that the final assault on the mystery boy had been covered up and removed from the records, if the incident had even been logged in the first place.

'Stace, I'm out of ideas,' he said honestly.

'Penn, I know for a fact that you'd keep looking for the proverbial needle in the haystack if someone told you it was definitely in there, but there's no guarantee here. You can keep looking or...'

'I can move on to one of the other twenty jobs the boss gave us.'

'Exactly,' Stacey said, closing the door behind her.

He decided to focus on the staff. Apparently Lenny Baldwin had hinted that there were skeletons in that particular closet.

He put aside the piles of paperwork that pertained to the boys and grabbed the box filled with his first miscellaneous pile. These documents had been quickly cast aside when there had been no obvious mention of the names he'd been looking for.

A third of the way down, he came across an official report carried out by the Health and Safety Executive. It was a document formed of twenty pages or more and focussed on an investigation into the safety of the north wing staircase. It wasn't a document he'd expected to yield any results, but now he looked at it a little closer.

He turned over the first page to reveal the name of the prison officer who'd been fatally injured due to falling down the north wing staircase.

He clutched the report, then tore out of the room and down the stairs.

For this he needed his colleague's help.

EIGHTY

'You're not going to tell me why we came here?' Bryant asked, pulling away from the kerb.

'Absolutely. Just as soon as you give me your best guess as to how Vik missed the Stacey shrine at Birch's house.'

Silence.

'Thought so. We'll just accept it was a welfare check, eh?'

'Good luck with getting anyone who's met you to swallow that one.'

Kim was saved from answering by the ringing of her phone. She held her breath. Anyone other than Keats was welcome.

'Go ahead, Stace,' she said, letting out the breath.

'Just been doing some further checking on the guys you're going to see, boss. Nothing new on Elliot, but his mate, Gordon Banks, seems to have disappeared from all the social-media platforms he used to be on. It's like he was never there.'

'Okay,' Kim said, frowning. She'd barely given the quiet guy in the Angels office a thought.

'Thanks, Stace,' she said before ending the call.

She turned to Bryant. 'How the hell did this guy escape our attention?'

'Cos his only crime was to not be very talkative in your presence. If we questioned—'

'Bryant, shut up,' she said, lowering her window.

The stench of burning had seeped into the car. They were less than half a mile away from the headquarters of the Black Country Angels.

'Just a coincidence, guv,' Bryant said, putting his foot down, belying his own words.

The smell grew stronger the closer they got.

A cordon was set up at the end of the road.

'Shit,' Kim said, jumping out and heading towards the police officers with her ID in her hand. She didn't need it, as they immediately stepped aside.

Two fire engines were aiming their hoses towards the premises of the Black Country Angels.

'You have got to be fucking kidding me,' Kim said, feeling the court order burning a hole in her inside pocket.

Elliot Reed broke free from the crowd and headed her way.

'Anyone inside?' she asked as Bryant caught up with her.

'God no. I got here to open up at just after nine. I wasn't even out of the car when I saw the smoke coming out of the place. Neighbour smelled it and called the fire service.'

'I have a warrant,' she told him.

He shrugged. 'You're welcome to whatever's left after these guys have finished.'

Anything not burned would most likely be waterlogged, and the joy of sorting through that lot would only come once the fire investigator had determined the cause.

'We did have a crappy heater that threw out the odd spark now and again,' Elliot offered, wiping his palm over his head.

'Who'd have been in there putting the fire on?'

He shrugged. 'Just guessing.'

'Where's Gordon?'

'I dunno. We only do the occasional shift together.'

'But you've got a number for him.'

'Sure,' he said, taking out his phone. 'You want it?'

'No. I want you to call him and ask him where he is.'

'Okey-dokey,' he said, pushing his curly black hair out of his eyes.

He looked back at the burning building as he waited for the call to connect.

'Strange. Straight to voicemail. Hang on, I'll try again and leave a message.'

'Never mind,' Kim said. 'What do you know about him?'

'Lives over on Hollytree. One of the tall ones. Let me think,' he said, scrunching up his face. 'Shakespeare House.'

'Doesn't exist,' Kim snapped.

The three tower blocks were named after famous writers, but Shakespeare wasn't one of them.

'What do you know about his past?'

Elliot shrugged again. 'We don't talk about stuff like that. I don't think he had a very happy childhood. Spent time in a kids' home, I think.'

'Kids' home or youth offenders institute?'

'Dunno. Could have been either. I think he was bullied wherever he was.'

Kim realised she was going to get as much information out of Elliot as she was from this conveniently burning building.

Regretfully she turned and headed back to the car.

'Ah, right on cue,' Kim said as she almost collided with Tracy Frost.

'Why, you want more help?'

'Nah, I was just thinking my day couldn't get any worse and yet here you are.' She turned to her colleague. 'Get the car started. I won't be long.'

'Anything from those names I gave you?' Frost asked while taking a look at the fire which was the reason for her presence. As soon as she knew there was no one inside, she'd most likely be on her way and not bother to cover it at all.

'Not really, and I don't think this'll make it into your next article.'

'Unlikely if there's no human element and especially because I might be on to something else. A bit closer to home for you to be honest.'

'Ah, Frost, what little lies are you making up now?'

Frost tossed her long blonde hair behind her. 'There are times when you really wish I wasn't very good at my job.'

'Luckily for me, those times don't come around very often. Now if you've—'

'See, I heard this rumour from a friend of a friend that you've been particularly interested in a hit and run from earlier this week.'

Kim felt the blood chill in her veins. She kept her face devoid of expression.

'It didn't take me long to realise the victim was a previous witness of yours, but given your inability to form emotional attachments, I knew it wasn't that simple. Turns out the man has quite the record for stalking; terrorised one family for a decade. Nope, that still doesn't explain your interest in his death. Gotta be more to it than that. And then silly me starts putting a few other things together, like you being off your game, except it's not you off your game, is it? So now I'm thinking that Birch turned his attention elsewhere, and then I'm thinking I've got a pretty good story here that—'

'Is completely fictional and the result of an underactive psychotic mind.'

Great, after all their efforts to protect Stacey's name, her worst nightmare had managed to put it all together. Damn it.

'Ah, it's true then. I got it right. You did the thing.'

'What thing?'

Frost shrugged. 'I'm not gonna tell you about the thing, cos then you'll stop doing the thing and I'll never be able to rely on the thing again.'

Kim stepped closer. 'You repeat one word of that bollocks to anyone and—'

'Stop threatening me, Stone,' she said, stepping away from the finger wagging in her face. 'There's an easier way to get what you want.'

Kim was reminded of an experiment Woody had done on her and Bryant a few years ago. He'd instructed her to open his fist. She'd tried to pry it open with her fingernails and brute force. It was when she'd reached for his paper knife that Woody had asked Bryant to do the same thing. Her colleague had simply asked Woody to open his fist. And he had.

'Frost, I'm asking you to leave it alone – please.'

'Okay, consider it done.'

'That easy?' she asked, raising an eyebrow.

'She's a good kid. I like her. Now, if it had been you...'

'Bye, Frost,' Kim said, turning and heading for the car. Her mind was already swinging back to the case.

She took out her phone, but the caller had beaten her to it.

'Penn, I really need anything you can get me on the kid that shared a cell with Eric and Paul.'

She'd learned that the majority of the bullying had been from those two, but he'd been seen as an easy mark for abuse. There could easily have been incidents including all six of them.

'I'll keep trying, boss, but there's something you need to know. The prison officer that fell down the stairs. He had a son. And we already know his name.'

EIGHTY-ONE

Today they had no such luck of bumping into the person they wanted as he left for his lunchbreak. Instead, they'd requested his immediate presence at the hospital reception desk via Belinda the receptionist.

With a surname as common as Jones, it had taken a while for Penn and Stacey to ascertain that Curtis Jones was definitely the son of Richard Jones, the forty-three-year-old officer who had fallen to his death down the north staircase at Welton.

'This bloody case has got more twists and turns than Alton Towers,' Bryant remarked as they moved away from Belinda's domain.

He wasn't wrong, Kim thought as she heard the familiar sound of Crocs on floor tile. This time they were heading down the stairs, and unlike when they'd arrived to speak to him yesterday, he made no attempt to offer an engaging smile.

She moved further away from the reception desk, already knowing how this was going to go.

'Inspector, these interruptions—'

'Would not be necessary if you'd told us the truth in the first place, Mr Jones.'

He offered a frown that wasn't as deep as it should have been. 'I'm not sure what you mean. I haven't once lied to the police.'

'You haven't exactly shared the whole truth either, have you?'

He said nothing, waiting for her to show her hand. She was happy to do so.

'You didn't think to mention that your father died at the institution where your love rival spent three years as a teenager; or that the group known as the Psycho Six was seen in the area where your dad fell?'

He shrugged, and Kim realised he was going to give them nothing for free.

'Did you know Eric Gould was a member of that group when you learned that he was Teresa's new boyfriend?'

'Not at first. I knew the name sounded familiar, but I hadn't given it a thought in years.'

'You hadn't thought about your dad's accident?' Bryant asked.

'His murder, Inspector,' he hissed as emotion began to loosen his tongue. 'My dad had run-ins with that group all the time. He was strict and he didn't take their shit. They hated him because they couldn't pull the wool over his eyes. They never managed to get one over on him, and he treated them like the scum that they were. Everyone else was scared to death of them – the kids, the staff, but not my dad. I'd hear him talking to my mum about them, and no matter what they did, he wouldn't be intimidated. So they decided to get rid of him altogether.'

Kim wasn't prepared to challenge his view on the incident quite yet. There were other questions that needed answers.

'I'm just wondering how you must have felt when you found out that one of the culprits had stolen your girlfriend,' Bryant said.

'I was sick to my stomach, but what exactly could I do about it?'

'He's dead,' Kim reminded him.

'And I'm not sorry.'

'Does Rufus know?' Kim asked. For some reason, the image of the two of them driving away in Rufus's little pet ambulance had lodged in her mind.

'About what?'

'All of it?' Kim asked.

Curtis coloured slightly. 'I'm not... I mean... probably. I've talked about different stuff to do with it, and—'

She could picture the two of them dissecting the whole thing after a few pints. It was no wonder Rufus had been unable to warm to Eric Gould.

'Did Rufus tell Teresa about Eric's past?' Kim asked.

Curtis shook his head vehemently. 'He wasn't going to risk losing her. He hoped the whole thing was just going to fizzle out.'

Or had he planned on eliminating Eric from Teresa's life in a more permanent way? Kim wondered.

'If you lot had just done your job in the first place—'

'The force did nothing wrong,' Kim defended, having had Penn read out the whole report to her over the phone during their journey. 'There was no crime to investigate. The boys had been seen in the area, but the real culprit was a faulty handrail.'

'He was pushed.'

'No he wasn't. The handrail came away.'

'They loosened it,' he insisted.

'It had been on the maintenance "to do" list for three days. It was a terrible, tragic accident that should never have happened, but they were not responsible.'

He shook his head. 'There's nothing you can say or do that will convince me they were innocent. They received no punishment for what they did to my dad.'

Kim opened her mouth to clarify once more that there was no evidence, but she knew she would be wasting her breath. This belief had festered inside him for fifteen years. She was more interested in the consequences of that fact.

'Did Rufus believe you or did he try and talk some sense into you? He's very protective, and now three of your sworn enemies are dead. You both have access to fentanyl, and—'

'Inspector, I don't know exactly what the hell you're trying to get at here, but—'

'Really? You're an intelligent, educated man. I'd have thought it was perfectly obvious.'

He held her gaze for a good ten seconds, the throbbing vein in his forehead giving her a good indication of the emotion he was suppressing.

'Please don't come here again. If you want to ask me any further questions, I'll be happy to oblige. In the presence of my lawyer,' he said before turning and heading back up the stairs.

The receptionist offered them a look of disapproval as they headed out of the hospital.

Kim was on the brink of deciding whether to begin the process of a formal interview with Curtis Jones when her phone rang.

'Go ahead, Penn,' she answered.

'Hey, boss. Lenny Baldwin's tip has turned into a bit of a goldmine. I'm still focussing on the staff at Welton like you asked, and you're not going to believe what else I found out.'

EIGHTY-TWO

Welton Hall looked no friendlier than it had a couple of days before. It was a hardened juvenile that would be brought here and not feel some trepidation walking through the doors. Maybe even the staff had the odd misgiving too.

'Josephine Kirk,' Kim said, showing her ID.

'I remember who you are. I was here the other day,' said the girl on the other side of the desk. 'But I'm not sure Ms Kirk is available.'

Kim understood that not everything could be dropped just because police officers investigating a triple murder turned up on your doorstep. But short of a full-blown riot or a suicide situation beyond those locked doors, Kim was unsure what trumped her presence.

'Please tell Ms Kirk it's urgent we speak with her. Now,' Kim said, stepping away from the desk, leaving no room for argument.

From the corner of her eye, she watched the girl make the call. It was short, and she said nothing to them once it had ended. She simply nodded towards the officer who'd completed the security checks, who beckoned for them to follow.

Kim could easily have found her own way, but she guessed that even police officers weren't allowed to roam freely around the facility.

The officer knocked on the door of Josephine Kirk's office and waited for her instruction before pushing the door open.

Kirk was dressed in what appeared to be a self-imposed uniform of white silk shirt and navy slacks. She didn't stand or offer her hand. Neither did she invite them to take a seat, but they did so anyway.

'Thank you for seeing us so promptly,' Bryant said.

'There was a choice?' Kirk asked, looking directly at Kim.

'Not really, but my colleague has better manners than me,' Kim answered.

Kirk didn't dispute it.

'Oh and thank you for sending over the records.'

'I didn't think there was a choice with that either.'

'Yes, quite,' Kim conceded. 'Although I'm sure we could have waited an hour or two for them to be sorted into order. Any order.'

Kim could swear she saw a hint of triumph in the woman's eyes.

'We understood it was urgent. Tidying up archived records doesn't take priority. We sent them as soon as we located them.'

Kim tipped her head. 'I suppose a cynical person might wonder if the lack of organisation was an attempt to hide certain details.'

'Then those people wouldn't understand that it would be against the law to withhold such information.'

'I didn't say withhold, Ms Kirk.'

The woman coloured slightly, and Kim was done playing.

'Enough of this dance. You had to have known that we'd find out that you were the young female officer attacked by the Psycho Six.'

Still she said nothing but swallowed deeply.

'Did you think we'd overlook the fact that three of your attackers are now dead? And is there any reason you didn't bother to tell us this yourself?'

Her hands gripped each other on the desk. 'I didn't see any relevance. It was a long time ago.'

'So you won't mind telling us what happened,' Kim said, sitting back in her seat.

'It was a prank. Just a stupid act by a group of immature boys.'

Kim wasn't sure whether she was playing it down for their benefit or her own.

'Six boys attacked you, held you down, stripped you naked and were poised to rape you.'

The woman moved some papers around. 'You're making it sound much worse than it actually was.'

'No, I don't think I am. It affected you enough to leave your job.'

'Well, of course it upset me a little at the time.'

'Ms Kirk, you appear to be the master of understatement. Those six boys stripped you and tried to rape you. They over-powered you and placed you in a vulnerable, terrifying situation. Why the hell are you acting as though they tripped you up while carrying your lunch tray?'

'Because I don't like to give it much thought, give *them* too much thought. To dwell on it gives them too much power in my present, not just my past.'

Kim was about to test how that was working out for her. She may have pushed the six to the back of her mind, but now they needed to be discussed.

'We need to understand the dynamics in that group better. Who was the ringleader during the sexual attack?'

'I c-can't remember,' she said, shaking her head.

'Was it Paul?' Kim asked. After all, Paul was a convicted rapist.

'I really can't remember, Inspector, and I'm not going to try too hard.'

'Bloody hell, you do realise you're being obstructive?' Kim asked, not even bothering to hide her frustration.

'My memory is my memory, and I'm not prepared to make things up.'

It was clear that the woman hadn't properly dealt with the attack and that they weren't going to get anything else out of her.

Because there had been no actual rape, it had impacted no one's life in a major way. Except for Josephine Kirk. To everyone else it was an 'almost' event. Something that could be pushed aside and forgotten about.

It seemed to Kim that Kirk had attempted to do the same. Everyone else had played it down, and so had she. She not only still worked in the same industry; she worked at the place it had happened.

Having never dealt with any of her own childhood traumas, Kim was the last person qualified to offer judgement. And knowing that she was probably one wrong question away from the woman refusing to speak without a lawyer, there was no point asking any investigation-related questions without doing her homework.

'Okay, Ms Kirk, we won't trouble you any further. If you think of anything that might help, please give us a call,' she said, before standing and heading for the door.

'Two of them...' Kirk said as she was about to leave.

Kim turned and waited.

'Two of them didn't want to do it. They were telling the others to stop.'

'Which two?' Kim asked gently.

'Dean Newton and Leyton Parks.'

'Thank you,' she said before closing the door behind them.

She stayed in her own thoughts as they were taken back to the entrance.

Was it coincidence that the ones who'd tried to stop the attack were two of the three still alive?

But more unnerving for her was the knowledge that balled up inside Josephine Kirk was a whole concoction of volatile emotions that reminded her of a chemistry experiment.

The woman was pushing her feelings so far down that they were going to find a way to break free sometime. It was going to happen whether she wanted it to or not.

EIGHTY-THREE

'Poof,' Stacey said.

'Not terribly politically correct,' Penn responded, taking a bite from his sandwich.

He'd surfaced from the meeting room to grab a spot of lunch.

'Poof as in magic, gone, disappeared,' she clarified. 'That is literally what's happened to Leyton Parks. He's on no social-media platforms, no business forums, no dating sites and he didn't re-offend after he was released.'

'Last known address?'

'Was a permanent travellers' site that was disbanded and sold for housing ten years ago.'

'He lived on the site with his parents?' Alison asked.

Stacey nodded.

'What happened to the other travellers?' Penn asked.

'Moved to other sites around the county. No record of who went where.'

'Christ, Stace, if he's from the travelling community you've got no chance,' Alison said. 'You're not going to find him registered anywhere.'

'How the hell am I supposed to locate him then?'

Alison shrugged and went back to her laptop.

Stacey turned her attention to Penn, who was throwing the last piece of sandwich into his mouth.

'Did you say you'd sorted everything to do with the boys into their own pile?'

'Yep.'

'Can I have Leyton's pile? There might be something in there to give me a clue.'

'Yeah, I'll go grab it. Gotta start moving out of there anyway. Budget meeting at four.'

He left the room, and Alison immediately pushed aside her laptop and rested her chin on her interlinked fingers.

'So, you going to tell me what that chat was about this morning?'

'Nothing to tell, except that we're good, kind of, maybe. Well, it's better anyway,' Stacey said, still feeling the relief of her earlier conversation with the boss.

She didn't think for a minute things were going to snap right back to how they'd once been, but at least now the boss could look at her, and she was back to calling directly instead of going through Penn.

The relief of that development paled against the euphoria she'd felt when she and Devon had walked back to their home hand in hand. There was no doubt they had work to do, but Stacey knew the depth of their love would see them through.

'And the text?'

'Jesus, Alison, anything you don't want to know?'

'Not really. I should be climbing right now. I'm not, so I've got to get my excitement somewhere.'

'Fair enough. It was the boss telling me that Devon was in the clear. Not that I needed telling, but Devon was relieved.'

'So, what's the boss know that we don't?' Alison asked.

'You know her aversion to detail. She didn't say, and I'm not going to ask.'

'More importantly, how are you feeling about it all?'

'Better,' she said honestly. The tension between her and the boss had added hugely to the surrealness of the last few days.

'Good. On that note, I'm going to book a B&B in Shropshire for the weekend and get out of here.'

'But the case,' Stacey protested.

'I was never needed for this one, matey, and you know it. I've offered every insight I can, so I'm just going to tidy my stuff up and get gone.'

Stacey was prevented from offering any argument by Penn charging back into the office. Not that she would try and stop her best friend from enjoying the last few days of her holiday.

Alison was right. She hadn't been needed for this one, but it had helped Stacey having her friend just ten feet away.

'Okay, here's everything on Leyton Parks. Not sure how much use it is. If he wants to hide, he'll be miles away, probably in a city somewhere.'

'Not necessarily,' Alison said, putting her laptop into her bag.

'Surely safety in numbers, the volume of people. Chaos. Anonymity. Even somewhere like Birmingham you can just fade against thousands of other people. I mean, I lost Lynne in the Bullring for an hour, and I know what she looks like.'

Stacey chuckled.

'It doesn't feel safe,' Alison explained. 'You feel vulnerable if you're hiding from something. It could sneak up on you at any second. The noise and the traffic and the crowds mean you can't look in all directions at the same time. It's exhausting. You'd feel like you need to be moving all the time. Hundreds if not thousands of cameras are watching your every move. Far too exposed.'

'Thanks for that parting shot, buddy,' Stacey said, wondering where the hell to start her search.

'Think of it another way: if we feel threatened or vulnerable, where do we head for? Where do we feel safest?'

'Home,' Penn offered.

'Yep,' Alison said, reaching for her coat. 'It's familiar. We know its strengths and weaknesses. We have exit strategies. We know who to ask for help. We know everything about where we are.'

'Yeah, well, he'd be in the middle of someone's living room if he'd gone back home,' Stacey pointed out, tapping the new houses on a printout plan.

'With that, I bid you both farewell. Stace, I'll give you a call over the weekend.'

'Okey dokey, and Alison?'

'Yeah?'

'Thank you,' Stacey said and meant it.

Alison waved in response before disappearing from view.

'Can I have a quick look at that, Stace?' Penn asked.

'Trust me, you can't afford these houses,' Stacey said, pushing the plan towards him.

'Hmm...'

'What?'

'I just want to check something on the planning application.'

'Penn, now is not the time to check if they followed building regulations.'

'Okay, cool,' he said, clearly not listening.

He tapped furiously, focussing on the screen.

She'd seen that look before, and she knew to keep quiet. A bald eagle could land on his head, and he wouldn't notice.

She jumped as the printer behind kicked into life. She reached for the sheet as it landed on the tray.

'One sec,' Penn said as the printer fired up again.

He came round to her side of the desk.

'Pick a property,' he said, looking at the two sheets of paper.

'We playing fantasy homes?' she asked.

'Just want the postcode.'

'Okay, got it.'

'Get it up on Earth,' he instructed.

Stacey did so and watched as the world turned and then deposited her with a bird's eye view of the ten new buildings.

'Turn it around,' Penn told her, putting his two sheets of paper on the desk and then wheeling over Bryant's chair to sit in.

'Look at this,' he said, pointing to the first page. It was an old aerial shot of the travellers' site prior to the housing development. The road accessed the site from a country lane just one mile out of Stourport. It then ran a straight line through the site with eight caravans on each side. The whole area was surrounded by a grove of mature trees thirty to forty feet deep, beyond which was a small reservoir which separated the site from the main road into the town.

'Okay,' she said, not sure what she was supposed to be looking at.

'This second sheet is the planning permission for the new project.'

'Okay,' she said again, fighting her frustration. Sometimes she wished Penn would just tell her straight out what he was thinking, but she knew he wanted her to follow his thought process to see if she arrived at the same destination.

'It's shorter,' she said, looking from one sheet to the other.

'Yep. Planning permission said the last house had to be at least a hundred metres from the tip of the reservoir.'

It was now clear to Stacey that the batch of trees separating the houses from the water was much thicker than it had been on the travellers' site.

'The developers obviously planted more trees at that far edge to keep continuity with the ones already there.'

'You don't think...?'

'Zoom in on the trees,' he said, moving closer to the screen.

Stacey moved to the left-hand side of the trees and zoomed in until she began to lose clarity.

She moved the mouse slowly an inch at a time, looking for anything that appeared out of place.

The room was completely silent as they both focussed on the screen.

'There,' Penn called out, stabbing the screen and frightening the life out of her.

But he was right, she thought, zooming back out just a bit. There was an irregularity in the uniformity of the trees.

She moved back in slowly, keeping the focus as she went.

'Stace?'

'Yep, I'm seeing it, Penn.'

Nestled beneath the trees, but unable to hide itself completely, was one single caravan.

EIGHTY-FOUR

Kim sipped at her coffee, trying to force order onto the thoughts in her head.

Seeing the concentration on her face, Luigi had called out, 'Extra strong coming up.'

They'd brought their drinks outside. The sound of the Mucklow Hill dual carriageway usually helped clear her head.

'I'm still not getting it,' Kim said. She'd sent a welfare check text message to Dean Newton, whose reply of 'fuck off pig' had confirmed he was very much still alive. 'What's so different about him?'

'His charm and boyish good looks,' Bryant answered.

Kim laughed before sipping her coffee again. The man possessed neither. She was saved from responding by the ringing of her phone.

'Go ahead, Stace,' she said, putting the constable on loud-speaker.

'Boss, we've got good news and bad news.'

'Desperately need the good news right now.'

'We think we've found him, boss. We think we know where Leyton Parks is living.'

'Go on,' Kim said, sitting forward.

'It was Penn who found it. Looks like he's living totally off-grid. Single caravan, no electrics, no gas, not a registered address and surrounded by a perimeter, maybe fencing, maybe barbed wire.'

'Okay, what's the bad news?'

'We think the Sentinel might have found him too. There's been another tweet. Just a minute ago.'

'Saying what?' Kim asked, feeling her heartbeat quicken.

'One word, "Gotcha",' Stacey answered. 'He may be talking about Dean Newton, but Penn is currently being told to piss off by the man himself.'

'Shit, can we get squad cars en route to Leyton?' she asked, realising that trying to protect Dean Newton was a lost cause.

'Whoa, easy tiger,' Bryant said. 'Scrub that last instruction, Stace, and send us all the information you've got.'

Silence fell while Stacey waited for that command to come from her.

'Send the stuff and I'll call you back,' Kim said, taking her phone back and ending the call.

'What the hell, Bryant?' she asked as he moved the extra-strong coffee away from her. 'We know where Leyton Parks is. The Sentinel might have tracked him too. We need to warn him.'

'Of course we do. But did you hear what Stacey said? He's not exactly rolling out the welcome mat. The man has chosen to live off-grid, isolated, without basic services. You send squad cars rolling in, you don't know how he's going to react. He may have weapons; there may be other people there. You just don't know how it's going to end.'

'Jesus, Bryant, it ain't Waco.'

'Guv, this guy lives this way out of choice. Either he's hiding from someone, in which case he's not going to be pleased to see us, or he's done something wrong and he's not going to be pleased to see us. Either way, he's not going to be offering us tea and crumpets. There's also the possibility he has mental-health issues. Not one of these scenarios is helped by a load of squad cars turning up. We're not always the first bunch of folks people want to see.'

'Okay, maybe you've got a point,' she said as both their phones tinged receipt of a message. 'But if the Sentinel gets there first, we're fucked.'

'Think about it, guv. If there's any truth to Stacey's *Minority Report* theory that the Sentinel is targeting people who are about to re-offend, surely he's more likely to go for Newton. There's no evidence that Leyton has put a foot wrong since being at Welton.'

She saw his point, but then why wasn't Newton already dead? He re-offended constantly.

She knew they were missing something. The revenge motive wasn't adding up. But right now the priority had to be Leyton Parks.

They silently viewed the information Stacey had sent them.

'Fair enough. For once you actually do have a point,' she admitted. Because the detail would be hard to decipher on the small screens of their phones, Stacey had added arrows and descriptions. 'Sure doesn't want any visitors.'

'We have to be as low-key and non-threatening as possible,' Bryant said. 'We need to appear friendly. It might be best if you stay in the car.'

She offered him the look.

'Look, ultimately we're strangers, and he's not going to—'

'Ooh, I have an idea,' she said, picking up her phone.

'Do not send in the SAS,' Bryant joked.

'I've got better,' she said, waiting for the call to be answered.

She thought it was going to go to voicemail, but Ryan West answered in the nick of time.

'Hello.'

His voice was barely a whisper.

'Are you free?'

'Not right now. I'm teaching an English class to a group of foreign exchange students.'

'When do you finish?'

'Half an hour. Why?'

'We've found Leyton Parks. He's going to need to see a friendly face.'

'I don't know. It's been a long time. He probably wouldn't even remember me.'

'Everyone says you two got on. We need to let him know that we're no threat.'

'Erm... is it dangerous?' he asked. 'I'm an English teacher.'

'Accompanying two police officers. You'll be fine.'

'Okay, do you want to pick me up outside Dudley College at five?' he asked.

'Got it,' Kim said before ending the call.

'Good idea,' Bryant said, raising his hand for a high five.

The disgust on her face killed the gesture like a wilting flower.

She pulled her coffee back from the edge of the table. Finally, they would be able to warn Leyton Parks that he was in danger.

Penn and Stacey had done a cracking job in locating him. She just prayed that their killer hadn't found him first.

EIGHTY-FIVE

As arranged, Ryan was waiting for them outside Dudley College's main entrance.

He removed his backpack before opening the rear passenger door.

'Thanks for agreeing to do this,' she said as he buckled himself in.

'It's okay. I've got an online tutorial at eight. Do I need to cancel it?'

'Not sure – we'll see how it goes.'

He looked behind them. 'Is this it?'

'We don't want him to feel threatened,' Kim said as Bryant put the postcode into his satnav.

'Got it.'

'Tell us about him,' Kim said. Any information they had could be helpful in getting him to open the door.

'I didn't know him for that long, but I felt like he didn't really belong anywhere. I knew he came from the travelling community, but he wasn't brash or tough. I think he was easily led by older kids and that's what got him into trouble. He followed suit at Welton and got in with some older, tougher kids and did what he was told. I just sensed something different in him. In my lessons, he appeared to be listening. It was like he wanted to learn. He hadn't had much education, and it was all like a new discovery for him. His reading and writing ability was far below the others.

'I offered him extra tutoring, to help catch him up. He accepted, but then his buddies found out and took the piss, so he didn't want to do it any more.'

Kim was saddened by the story. Welton could very easily have been a success story for Leyton Parks. The facilities and opportunities had been there to give him a brighter future, but peer pressure had destroyed that hope. And now he lived in a battered caravan isolated from the rest of the world.

'I'm going to cancel it. Just to be safe,' Ryan said, taking out his phone.

Kim took out her phone at the same time. She needed to study what they'd received from Stacey and work out how they were going to reach him.

From the photos, there was no way they were going to get a car anywhere near the place.

She was guessing that when he left his secluded spot, he didn't scale the fence and use the road that ran in front of all the new properties. A man who'd worked so hard to protect the secrecy of his location wouldn't walk so blatantly close to these houses. She'd bet he'd stand out by a mile, and anyone who saw him would question where he'd come from. That direction of travel would also take him away from the town and necessary provisions.

She moved her focus to the open fields that flanked the reservoir and led onto the main road.

Somewhere there had to be a path.

She zoomed in and finally spotted a line that travelled in a diagonal direction from the tip of the reservoir down to a field gate on the road. Not an official path but what she guessed was a route worn by people coming to look at the water or feed the ducks.

From the aerial view, it appeared there was no way to walk around the reservoir, but she'd bet that someone who knew where they were going could easily make their way to the edge of the trees and skirt around the reservoir to join the path at the end.

If they were right, the man had chosen to live in a caravan that lacked even basic amenities. There was no vehicular access, so any kind of delivery was impossible.

If he was alone, he was isolated and detached from any kind of community. He had a mile walk to pick up the most basic of provisions and he'd surrounded himself with some kind of barrier.

The most prominent question in her mind was why.

EIGHTY-SIX

It was almost six when Bryant pulled up at the field gate. Although it was only twenty miles away, rush hour had added a good twenty minutes to the normal journey time.

As he switched off the engine Kim turned to him.

'Bryant, I...'

'Yeah, I was thinking the same thing,' he said, holding up his hand.

'What?' Ryan asked from the back seat.

'Bryant needs to stay here in case we spook him and he tries to get away.'

'I can wait here if you like,' Ryan offered.

Kim was starting to understand why he hadn't lasted very long at Welton. 'I need you with me so that if we make it to his front door, he sees a face he knows.'

'Okay,' he said, getting out of the car.

'Every five?' Bryant asked, talking of one of their usual safety tricks if they were separated.

Bryant would ring her phone at regular intervals. If she didn't answer, he knew to leave his post and come looking.

'Make it ten,' she said, opening her door and stepping out. 'I don't want to be right outside his front door and have my ringing phone set him off.'

'Okay. Be careful.'

'I'll be fine. Ryan here will protect me if we meet any trouble.'

'Wh-what?' he asked, shrugging his backpack onto his shoulders.

'You could leave that here,' she suggested.

'Water and hay-fever meds. And I don't go anywhere without my inhaler,' he said, patting the fabric.

'Cool,' she said, climbing over the metal gate. They were hardly hiking to the top of Ben Nevis.

He seemed unsure so she offered him a steadying hand.

Once on the other side, she pictured the photo in her mind. On the satellite image, the field had looked smaller, and it hadn't been filled with a crop of some kind.

The path was barely visible, and the plants were up to their thighs.

'Rape,' Ryan said, from behind.

'What?'

'Rapeseed,' he said. 'That's what we're walking through.'

'Good to know,' she said, trying to keep her bearings. The field was a good eight to ten acres and they had to travel across it diagonally. As the field rose up, obscuring her view, she had to just hope she was heading towards the tip of the reservoir.

'It's the third-largest source of vegetable oil and the second-largest source of protein meal in the world. The by-product is an animal feed used for cattle, pigs and poultry. Rapeseed oil is also used as diesel.'

'Ryan,' Kim interrupted.

'Yeah.'

'Shut up,' she said, feeling that she knew him well enough to be that candid.

'Got it,' he said as she reached the brow of the hill.

It was a mixed blessing. She could see the tip of the water and the trees to the east, but they were barely halfway across, and the trudging motion to get through the crop was already telling on her thigh muscles.

She had the sudden urge to rub at her eyes.

'Keep moving,' Ryan said, walking past her. 'We need to get out of here.'

'Why?' Kim said, pointing in their general direction of travel.

'Allergies, itchy eyes, coughing and breathlessness. I'm going to shut up now.'

Kim was thankful. With Ryan taking his turn in flattening the crop, they made it to the tip of the reservoir as her phone began to ring.

'I'm fine,' she said breathlessly.

'Jeez, you sound rough. How far are you?'

'Over the field.'

'Is that all?'

Kim was tempted to give him a mouthful, but the energy was better spent trying to get her breath back.

Why the hell did Leyton Parks not just have a bloody phone?

'Fifteen,' she said to Bryant before ending the call. The ten minutes they'd agreed wasn't long enough. She'd really hoped she was going to be further.

'Right, that was the easy part,' she said, entering the woods. It wasn't going to be as straightforward keeping her bearings amongst the dense crab apple and bay trees.

'Damn,' Kim said as something wrapped itself around her ankle.

'Blackberry thorns,' Ryan said, stamping on it and holding it down so she could free her ankle.

She knew one of the little blighters had punctured the

fabric of her trousers. She resisted the urge to rub it and carried on moving.

'Be careful of those dwarf nettles as well. They sting like hell.'

'Will do,' Kim said, following where he pointed. She wasn't sure how they were going to avoid them. Damn things were everywhere.

'Did you know that thorns exist on plants to deter animals from eating them?' Ryan asked.

'Nope, and I'm sure it's not a fact I'll ever have cause to repeat.'

'I notice that you're prone to sarcasm,' Ryan observed.

'Really, and here I was thinking I hid it very well.'

'See, you just did it— Oh, okay, you got me.'

Kim smiled. It wasn't all that hard.

As they moved further in, she noted the change in trees as they became more coniferous, providing better cover.

'I think we're almost there,' she said. The trees looked less dense twenty metres in front.

'Oh shit,' Ryan said, clutching his ankle. 'One of those dwarf nettles stung me.'

He pulled down his sock to reveal a red mark.

His face was contorted in pain, and Kim realised just how much of a baby he was.

'Shall I get you a dock leaf?'

'Any leaf,' he said, lowering himself onto a fallen log.

She plucked a couple and handed them to him. He scrunched them up in his hand and then rubbed them over the affected area.

'It's the sap that helps. Doesn't need to be dock.'

'You know, you sure know a lot of useless—'

She stopped speaking as her phone rang.

She answered it quickly.

'All okay, fifteen,' she whispered before ending the call.

With one final rub, Ryan jumped to his feet. 'All good.'

Kim continued forward, and as she'd thought, the trees began to thin.

In the distance, she could make out a three-tier barbed-wire fence.

They approached it cautiously, looking all around them as they moved. Kim wouldn't have ruled out animal traps and, damn him, Bryant's words about the man's possible reaction were now lodged in her head.

The whole area was encircled by hostile fencing with a one-metre cut-out to access the caravan. She could see a small window with the curtains closed.

Kim took a good look around, noting piles of metal, wood and rubbish. The caravan was placed where the end of the old road of the travellers' site would have been.

A feeling of trepidation stole over her.

The air around her was tense, charged.

She'd come here to warn a man that his life was in danger, but she had the sudden, inexplicable fear that her own life was now somehow hanging in the balance.

EIGHTY-SEVEN

'Thanks for this, Stace,' Penn said, trying to re-sort his piles.

The two of them had got so caught up looking for Leyton Parks, he'd forgotten about the budget meeting in the boardroom, until Woody had called and told him in no uncertain terms to get the stuff shifted.

Stacey had run up the stairs with him to collect everything together into one big pile and just get it out of there.

'No probs,' she said, tapping her fingers on the desk. 'Still waiting to see if I need to carry on looking for Leyton Parks.'

Penn was dying to call the boss to see if their theory had been proven correct.

'Doesn't feel like a Friday,' she mused.

'That's cos we're not getting the weekend off, Stace. No way is the boss releasing us for two days while we've got a killer on the loose.'

'Fair point. I'm gonna carry on trying to see if I can find out any more about this Gordon Banks character. It's a bit suspicious he's disappeared after the place burned down.'

Penn continued sorting his paperwork. They were no closer

to finding the murderer so his work wasn't done. All they'd uncovered so far was the location of another potential victim.

'Right, you go on that pile with the other...' He felt the words die in his mouth as he examined the single piece of card in his hand more closely.

'Err.... Stace, we've got a problem.'

'What's that?'

'An invitation to a memorial service for one of Welton's former staff members.'

EIGHTY-EIGHT

For Kim, three things happened at once.

Her phone started to ring.

Leyton Parks appeared to the side of the caravan.

Ryan West grabbed her round the throat.

In the second it took her to register what was going on and instruct her brain to resist, he'd positioned himself behind her with his thumbs at the base of her skull and his fingers pressing on her larynx.

Leyton Parks made no move to come to her aid. His face was frozen in fear, staring at the man behind her.

'I knew you'd find me,' he said quietly.

'I promised you I would, and you know I keep my promises. You gave me a hard time finding you, but lucky for me, this nice police lady led me right to you. She even gave me a lift.' He laughed pleasantly. 'And because of all her help, I'm not going to kill her yet.'

Kim could feel the panic rising within her, but she dared not move a muscle. Ryan was already applying light pressure to her throat.

She had to be patient and wait for the right moment.

'Where are the others?' Leyton asked.

'Dead.'

Leyton nodded as if that was the answer he'd been expecting.

Kim wanted to scream at him to run, to disappear into the trees until help came. But it was as though he couldn't move.

'Inspector, I'd like to thank you for allowing me to tag along, but you're no longer needed. Leyton and I are going to have a nice walk and conduct our business. I'm going to apply enough pressure to render you unconscious for a while but not kill you. This will give me the chance to do what I came here to do. If you try to come after us, you will not get that same consideration twice. Do we understand each other?'

Chilled by the perfectly reasonable tone, Kim nodded slowly, aware that it had only been a couple of minutes since her last call with Bryant. Ryan had timed his nettle sting perfectly so that another check had been made. Bryant wasn't going to be budging from the car any time soon, and even when he did, he'd take a good twenty to twenty-five minutes to reach her, if he could find her at all.

Physically, she was unable to fight the strength she could feel in Ryan's hands. So she had to make each second count.

Her mind was still trying to understand why Leyton was so scared of his old English teacher, and why the English teacher was trying to kill them all.

'You're not Ryan West, are you?' she croaked as the pressure on her larynx began to increase.

'Bravo, Inspector. Top marks.'

The stars started to circle around her head, and her vision began to cloud at the edges.

'Y-you're that kid. The one they bullied,' she said, feeling the life leaving her body.

'Yes, Inspector, that's exactly who I am,' he said, offering a final squeeze before dropping her to the ground.

EIGHTY-NINE

Bryant checked the clock. Nine minutes. He turned up the air conditioning for a blast of cooler air. It wasn't that he was particularly warm, but the cold air would help keep him awake. Just sitting in the car watching the clock roll around to check-in time was adding weight to his already heavy lids.

Losing four hours of sleep and then racing around on another twelve-plus-hours shift had him silently yearning for a cuppa and bed. Not that he'd ever tell the guv that. She had enough fodder for mocking.

He checked the clock again.

Seven minutes.

His phone rang. 'Hey, Penn, you've got around six minutes to entertain me until I—'

'Bryant, where the fuck are you?'

Bryant sat up straight. Penn never swore. 'In the car. At the farm gate. The guv wanted me to keep watch while she and Ryan—'

'He's not Ryan,' Penn screamed as Bryant turned off the engine.

'What the hell are you talking about?' he said, getting out of the car.

'Ryan West died years ago. He was fifty-seven years old.'

'Then who the hell is she with?' he demanded, jumping over the field gate.

'We think it's the kid they bullied and put in the hospital, but because it was all hushed up, we don't have a name. There's no official record.'

'I'm heading towards her location,' he said, trudging through the field. The adrenaline had kicked in and he was chewing up the metres.

'Bryant, she's not answering her phone. What do you want me to do?'

'Backup coming?'

'Oh yeah.'

'Then pray. Just pray that she's safe.'

Penn ended the call, and Bryant growled to expel the rage in his stomach.

Not only had they led the killer right to his next victim, but they'd put the guv in danger in the process. All kinds of scenarios were playing through his mind.

He picked up speed and called her number again.

He was totally awake now.

NINETY

Kim heard the ringing of her phone, but it sounded as though it was underneath the bedcovers.

As her mind began to clear, the throbbing in her throat brought back the memory of what had happened.

She had no idea how long she'd been unconscious, but Ryan had made good work in the meantime by tying her hands and feet together. They weren't particularly good knots, and she was able to free her feet quickly by rubbing the rope on the ground and twisting her ankle around.

Ryan, or whatever his name was, had been clever in orchestrating the nettle sting to delay meeting Leyton until that second check call had happened. Once she'd confirmed her safety to Bryant, he'd known he had a full fifteen-minute head start without interruption.

She got to her feet and headed for the barbed-wire fence. The rope was tight against her wrists, and she realised quickly that the tiny spikes would take far too long to have any impact. She'd rip her arms to shreds before getting through the twine.

She looked around and headed towards the rubbish pile she'd spotted. Seeing nothing of use on top, she started kicking stuff out and struck gold when she found an empty tin of beans with the jagged lid still attached. She picked it up with both hands and managed to bend the lid up. Then she sat on the ground, placed the can between her knees and rubbed the rope back and forth on the razor-sharp metal, taking care not to get too close to her wrists.

Immediately, she could see the rope fraying. It was doable, but it was going to take a bit of time. And it was time that Leyton Parks didn't have.

Her phone stopped ringing and then started again immediately.

'I can't bloody answer you,' she croaked.

Whoever was ringing her was going to be alarmed at her failure to respond. They would bring backup.

That didn't help Leyton Parks, who was probably minutes away from being jabbed with a needle full of fentanyl.

'Quicker,' she shouted at the rope as she increased the speed of the movement.

The fraying was happening faster, and she could feel the twine weakening.

'Yes,' she cried in triumph as the rope gave way.

She jumped to her feet, reached for her phone and wasn't surprised to see the missed calls were from Penn and Bryant.

She called Bryant back.

'Thank God,' he answered. 'Are you...?'

'Where are you?' she asked, heading towards the caravan.

'Coming your way.'

'Ryan isn't Ryan. He's the killer. He has Leyton.'

'I know. Just wait there and—'

'There's no time. Have you reached the tip of the reservoir?' she asked.

'Right there now.'

'Go west instead and come around the reservoir from the

other direction. I'll head that way and we can meet in the middle.'

'Guv, I think I should—'

'Just do it,' she said, ending the call. Bryant's first instinct would be to come straight to her, to check she was okay, but Leyton didn't have that kind of time.

A quick look around the deceptively spacious caravan confirmed they weren't there.

She circled back around and headed in the opposite direction to which she'd come with Ryan.

She hoped that Leyton had tried to make his escape and was giving Ryan the runaround. Anything that would buy her a bit of time to find them. Judging by her phone, she'd only been unconscious for a few minutes, so she was praying she wasn't too far behind.

She entered the woods that would eventually lead to the wider end of the water. Stacey had said the tree depth was approximately eighty feet, so she'd have to move slowly and listen carefully.

Once inside the woods, she saw that she had better visibility than on the approach to the caravan. She was walking through trees that were a mixture of old ones that had been here for a hundred years and new ones planted by the developers that hadn't yet fully matured.

If she looked to her right, she could just make out the new houses. If she looked to her left, she could see the distant shimmering of the water.

Kim heard a voice up ahead and froze.

She listened hard. Was it someone who'd veered away from the fishing points?

No. The voice was raised, agitated and it was close to the water.

She took out her phone and keyed in a quick text to Bryant.

Near the water line

She carried on towards the voice.

A groan of pain told her Leyton was still alive.

She breathed a sigh of relief as she moved closer, even though right now Ryan had all the power.

Two more steps and she could see Ryan straddling Leyton at the edge of the reservoir. Both were muddied and dirty, and Kim was gladdened that Leyton had been fighting for his life. The not so good news was the fact Ryan was holding a syringe in his hand.

She moved close enough to hear what Ryan was saying.

'If you break a promise, you have to pay the consequences. I told you all what would happen if you broke your word.'

Snippets of the week slammed into her head all at once. The pieces that had been scattered in her mind floated together and formed the picture she'd been missing.

She stepped forward. 'Put the needle down, Ian.'

She finally knew who he was. Not the kid who'd been bullied but the ringleader of the Psycho Six.

'Fucking hell, not you again,' he said, rolling his eyes. 'But at least this time you got my name right.'

'You really want to do this?' she asked, nodding towards Leyton.

'I have to do this. I know them better than anyone. They're not going to change. They're all going to do bad things, and I'm stopping them before they do it. I would have thought you'd have worked that out by now,' he said with disgust.

'Oh, we worked that out ages ago. You left us enough pointers. Maybe too many.'

He frowned at her, but she'd heard what he'd said and now everything made sense.

'You killed Eric because you felt he was about to assault his girlfriend, correct?'

'The signs were there. I saw that photo with the bruise on her face.'

'And you killed Paul because he was about to commit rape?'

'I literally pulled him off her, so yeah, that was gonna happen, and before you ask, yes, I know that Nathan was going to volunteer to work with kids. I've been doing you guys a favour. You should be congratulating me. These people are off the streets because of me. They'll never get to commit those terrible crimes. I've saved lives.'

'Oh, how very fucking noble of you,' Kim said, crossing her arms and rolling her eyes. During his little speech, she'd had time to consider her attitude and find the one that was going to keep the syringe away from Leyton's flesh. She was taking a gamble with a man's life at risk, but Ian was a psychopath and a bully. She had to speak his language.

'Do you actually believe that bullshit or are you more self-aware than you act?'

His gaze narrowed. She had him engaged, and the needle was still in his hand.

'I mean, it's all very honourable of you, but if you're telling the truth, why isn't Dean Newton dead? He's a prolific offender. He's never stopped. So why isn't he dead? Why not go all *Minority Report* on his ass?'

'He will be. He's next.'

'No he's not. You've had plenty of time and opportunity, and he's still going strong. He's hardly hiding.'

He glared at her.

'You're full of shit, Ian. It's not a coincidence that Dean Newton was the only one who re-offended, is it?'

Ian's face filled with rage. She continued, 'He's the only one that came back. They all agreed to, but only Dean kept his promise.'

His words about promises had brought back everything

Alison had said about dynamics and hierarchy. The tweets that had a parental feel, the right to punish.

'You destroyed your own family, so you made another in your mind. Eric, Paul, Nathan, Dean and Leyton were your new family, and they all left you one by one. They all promised they'd come back and see you, and they didn't.'

Kim could see his hand trembling with anger.

Come on, Bryant, she silently prayed. She'd committed to a certain play and she had to see it through.

'You big fucking baby,' she said, shaking her head in disgust. 'Didn't you realise you were a means to an end? You gave them all protection while they were at Welton, and once they left, they didn't give you a second thought.

'Did they even know that you weren't sexually abused by your brother, that you killed him over a game? Or was that something you shared only with Dean Newton when he kept his promise and got himself put back inside?'

'He told you?'

'Fuck's sake, Ian. When are you going to understand that none of them give two shits about you? Dean was happy to tell us what you're really like. They promised they'd come back, and they didn't. They disappointed you. Boo fucking hoo. They were not your family.'

'So what's to stop me sticking him right now?' Ian asked, clenching the needle in his hand.

She shrugged. 'Do it. He's no loss to me. But the second you do, you lose your power. Once that needle touches his skin, you gotta hold it in place to do the job, and I've got nothing left to lose. I'm coming right at you.'

His head straightened as he heard the same thing she did.

'That's backup, Ian, following me. In about five minutes' time, you're not going to be able to move in these woods without tripping over a police officer.'

A movement beyond him caught her eye.

'You hang around long enough to jab him with that needle and I've got you. Run now and you might get out in time. You're bright enough to know that's the only chance you have.'

He hesitated, but she needed him to make the right decision.

'Your call, Ian. Prove your point and spend the rest of your life in prison or make a run for it. Who knows, maybe you'll outwit me and I'll never find you. Unlikely, but at least you've got a chance.'

He fixed her with his stare. There was nothing left of the affable, helpful English teacher. His eyes were cold and full of hate.

She held her breath as she stared right back.

He leaped up from his position straddling Leyton Parks and darted for the tree line.

Right on cue, Bryant stepped from the shadows and knocked him to the ground.

'And where do you think you're going, sunshine?'

NINETY-ONE

Kim leaned across to the passenger seat and stroked Barney as she waited for the others to arrive.

It was 9 a.m. on Saturday morning and the sun was already warming up. It was going to be a good day for what they planned to do.

It was less than twelve hours since she'd left the station after interviewing Ian Perkins. After some direct questioning, he'd admitted to the murders of Eric Gould, Paul Brooks and Nathan Yates. The charge of attempted murder of Leyton Parks was still being challenged by the CPS, as other than a roll in the mud, the man hadn't been harmed in any way. There were lesser charges in connection with his attack on her, so even without the charge on Leyton Parks, Ian Perkins was unlikely to ever see freedom again.

Kim was unsure how hard Leyton would want it pushed. She was guessing he wouldn't welcome the court appearances and public scrutiny. He'd lived his solitary lifestyle for so long she wasn't sure how he'd handle the public scrutiny.

Ian Perkins had occupied her thoughts for much of the time since she'd left the interview room. When he'd talked about the love of education in relation to Leyton Parks, he'd really been talking about himself. Since leaving prison, he'd taken every opportunity to educate himself and develop a brand-new persona. She'd taken a moment to look at his photo on the system, and even though Stacey hadn't shown it to her during her background checks of the Psycho Six, she wouldn't have recognised him if she had. Back then he'd had buck teeth, bad skin, bushy eyebrows and a wild, almost feral look in his eyes. The photo bore no resemblance to the groomed and knowledge-able person he'd presented as Ryan West. The full beard and his time in prison had aged him, and there had been no hint of a reason to suspect he hadn't been genuine. The psychopath in him had ensured he could exude charm and likeability. His need for control had prompted him to insert himself into the investigation at the earliest opportunity. He'd left enough crumbs about his knowledge of the boys and waited for them to follow the trail. His aim from the outset had been to use them to find Leyton Parks and they had duly obliged. Of course he'd been able to answer any question about the Psycho Six. He'd been their leader.

When Leanne had carried out her checks on Ian Perkins, she'd found him to be living a respectable, quiet life under the new name he'd been given. It was only to them he'd identified himself as the old English teacher as a ruse to get close to the action. His activities hadn't been detected by the protection officers, as most of the 3,000 members of the witness protection programme were monitored much less frequently than the serious cases where lifelong anonymity had been granted. And yet all those ways he'd worked on himself had resulted in surface changes only. His gleeful admission that he'd sent the letter to Mrs Baldwin about the porn on Lenny's computer, just because he could, showed that he was still the selfish, vicious person he'd been in his youth.

An ordinary silver Ford Focus estate car registered to his

new identity had been recovered from Dudley College car park, where he'd driven to be collected by them in order to keep the charade going. She had no doubt that trace evidence of all three victims would be found within the vehicle once Mitch had finished with it.

She now knew that Nathan Yates had been trying to communicate something and she'd missed it. His thumb had been tapping against his middle finger. Sign language for the letter I. How the hell had she missed that? In fact, how the hell had she missed the signs of the psychopath? It wasn't like she hadn't had the practice of being in their company.

She admitted that he'd been both clever and meticulous. Everything had been carefully orchestrated. The social-media accounts were for his own personal vanity as well as causing havoc and disruption, but ultimately he'd revealed the name of the second victim to give himself the opportunity to make contact and profess a link to both men.

While Ian had admitted to the murders, he'd maintained he'd done it to stop them from re-offending, and not because he'd turned them into some kind of pseudo-family who'd ultimately disappointed him. She was unsure why he'd waited so long to exact his revenge. She suspected that his need for control had required meticulous planning and research and that he wouldn't have allowed himself to rush.

The Black Country Angels were currently reassessing their position within the community. With no premises and a lacklustre group of volunteers, she suspected they wouldn't re-form. Fighting injustice was hard enough for police officers; maintaining that passion and righteousness around full-time jobs and family was a big ask. The cause of the fire was yet to be determined, and Gordon Banks had vanished into thin air. Was he the boy who'd been bullied mercilessly by the Psycho Six at Welton and had found a place in a group that fought for victims? Or had he been completely unrelated to the case but had something else to hide? Between the poor Welton records and a cover-up, she suspected they'd never know.

Her thoughts turned to the staff, old and new, from Welton. She hadn't warmed to the woman who now managed the facility, though she had a grudging respect for her ability to not only stick with the profession she'd loved but to advance in it. Whether Josephine Kirk had ever really dealt with the trauma of the attempted rape was another matter entirely.

Then there was Lenny Baldwin, who'd allowed himself to be blackmailed to prevent his wife finding out about his predilection for watching pornographic videos of gay sex, and so given too much power to the Psycho Six. There were many ways the man could have handled the situation, but all would have included him telling the truth. His actions hadn't contributed to the murders, but they'd shown how far he was prepared to go in order to protect his secret. It had done him no good in the end anyway.

She was hard-pressed to find any sympathy for the victims of Ian Perkins. Their actions at Welton had terrorised staff and other inmates alike. More than one person was going to have to live with the consequences of their despicable actions for the rest of their lives. There was no doubt that Eric had been about to embark on a journey of domestic abuse. The signs were there, and the escalation had begun. Who knew where that might have ended?

Paul Brooks had been seconds away from raping a woman. His past history and his disgusting selection of pornographic material indicated that it had been in his mind for a while and had only been a matter of time.

Nathan Yates had been trying to find an inroad to working with children, and despite his marriage and its dubious connotations, there had been a hunger within him that he'd been trying to satisfy.

Ian Perkins had claimed that none of them had changed

from when they were teens, and Kim had to wonder if he was right. Every one of them, except Leyton, had continued on the path they'd started as teens. If the success rate for rehabilitation was a paltry one in six, the system needed a serious overhaul. But ultimately, whether he was right or not, that hadn't been Ian's motivation for killing his former friends. He'd formed a family and they had disappointed him. It was no more complicated than that. So, although she struggled to mourn the loss of Eric, Paul and Nathan, she knew that Teresa Fox and Katie Yates would be affected by Ian's actions for the rest of their lives.

Curtis Jones would never believe that the Psycho Six hadn't been responsible for the death of his father, but having read the report in full, Kim was in no doubt that it had been a tragic accident. She hoped that over time Rufus would help ease him of the bitter burden he carried. At one point, when she'd seen the two of them driving off for lunch, she'd briefly wondered if they'd been in this thing together.

Rufus Fox had bonded with Curtis, had known of his terrible loss and had taken on that fatherly role in his life. He'd been desperate to welcome the man into his family as a son-in-law and had maintained that relationship even after the romance with his daughter had ended. She would imagine he'd now be pulling at his daughter's every heartstring to reunite with the man so he could have the family he wanted.

The irony of her own struggles with Stacey this week weren't lost on her. Was she guilty of doing the same thing as Ian with her team? Maybe. Would she kill them if they disappointed her? No. She'd just shout at them and not acknowledge their existence for a week.

Heat warmed her face. Looking back, she wasn't proud of the way she'd treated Stacey upon finding out her secret. Yes, she'd been angry. Yes, she'd been hurt. And yes, she'd eventually realised that Stacey had suffered greatly and had been a victim of a very disturbed individual. She should just have realised that fact sooner.

Ultimately, family had been at the heart of everything this past week. The focus had been on the families you make.

Mrs Danks had risked everything to spend time with her daughter again. She'd had experience of the cruel disease she suffered from, and she knew what was coming. She knew she was in the early stages where the good days outnumbered the bad. Every day that passed, that balance might tip against her, and she'd be unable to do anything about it. Of course, it was only suspicion on Kim's part that the woman had been out driving her small light-blue car on the night of Terence Birch's accident. Anything more would have obligated her to make a call to Vik. As far as Kim was concerned, Mrs Danks had already missed out on years with her daughter, so any suspicion would remain purely in her head.

But that same suspicion and her own actions had led her to question her own beliefs in vigilantism. Prior to this case, she had been resolutely against any form of members of the public exacting their own justice. But how much more were the Danks family supposed to take? They'd been placed in a horrific situation where, tied by the hands of the law, police officers had been unable to help. And wasn't she herself somewhat guilty of taking matters into her own hands this last week?

Without doubt, she should have told Vik everything she knew about Stacey's involvement with Birch. She'd done her utmost throughout her career to never enter the grey area of policing, but when it had come to protecting one of her own, she'd withheld information, illegally gained entry to a dead man's home and lied to her boss. The voice that shouted loudest in her head still said that no one had the right to take the law into their own hands and that punishment was decided by the justice system. That voice just wasn't as loud as it had once been. That fact and the grey area into which she'd slipped would all be sealed in one of the many boxes in a dark corner of her mind.

She pulled herself back to the present as the Astra Estate entered the car park. Her colleague and friend, Bryant. Even his moral compass had malfunctioned briefly this week. Somehow, they'd formed a silent agreement. He wouldn't ask her about the Danks family, and she wouldn't ask him about the disappearing shrine at Birch's house. He'd faced his own family issues this week. He'd been forced to accept that his was about to grow and that it would never be just the three of them again. He would eventually come to see that having Josh in the family would be a blessing not a curse.

Next to arrive were Penn, Lynne and Jasper. They stepped out of the car, and Kim was pleased to see Jasper carrying a sizeable Tupperware box. None of them were going hungry today.

Penn and Lynne had reached a milestone in their own little family this week. There was no question the two of them were in love, and it was clear that Lynne had a special place in her heart for Jasper. She accepted everything about Penn: his weirdness, his social awkwardness and his lifelong commitment to Jasper. They both had demanding jobs, and Kim just hoped their feelings could outlast the challenges ahead.

Last to arrive was the small blue car that had caused her to lose sleep for much of the week.

Devon and Stacey got out and moved towards the small group that was forming. A smile tugged at her lips as Kim saw something that gave her hope they could weather their current mistrust and rebuild their relationship. The distance from their car to the rest of the group was thirty feet, but their hands reached for each other and held for the time it took to cross the short space.

She felt sure that their small family would survive.

'And we're okay, aren't we, boy?' she asked, giving Barney's head a ruffle.

For some reason, the image of Leanne came to her mind. She had no idea why except for the fact that she too existed alone, committed to a job that demanded it. No colleagues, no friends, just people who needed her protection.

She pushed the image away. It was unlikely the two of them would ever meet again.

Kim unclipped Barney's seat belt and attached his lead. She opened the car door, and Barney followed her out.

They all turned her way and smiled widely. Barney instantly started pulling her towards Bryant.

'Here, take him,' Kim said as her gaze rested somewhere else.

Bryant took the lead from her hand and produced an apple from his pocket.

'Devon, got a sec?' she asked, moving away from the group. Devon followed.

Kim took a breath. 'Listen, about the other day—'

'You know, it was really a shit week, wasn't it?' Devon said, cutting her off.

'Oh, yeah,' Kim agreed. 'But that didn't give me the right to—'

'Of course it did,' Devon protested. 'Given the evidence, how could you not question me? I'm not proud of my actions. I shouldn't have hit him, but I'm not sorry he's dead.'

Kim didn't disagree.

'But I need to say something,' Devon said, biting her lip. 'I should never, ever have questioned your loyalty to Stace. I know how much you think of her, and that was unforgiveable. I'm sorry.'

'Thank you, but—'

'Listen, enough of this. I'm good. You good?' Devon asked with an engaging smile.

Kim laughed. 'Yeah, we good.'

'Great. Let's garden the shit out of this place.'

Kim followed her back to the group, where the attendees had been busy removing tools from their car boots.

'Bloody hell, folks, looking a bit like *Ground Force* right now,' she observed as they walked towards the entrance gates of Three Oaks Primary School.

She'd foregone all the red tape of a full-on police initiative to repair an unusable plot of land. As she'd suspected at the beginning of the week, planning was still ongoing.

Instead, she'd called the school and asked if she could bring some friends along to tidy up the space a bit.

The offer had been accepted with overflowing gratitude.

A woman in her early fifties wearing jeans and a tee shirt appeared at the gates.

'I'm Leslie Stubbs, head teacher, and I'd like to thank you so much for this. You have no idea.'

'Put us to work,' Kim said as they all piled through the gates.

'This way.'

They followed her to an area that was probably a quarter of an acre but was overgrown with weeds and brambles.

'The whole thing needs strimming,' Leslie said apologetically.

'Sounds like a job for us,' Bryant said, nodding towards Penn. Both were carrying battery-operated strimmers.

'This line of pavers needs to be levelled. It's a trip hazard for the little ones,' she said, pointing to a path that led to the broken-down vegetable garden.

Lynne looked at Jasper. 'You lift and I'll level?'

'Cool,' he answered and followed her to the first slab.

'And the vegetable garden desperately needs those loose strips of wood re-attaching.'

'I have a hammer and nails,' Devon said, patting her tool belt and heading towards the beds.

'And this over here was once a lustrous, thriving wisteria. It was strong and healthy, but the chickweed has managed to damage it. With some tender loving care and a bit of effort, it can be just as strong again.'

Kim met the gaze of her detective constable and smiled. 'Sounds like just the job for you and me, eh, Stace.'

A LETTER FROM ANGELA

First of all, I want to say a huge thank you for choosing to read *Bad Blood*, the nineteenth instalment of the Kim Stone series, and to many of you for sticking with Kim and her team since the very beginning.

This wasn't an easy book to write following the sudden and unexpected loss of my mum earlier this year. There were times that it was difficult to free up my mind to allow the creativity to roam free, and yet once I did, writing became what it has always been, my best friend and my escape. Immersing myself in Kim's world allowed me the space and time to accept my loss.

As many of you know, I love to present Kim with new situations, and in this book, I wanted to force her into a grey area of policing. How would she act when one of her own had been threatened? How closely would she adhere to the rules that she passionately upholds and lives by? How far is she prepared to go to protect the people she cares about, and what are the consequences of those actions? I really wanted to explore the dynamics that happen in the families that we make.

As ever, it was fun to bring back Alison, and the scene between her and Kim at the rock face was one of my favourites to write. Her insight into the case as well as the relationships between the team were enjoyable to explore through her eyes.

I thoroughly enjoyed writing *Bad Blood*, and if you enjoyed it, I would be forever grateful if you'd write a review. I'd love to hear what you think, and it can also help other readers discover one of my books for the first time. Or maybe you can recommend it to your friends and family...

I'd love to hear from you – so please get in touch with me on social media or through my website.

And if you'd like to keep up to date with all my latest releases, just sign up at the website link below. Your email address will never be shared, and you can unsubscribe at any time.

www.bookouture.com/angela-marsons

Thank you so much for your support – it is hugely appreciated.

Angela Marsons

www.angelamarsons-books.com

ACKNOWLEDGEMENTS

As ever, my first acknowledgement is to my partner in crime and life, Julie. Every single book is a different journey that at some stage in the process I feel I'll never finish. Unfailingly, she is there for the hard times, the self-doubt and the mid-story wobbles, and although we've been through these things many times before, her patience is limitless, as is her passion and enthusiasm. I couldn't do what I do without her.

Although no longer with us, my eternal thanks goes to my mum, who would tirelessly spread the book news to anyone who would listen.

Thank you to my dad and to my sister Lyn, her husband Clive and my nephews Matthew and Christopher for their support too.

Thank you to Amanda and Steve Nicol, who support us in so many ways, and to Kyle Nicol for book spotting my books everywhere he goes.

I would like to thank the growing team at Bookouture for their continued enthusiasm for Kim Stone and her stories.

Special thanks to my editor, Ruth Tross, who helped me navigate a new creative space after a sudden and unexpected personal loss. I have truly appreciated her passion and enthusiasm for the Kim Stone stories and especially the creative input she's allowed me in all areas of the process. I should also note that her little messages throughout the manuscript have made me laugh out loud and ensured that the editing process is as positive and painless as possible. Looking forward to working on the next.

To Kim Nash (Mama Bear), who works tirelessly to promote our books and protect us from the world and has offered a much appreciated helping hand through this one. To Noelle Holten, who has limitless enthusiasm and passion for our work, and to Sarah Hardy and Jess Readett, who also champion our books at every opportunity.

A special thanks must go to Janette Currie, who has copyedited the Kim Stone books from the very beginning. Her knowledge of the stories has ensured a continuity for which I'm extremely grateful.

Thank you to the fantastic Kim Slater who has been an incredible support and friend to me for many years now and who, despite writing outstanding novels herself, always finds time for a chat. Massive thanks to Emma Tallon, who keeps me going with funny stories and endless support. Also to the fabulous Renita D'Silva and Caroline Mitchell, both writers that I follow and read voraciously and without whom this journey would be impossible. Huge thanks to the growing family of Bookouture authors who continue to amuse, encourage and inspire me on a daily basis.

A special thanks to a lovely lady named Chell Simpson who shared her own experiences of Lewy body dementia with her lovely mum and allowed me to share her stories.

My eternal gratitude goes to all the wonderful bloggers and reviewers who have taken the time to get to know Kim Stone and follow her story. These wonderful people shout loudly and share generously not because it is their job but because it is their passion. I will never tire of thanking this community for their support of both myself and my books. Thank you all so much.

Massive thanks to all my fabulous readers, especially the ones that have taken time out of their busy day to visit me on my website, Facebook page, Goodreads or Twitter.

Made in the USA
Thornton, CO
11/09/23 02:46:18